Intrusion

by

Arlene Kay

Dedication

For my husband Kent

and for Marilyn S. Miller (RIP)

One

I was dreaming of Kai when the phone rang. Its harsh tone buzzed through my brain like an angry bee, stinging me awake. I pried open my eyes and stared blearily at the alarm clock. Midnight. Thank God for Lasik surgery. At least I could see the damn thing now. My fingers reached blindly for the cell phone on my nightstand. Who the hell would bother me at this hour?

"Hello." I mumbled into the receiver.

"Betts. Wake up. You've got to hear this."

It was Candy's voice, bright and bubbly just like always. No one else called me Betts, not even Kai. Lizzie Mae. That had been his name for me. I'd just settled into REM sleep, and she'd spoiled it. I hated her.

"Go away. I'm sleeping." I disconnected, burying the cell phone under my pillow. She'd done this before. Couldn't wait to thrill me with her latest conquest. Screw that. Girl talk should be mutual, and I had nothing to trade. Why else would I clutch my pillow on a Saturday night instead of curling up with him? Those days of cuddling and kisses were long gone. They say that abstinence is good for you, builds character. Phooey. If I really tried, I could feel Kai with me, holding me tight, whispering softly in my ear, lulling me to sleep. I drifted into fantasyland with a smile on my face.

The pounding wouldn't stop. It wasn't a migraine. It wasn't even in my head. Some idiot was battering down the front door. My mood was less forgiving than a mama grizzly's. Even my dog Della stayed sacked out in her crate to avoid my wrath. I grabbed a robe, belted it and lunged for the claw hammer. Not much of a weapon, but a woman couldn't be too careful. Boston lawmakers coddled killers, not vulnerable females. I took a chance and used the peephole. Killers cap you right between the eyes if you're not careful. All the books said so.

"Let me in. Come on, Betts."

I'd finally get the chance to use that hammer when Candy put her perfectly pedicured toes into my house.

I switched off the burglar alarm and flung open the door. Something was very wrong. Candy was shivering, oblivious to the mascara ringing her eyes. They were her best feature, those green cat eyes. Her legs weren't bad either. She wore a thigh-high silk dress with kitten heels. That didn't improve my mood any. I'd wear a burqa if it covered my bony legs.

"What the hell is wrong?" I asked. "You're a mess."

She staunched the tears coursing down her cheeks. "Oh, Betts, he's gone."

"Who? You're not making sense." I clutched my hands to keep from shaking her.

"Tommy," she cried. "He's dead."

We only knew one Tommy, Tom Yancey, our college buddy, confidant and court jester. He wasn't dead. Impossible. I'd spoken to him only last month. A wave of guilt assailed me. He'd left messages on my machine, sent emails, too. Nothing urgent, just needed to touch base. I'd ignored them, shuffled them off to my pending list. He'd understand. We had all the time in the world.

"It can't be," I said. "What happened?"

Candy hiccupped, an open portal to hysteria. She'd be incoherent soon unless I did something.

"Here, follow me."

I signaled Della to join us, since her people skills easily surpass mine. When Candy dissolves into a quivering mass, I get violent. Della licks her hand. Chalk it up to generations of herding instinct.

I filed into the kitchen and found the teakettle. British wisdom triumphed: nothing beats a nice cuppa when disaster strikes. Candy loved the soothing taste of Chamomile. Tommy insisted ... I shook my head. No time for that kind of stuff. I blinked to keep from seeing him, long legs wrapped around the bar stool, sipping his mug of Earl Grey. "Real man's brew," he'd called it, making a muscle. "Strong like bull."

Candy grasped her teacup like a talisman. I didn't offer food; I knew better. That size two shape was no accident. She counted calories with nuclear precision.

"Got any Xanax?" she asked. "Or something stronger?"

"Later. Right now I need information." I found a bottle of Glenlivit tucked away in the cupboard and poured a dollop into her cup. "OK. Tell me."

Candy's cloud of hair gave up the ghost and escaped its clip. She raked her fingers through it, gulping. "They called. The cops. You never answer your cell phone, so they got me."

"When?"

She checked her watch. It was way too large for her, a legacy from her dad. "About an hour ago. Right before I called you. Someone, a detective I guess, said Tommy was dead." She sobbed. "They wanted an ID, Betts. Like at the morgue. I can't do that."

Morgue? Just the thought gave me the willies. I'd seen that hellhole once before. Just once. My skin felt clammy, and my breathing slowed. *Not again. I can't do it either. Not again.*

Candy gulped her tea and looked for more. I made this one stronger. Half the cup was pure scotch. She didn't even notice.

"Maybe they're mistaken," I ventured. "Tommy might be fine." Candy's grim face called me a liar. She shook her head.

"They have a picture from his wallet. You know the one. Us three and Della."

How could I forget that day? It was three months ago. I'd been cowering in my bedroom, missing Kai with all my heart, praying he'd come back. Back from the dead. I saw his cheeky grin and sparkling eyes, felt his strong arms holding me.

Just like that, they'd invaded my space. Tommy was a mess in torn jeans, sloppy tee and sandals. He'd stuffed his thick crop into a Red Sox cap just to annoy me. Candy looked much better. She'd paid good money for her torn jeans and faded blouse. Those honeyed blonde streaks cost her plenty, too.

Since Kai's death, I'd seldom ventured outside except to work and walk Della. Couldn't recall my last meal or decent night's sleep. Didn't really care.

Tommy dangled a key under my nose. "This is an intervention. Get dressed, Mrs. Buckley."

I flinched. Hearing that name, *his* name, made everything surreal. Elisabeth Mae Buckley. Mrs. Kai Buckley. Aren't there naming conventions for widows? Can I still use his name?

They camped out on the bed until I surrendered. With ill grace, I snatched an outfit from my closet and stomped into the bathroom. Tommy chattered nonstop until I reappeared.

"Well. That's much better." His smile was just short of a smirk. "Now, grab your things, leash Della, and follow me."

"Where are we going?" I sounded peevish, unlike the vibrant Betts of old. "This seems more like an intrusion, an invasion of privacy."

Candy tugged my arm. "It's a secret. Come on. Take a risk. Live a little."

That's what Kai always said. Climbing Mount Washington exhilarated him. He couldn't understand my reluctance, called me a chicken. I could still see him and Tommy strutting around the room, arms flapping, clucking like fools. Oh, God.

"What should we do?" Candy moaned. "He's expecting us." She pinched her skirt into a sodden mess, hiking it up to an alarming level.

"Who's expecting us? You're not making sense."

She fished a tattered card out of her pocket and thrust it at me. It was an unimpressive government issue with name, rank and organization: Sergeant Mark Andrews, Homicide Division.

I shook Candy like a rag doll. "Homicide! Tommy was murdered? Why didn't you say so?"

She cowered beside Della, whimpering. "I thought I did. The cop said someone ran Tommy down. Didn't stop. Right outside his office." Her tears aroused my guilt and a sneaky sense of pleasure. I'd morphed from dishrag to bully in five minutes flat. Kai would be proud.

"I'm not leaving now. Forget it." I folded my arms and stared Candy down. Della hovered around her, eyeing me. "Besides, he's probably gone home. Best to wait until tomorrow." That seemed to placate her. Deferred action but a glimmer of hope.

I found a Xanax in my pocket and held it aloft. Candy's eyes gleamed as she reached for the magic pill. Midway through she stopped, hiding her face under a mass of tangled curls.

"Maybe I shouldn't," she said. "You need it more than I do."

"Don't worry. I have plenty." I'd stockpiled enough pharmaceuticals to pacify all of Cambridge. Those capsules had been my boon companions since Kai died. I'd had to hide them from Tommy. He didn't approve of masking pain and threatened to flush every one of them down the drain. "Face reality. Let it all hang out." Tommy was big on slogans.

Candy washed down the tranq with an alcohol chaser. To hell with consequences, desperate times called for bravery. She curled up on the couch, pulled the cashmere throw around her and sacked out with Della at her feet. I envied that childlike sense of detachment. Sleep claimed her like a lover, while it only flirted with me.

I set the alarm, slipped into my bedroom and snuggled back under the sheets. Maybe if I closed my eyes he'd find me again.

~

Sunlight filtered slowly through my solar shade. I lurched out of bed, wondering if it had really happened. Had I dreamed it? Maybe it was just another convoluted nightmare. I checked my clock. Nine o'clock. Jesus, Lord! Della would be desperate by now. I tore into the living room and saw my best friend calmly reading a paperback. No more hysteria. Candace Ott, beauty guru and confidante of the stars, was in the house.

"It's true then," I said, scanning her perfectly groomed person. She'd shed the minidress for one of mine and smoothed her French braid. No mascara trails today.

Candy nodded. "I called Sergeant Andrews. We're meeting him at noon." She pointed toward the kitchen. "Espresso over there, and don't worry about Della. We already took a run around the Common."

I staggered toward the caffeine. "Nothing's changed. I won't go to the morgue. I can't."

She waved her arms dismissively. "Not a problem. He's coming here."

"Here!" My synapses weren't firing yet. I couldn't bear that police presence, the bland, meaningless phrases like, "We're so sorry for your loss, Mrs. Buckley," invading my home again. "No," I sputtered. "Call him. Cancel everything."

Candy masked pity with a mile-wide smile. "Sorry, Betts. No can do. He's on his way now." She checked that ridiculous watch again. "Oops. Better get in gear. Your hair could use a shampoo."

My hair! I'd always pampered it, obsessed about it actually. Not many natural redheads around these days, Kai always said.

"You're right," I said. "After all, I'm supposed to be a makeup maven, aren't I?"

"Exactly. You have time to deep condition, too, and a face masque wouldn't hurt." Her smile never wavered. "Tommy would approve. You know how he was about appearances. Kai, too."

Did I ever. The three of us had shared a college flat in Georgetown. Money wasn't plentiful, so Candy whipped up mayonnaise hair masks, oatmeal facials and God only knew what else. Tommy was a good sport about it. We'd slopped that goop all over him, too. Whenever he brought a girlfriend home, we flaunted pictures of him wearing our handiwork. He swore that's why he'd never married.

Armed with a dizzying array of products, I stepped into my shower. It boasted a collection of knobs, nozzles and gadgets that I'd never quite mastered. My birthday surprise, a sybaritic combo of marble, bronze and river stones fit for a monarch. Kai's queen. I stemmed the tide of self-pity, applying myself to the beauty rituals I loved. There's comfort in the scent of lavender and the soothing glow of honey cream. I emerged, scrubbed, perfumed and pampered, an almost believable visage of city chic. Candy's amazing camouflage cream masked the circles under my eyes. Vanity aside, my eyes were my best feature. Deep hazel. My auburn locks looked shiny again even though I didn't blow them dry this time. Let Johnny Law see me *au natural*.

One spritz of Creed and I was ready. I chose his favorite, Silver Mountain Water. Every time he used it, Kai heaved a giant sigh, closed his eyes, and swore he was back in the Alps. He'd loved the mountains, loved them to death.

Candy nodded at my buffed-up image. "You clean up nicely, Mrs. B."

My smile was wan at best. "Thanks. Listen, Candy. Just one thing. Cops can be ruthless. Nothing's off limits when murder's involved. Stay on your guard."

She cocked her head. "Why? I certainly didn't kill him. I loved Tommy. So did you."

The buzzer ended our sparring. Della charged the door as I let in the law.

Two

Sergeant Mark Andrews was nobody's fool. His sharp grey eyes did a quick assessment of his surroundings as he performed the greeting ritual, refused coffee and settled into a leather wingchair.

Our home, mine now, had once been a source of particular pride. We'd bought the flat from a tart-tongued dowager who was downsizing. She'd dismissed me out of hand, but oh, how she'd warmed to Kai. Women always did. Even after we'd gutted the entire place, obsessed over paint chips and scrutinized every purchase, it still bore her imprint. Maybe class and elegance were things you were born with. Kai had them, but I was a pretender. He had carefully and lovingly chosen every object in the house. I'd helped, of course. I made a great sidekick. Always second chair to the lead counsel.

Andrews probably calculated the cost of each square foot with that cash register he called a mind. Probably wondered if something illegal funded the opulence.

My first thought was crazy. Andrews had the raw-boned look and ungainly stature of Ichabod Crane. He'd brought a sidekick, too, a twenty-something rookie named Francie Cohen. Andrews flashed faux sincerity worthy of a politician; Francie checked her emotions at the door. She nodded briskly and faded into the woodwork, busying herself with note taking. Candy stared at her with maddening intensity. I knew she was doing a mental makeover of Ms. Cohen, applying foundation, shadow and a hint of blush. Naturally, that mound of helmet-hair would have to go.

Andrews surprised me. He skipped that usual line of cop patter and got right down to business.

"Tell us about your friend, ladies. You should know that we have no suspects and no motive." He crossed his rather elegant long legs. "Of course, it's early days yet."

Candy and I exchanged puzzled glances. I cleared my throat.

"What exactly do you want to know? Tommy was our closest friend since college days. We did everything together." I choked back a sob.

Andrews donned reading glasses and scrutinized a folder. His silver hair was remarkably lush for a man in his fifties. "Mr. Yancey was your business partner as well, I understand." Somehow that sounded like an accusation.

"Yes," Candy chirped. "That is, he used to be."

Andrews raised thick black brows. "You had a falling out? Let's see, you are the founder and CEO of Sweet Nothings, a cosmetic company."

From the bowels of the back room, Francie Cohen piped up. "Oh, no, Sarge, not just a cosmetic company. Sweet Nothings is a beauty empire." She ducked her head, mindful of the daggers Andrews shot her way. Of course, Candy was delighted. She brightened immediately and was all smiles as Francie's stock vaulted to the top of the chart.

"What part did Mr. Yancey play in this beauty empire?" His head swiveled back to me. "I understand you and your husband, Kai Buckley, are part of this enterprise, too."

That caught me unaware. To my horror, renegade tears slid down my cheeks. I turned away for a second and wiped them. "My late husband and I were CFOs of the corporation. Tommy and I met him in business school."

Andrews grunted. "You attended Harvard Business School?"

I nodded, fighting for control. "All three of us did."

"Not me," Candy said. "Not my style, not the academic type. By the time Tommy graduated he was sick of school, too. Betts and Kai kept on going straight through law school."

"Back to basics, ladies." Andrews uncrossed his legs. "Why did Mr. Yancey leave your company? He hooked up with this CYBER-MED firm a year ago. What was that all about?"

My response was measured. Andrews hadn't told us one thing yet. "I'm not sure of the details. Tommy was excited, said it was the wave of the future. Something about virtual care and enhanced communication. Frankly, I kind of tuned him out."

Andrews raised a furry brow. "I thought he was your dear friend, Mrs. Buckley."

I stammered a response. "Things were difficult then. My husband ..."

"Cut her some slack, Jack." Candy's voice dripped with contempt. "We all loved Kai. Besides, Tommy pulled out of Sweet Nothings last year. He wanted the cash, said he needed it for something big."

"Kai, my husband, offered him a loan instead. Everything was trending upward. We knew the business was bound to take off." I sighed. "And it did. We've turned a profit three quarters in a row."

Andrews had a face as blank as slate. He shuffled his papers, spending an inordinate amount of time studying something. "Looks like you're pretty well fixed," he said, glancing around the room. "Commonwealth Ave is as good as it gets."

I was proud of my home, our home, but it didn't define me. A shack would seem like a palace if Kai were alive.

Anger flamed my face. "I fail to see what that has to do with my friend's death."

He leaned forward. "His murder, Mrs. Buckley, don't forget that. We have a witness who swears Mr. Yancey was targeted. This was no accident. That car hunted him."

Candy clutched her throat, uttering a strangled cry. "Why? Why would anyone hurt Tommy? Everybody loved him."

Waves of cynicism wafted out of Andrews. "You'd be surprised how often people tell me that. If victims were all so lovable, I'd be out of a job."

Francie Cohen gasped, ducked her head again and quickly recovered. Her time with Andrews would be short if she kept that up. Most homicide cops considered compassion a waste of time and energy unless it helped induce a confession.

"Were you estranged from Mr. Yancey?" Andrews hurled that one at me.

"Certainly not. He was family, best man at my wedding. We cared about each other."

Andrews shuffled papers again. Hadn't that man ever heard of order? He patted a wing of white hair and smiled. "You forgave him then, I suppose."

I shivered. Scores of nature videos flashed through my mind. The helpless prey unable to escape. The relentless predator extending his claws.

"He was there when your husband died, Mrs. Buckley. At least that's what this report says. Cited for reckless conduct, almost charged by the authorities in New Hampshire." Andrews tapped a cheap plastic pen on the arm of the wing chair. "He caused your husband's death, didn't he?"

My throat closed. I swallowed, hoping to avoid a coughing spasm that would savage my carefully applied mascara. Candy saved the day by pressing a goblet of Pellegrino to my lips.

"Here, Betts," she said, "take a sip. Maybe we need our attorney." She squeezed my shoulder, recalling too late that Kai had been our lawyer. "I thought you wanted our help. We can't do that if you tromp all over us like the Gestapo."

For a petite, ultra - girly person, Candy stood ten feet tall when her hackles were raised. She gave Andrews a ferocious glare. "Now, can we have a civilized conversation or not?"

I recovered quickly, fueled by an intense desire to kick Mark Andrews' ass. He reminded me of every smug professor who'd eyed my breasts instead of appreciating my intellect. They'd changed their tune, and so would this guy.

"Sorry for the lapse, Sergeant," I said. "For the record, I never blamed Tommy for anything. My husband was a daredevil. He thrived on it. Tommy just went along for the ride."

He didn't believe me, the rigid set of his shoulders told me that, but he had a job to do. Plenty of questions to ask. Francie Cohen stole a glance at me and quickly receded to the background. Andrews stood, angling his body away from Candy.

"If your offer still stands, I'd like some of that Pellegrino." He seemed proud of himself for remembering the name. Candy flashed her party smile and quickly filled another goblet. "How about you, Officer?" she said to Francie. "Taking notes is thirsty work."

A fleeting smile and half nod were her answer. I steeled myself for the next onslaught, taking care not to underestimate my adversary.

"What did Tommy tell you about his new job?" Andrews asked, an open-ended question for either one of us. Candy galloped to the rescue.

"He was excited. Tommy said that a start-up like CYBER-MED was right up his alley." She shrugged. "With his MBA and all, they really wanted him. He could be his own man there, not standing in someone's shadow." She lowered her eyes, knowing that we'd all stood in Kai's shadow.

"I'm still unclear about something. What exactly does this company do, this CYBER-MED?" Andrews must have boned up on old Colombo episodes. His simple flatfoot schtick needed some serious work. I'd bet our third quarter profits that he'd already devoured the corporate prospectus. Probably inhaled the profit and loss while he was at it.

Candy wasn't the only charmer around. I polished my Ivy League gloss and answered the man. "Think of CYBER-MED as a security company, you know, like ADT or Brinks but for health use. They monitor wireless medical devices, the implantable kind."

This time his reaction seemed genuine. "I didn't know there's any demand for stuff like this. Real science fiction, isn't it?"

"Well, it's in its infancy now, but hey, technology is the wave of the future." I smiled, recalling Tommy's glowing face as he described his new duties. "Boston is a hub for high-tech gizmos." I shrugged. "All those medical facilities, you know."

Candy leaned forward and asked what I'd been wondering myself. "Why come to us with all this stuff? Shouldn't you be badgering Tommy's business partners or following clues? They'd know the right things to tell you. Unless you want the low down on wrinkle creams?"

Something like a low growl escaped Andrews' throat. "The victim, Mr. Yancey, listed you two as his next of kin. His heirs, too. You're the executrix of his estate, Mrs. Buckley. In most cases, that means something." He motioned to Francie Cohen and collected his things. "If you think of anything, call me."

A thought popped into my mind. "Sergeant, wait. Couldn't this be a regular hit and run? You know, some drunk panics and flees the scene. Lots of bars in that area, aren't there? I just can't believe it was murder."

Andrews whirled around, pointing a bony finger my way. "Maybe you can't face the truth. I get it. You've had a tough year, but your friend had an even worse one. That car threw him twenty feet." He shoved his hands into his pocket. "One more thing. Mr. Yancey was on the sidewalk. Someone went over the curb after him."

My hand shook with a kind of palsy that was foreign to me. I pictured Tommy's last moments as adrenalin surged and he ran for his life. He was an athlete, fast and agile. Maybe it was instantaneous. They'd said that about Kai. No pain, Mrs. Buckley. Naturally, they'd tell his wife that.

Candy escorted them to the door, engaging Francie Cohen in a lively discussion of lip gloss while I tidied up. Andrews was slicker than I thought. He'd wedged two business cards under the goblet of Pellegrino.

Three

I loathe shrinks. They strip you bare, load you up with drugs and charge a fortune. Next day, you're pretty much the same except for that gaping chunk of soul you shared with a stranger. Oh, yeah, shrinks are big on sharing but it's a one-way street. Candy, on the other hand, adores them. She's always in one stage or another of self-discovery—Freudian, Jungian, whatever. When Kai died, she dragooned me into seeing a therapist for one session. Total disaster. Despite the urging of Dr. Gayhart Dale, an arctic bitch with a perpetual sneer, I refused to abandon my husband. As long as he was alive in me, Kai would never die. Metaphysics 101. It's as simple as that.

As soon as the police left, Candy started babbling about her therapy session. I zoned out until she mentioned Tommy's name.

"What's this about Tommy and your shrink?" I leaned forward in my chair and swiveled toward Candy.

She twirled a sun-streaked curl and glared at me. "I knew it. You weren't listening. I swear, Elisabeth Mae Buckley ..."

"Cool it," I said. "Just tell me."

Candy shrugged. "No biggie. Tommy was seeing Dr. Langdon, my shrink's partner. I ran into him one day just as he was leaving."

"You never once mentioned it, either one of you." Betrayal swamped my voice.

"He made me promise. Tommy knew you'd make a scene. Besides, he only started going last month. He was troubled." She dabbed her eyes with a dainty lace handkerchief. "I still can't believe it. Why would anyone kill him?"

I shrugged. "Andrews was right on top of things. How did he know about Tommy's will and such? Kai drafted it for him last year." I snapped my fingers. "I'll bet he already searched Tommy's place. You know how tidy he was. Tommy, I mean. Who knows about Andrews?"

Candy snorted. "Tidy? Obsessive, I'd call it. Typical Virgo. Probably had a file tabbed LAST WILL AND TESTAMENT with an arrow pointing to it. Remember, Kai had your neighbors witness it."

"That's right! No wonder. If we were his beneficiaries, we couldn't do it." I jumped up and headed for the office. "Hold on. I'll bet there's a copy in Kai's desk."

I felt pity oozing from Candy's pores. No, I'd never emptied Kai's desk. It sat opposite my own bureau plat, just as he'd left it that last day. The library's walnut paneling, shiny oak planks and subdued lighting made the room cozy. A thick Sarouk rug and a small chandelier made it elegant. I spend a lot of time in there; it comforts me.

"For Christ's sake," Candy moaned. "This place is a mausoleum, not an office." She slipped into Kai's office chair. "I can still smell his cologne. What do you do, spray Creed in here every day?"

"Move." I unlocked the fruitwood console that served as his filing cabinet. "Obviously, it's on a disk, but Kai always kept a paper backup. Several, in fact."

She rolled those cat eyes my way. "You mean you don't know? Jesus, Betts, what's wrong with you? You're a lawyer, too, for heaven's sake. What if something really important fell through the cracks?" Candy put her arm around me. "Let it go. He's been gone for over a year."

She didn't get it. No one did. I died too when Kai was killed. Kai and our child to be. I now drifted through life on autopilot, pretending, following my routine, not caring much for anything or anybody except Della.

Tommy's file was easy to find. I took a breath and read the document linking the two men I'd loved. Everything was in order. It was signed, witnessed and embossed. No surprises other than bequests to Candy and me. Kai had been the primary executor. As in life, I was his backup.

Candy rifled through my desk while she waited. In anyone else, it would be inexcusable. For her, it was typical behavior. She'd done the same thing in college.

"Wait a damn minute!" Her voice shook as she thrust an envelope under my nose. "Here. Look."

How many times had I seen that writing? We'd kidded him mercilessly. All those perfectly formed letters looked so girly. Tommy blamed it on the nuns, claimed they'd beaten the Palmer Method into him. Now it lay there, unopened and ignored like an intrusive guest.

"He sent it to you," Candy growled. "You didn't even open it. What's wrong with you, Betts? Tommy reached out, and you brushed him off." She started sobbing, but this time I couldn't blame her. It was postmarked last week, right after he'd called me. Another call I'd ignored.

"He was your friend, for God's sake. How could you?" Candy folded her arms, hugging herself as she turned toward the limestone fireplace. A sense of calm swept over me. I'd felt that way in law school right before Moot Court. Just like magic my nerves evaporated and training took over. I slit the envelope with Kai's bronze opener. It was exquisite, just like all his things, part of an Art Deco desk set signed by Louis Comfort Tiffany himself. I took care not to stab myself. Age hadn't blunted the rapier sharp tip.

Candy plucked the envelope from my hands and stood there with a puzzled look on her face. "What's going on? It's just some old newspaper clippings."

I leaned over her shoulder. That was easy. I towered over Candy by at least six inches.

"That's funny, they're obituaries. I've never heard of these people."

Why the hell would Tommy send these to me? It seemed more like a kid's game than a high stakes path to murder.

Candy mopped her eyes and flipped through them. "Judge Jacob Arthur. What a meanie he was. Big Boston Brahmin. You remember him on TV. Huge scowl, always ranting about crime." She considered it briefly. "Good hair, though. He used our conditioning pack, you know."

"No, I don't know. Who cares anyhow? It says he died of a heart attack during a tax fraud trial. Sad, but hardly a personal tragedy for Tommy." I frowned, even though every beauty guru in the world advised against it. "I remember this next one. Mary Alice Tate."

"That ditzy socialite?" Candy was on home turf now. She stopped the tears and became all business. "I knew her. She was a platinum patron of Sweet Nothings. Great product placement. Lovely skin. Botoxed, of course, but who isn't these days?"

"I'm not, and I hope you're clean, too. We're not even thirty yet, for God's sake, too young to inject poison into our faces. Didn't this socialite commit suicide?"

Candy put on her thinking cap. "Yeah. Word got out that she wasn't biologically connected to the Tate family. Some kind of under-the-blanket stuff. They cut her off without a cent, and believe me, that destroyed her. Mary Alice lived for money."

A third clipping fluttered to the floor. It featured the photo and obituary of a buff young man clutching a barbell.

Even I remembered that story. Ian Cotter, trainer to the stars, died when his implanted defibrillator malfunctioned. His family cried foul, but the medical community stood shoulder to shoulder on this one. I didn't recall the details except that Ian was reputed to be a major hound dog, sniffing after any nubile or ambulatory client who wandered his way. When it happened, Tommy was still with Sweet Nothings. We'd joked about it, saying that at least Ian died with a smile on his face.

The final one was a real puzzler. It featured a lengthy article about diabetes with examples of celebrities who had thrived despite its ravages. The public face was very familiar, none other than Secretary of State Richard Chernikova.

"Hmm. I didn't know he had diabetes. He sure keeps an active schedule." I ticked off some of the hot spots Chernikova had visited. "The man gave new meaning to shuttle diplomacy."

"He's not dead, is he?" Candy asked. "We would have heard something by now."

Sometimes her antics astound me. You'd never guess that Candace Mary Ott was an incredibly savvy businesswoman, as lethal as a shark. She might not know the Secretary of State, but mention eye creams, and she's brilliant. Would-be competitors found that out immediately. Threaten Sweet Nothings, and you die.

"What's he doing here anyhow?" Candy asked. "Doesn't he live in D.C.?"

I scanned the article. "He has his medical work done here at the Joslin Clinic. Apparently, he had one of those insulin pumps implanted last month."

Candy yawned. "Big deal. Why all this interest from Tommy?

He hadn't left a note, just the clippings. Tommy wasn't usually that cautious. He had approached life like the workout fanatic that he was. Always time for one more pushup.

"I don't know. Maybe I'll find out tomorrow when I visit CYBER-MED."

"What? Way to go." Candy gave me a girly fist-bump. "Of course, I'll join you. It's only right." She was probably coordinating her outfit as we sat there.

"Wait a minute," I said. "Who's minding the store? Sweet Nothings depends on you."

Nothing kept Candace Ott from her appointed rounds. She bounced right back without losing a step. "I read Tommy's will too," she said. "You and I jointly own thirty-five percent of CYBER-MED now. Right, Mrs. Buckley?"

Math was never Candy's strong suit. I slipped into lawyer mode, giving her a cautious nod. "Actually, it's 51% total, just enough for controlling interest. Tommy made sure of that."

Candy snaked her arm around my waist. "It's not about money. You know that." She glanced around the room. "After all, Kai left you a boatload of bucks. You'll never have to work again unless you want to. I'm not so lucky. Sweet Nothings is everything to me. Now I guess that includes CYBER-MED. I'm doing this for Tommy, too."

I closed my eyes, forcing a blank expression on my face. I'd stayed home with Della the day Kai died. He'd insisted. Those Kona eyes shone as he teased me about my condition. Mountain climbing was for he-men, not pregnant women.

"Don't worry, Lizzie Mae," he had joked, kissing my wedding ring. "I'll never leave your side. You can't get rid of me."

That boatload of bucks meant nothing without him.

Four

Boston is a high-tech hive with a constant flow of worker bees streaming out of MIT and its environs. We found CYBER-MED nestled behind the imposing shadow of Mass General Hospital and the many tributaries that service it. The building wasn't opulent, far from it. Respectable, that's what I'd call it, a well-preserved Back Bay matron that had weathered a few decades with reasonable dignity and minimal cosmetic work. Tommy had bragged about it. He was an aficionado of traditional architecture, although he'd found the pervasive ivy at Harvard rather cloying. I had never been inside CYBER-MED despite his urging. He was proud of CYBER-MED, even offered me the full tour. "Later," I'd said, "when I'm feeling up to it."

Candy was definitely feeling up to it. Her costume *du jour* proved that: hair skinned back into a demure twist, knee-grazing navy suit, discreet jewelry and minimalist makeup, all part of the corporate image as interpreted by *Vogue Magazine*. I chose a different path: I dressed like a lawyer. It had been a while since I'd graced a courtroom, but boardrooms were another matter. We'd seen plenty of them during our funding quest for Sweet Nothings. Kai, Tommy and I had pounded many miles of pavement doing the corporate square dance. It had puzzled me at first. Why beg strangers when Kai could have financed everything by writing one check? He'd sighed when I'd asked that. "Darling," he had said, "You never risk your own money. That's how the rich stay rich."

We had saved Candy for the *coup de grâce*. She would sweep into the meeting, wowing the mostly male moneybags, turning on the old charm machine. By the time it was over, our hosts were our investors. They'd done very well by us.

"Come on, Betts. Step lively." Candy snapped her alligator clutch shut. "And use some lipstick, for heaven's sake. Tommy liked women to look good."

I ignored her. It was easier that way. I handed the young receptionist my card and settled into the no-frills waiting area. Not many firms hired a man for the front desk. I smiled at him, thinking what a nice change he made from the usual eye candy.

We didn't wait long. I felt Candy's elbow jab me in the ribs and looked up into a smiling male face with smooth brown skin and perfect, very white teeth.

"Mrs. Buckley, Ms. Ott. Welcome. I'm Arun Rao."

I'd already done some checking on him. Dr. Arun Rao had a slew of credentials and an enviable family pedigree. Like many of the high-tech tribe, he was an MIT man specializing in Theoretical Cryptography, a field I'd never heard of.

"Glad to meet you," I said. "Tommy spoke a lot about his colleagues." I almost made it without breaking down. I'd practiced that stiff little speech all morning. Something about saying his name to a stranger made Tommy's death, his murder, seem more real. Candy squeezed my shoulder and flashed her mega-watt smile at Arun Rao. It helped that he was personable and attractive, defying the MIT stereotype of the clueless nerd with taped eyeglasses.

"Dr. Cahill is waiting for us. Are you ready to meet her?" Arun's eyes twinkled as he surveyed my partner. His English was flawless. No accent, no indication that Rao's family had rather recently come from India. According to his CV, they had sent their only son to prep school, college and graduate school in New England. No wonder he blended so seamlessly into his surroundings.

Before pressing the elevator button, Arun Rao hesitated. "I knew Tommy for only a short time. Nothing like you two ladies." He stared at the floor, seeming to gather his courage. "Still, I considered him my friend, a good friend. I want you to know that I'll do anything in my power to help the police." He spun around and held open the elevator door.

"That's very sweet. I guess we're all family now." Candy had an odd way of constructing family units from total strangers. I loathed it, but it worked for her.

"Dr. Cahill feels the same way," Arun said, "but she's reserved, like most physicians. Doesn't let her emotions show." He guided us toward an oblong conference room in the middle of the corridor. "Make yourselves comfortable. I'll find Dr. Cahill."

There was nothing opulent about the room. Sweet Nothings has stylish furniture, warm yellow walls and plenty of vivid artwork. CYBER-MED was all business, shapeless chairs in Parcel Post brown, a faux wood conference table and walls lined with every imaginable computer device and video screen. As an owner, I should have felt gratified. Instead, I found the austerity chilling. Hard to imagine vivacious Tom Yancey toiling in this mind-numbing place.

"Ugh," Candy said. "What a dump. I don't see one personal touch in here." She dimpled at a sudden thought. "I wouldn't mind getting a personal touch from Dr. Rao, though. What about you, Betts?"

"Me? Certainly not. He seems nice enough, though. I'm glad Tommy had a friend here."

"He's nice and tall. As tall as Tommy, wouldn't you say?"

"Who?"

Candy sighed, one of those deep, theatrical gestures. "Oh, for Pete's sake. Focus, Betts. I'm talking about Arun Rao." She tapped her pen on the table. "Good hair, even though it's receding a bit. At least there's no grey in it like Kai had."

That got my attention. "Wait just a minute." Kai's hair had been gorgeous. Thick, glossy, perfect. Those grey streaks in a young man's hair made him more irresistible.

The door swung open, sparing Candace Ott from certain death. I trained my eyes on the cardiologist who glided into the room and sat at the head of the table. Dr. Meg Cahill was a presence in the Boston medical community. She was older than us, closer to my mom's age than mine, but you'd never know it by the wall of energy that surrounded her. The woman had her own magnetic field.

"Mrs. Buckley, Ms. Ott." She leaned over and shook our hands. "I want you to know that I liked and valued Thomas."

Candy and I exchanged puzzled looks. Finally, it dawned on us. She was talking about Tommy.

Meg Cahill shook perfectly styled platinum hair. Even I knew a superior cut when I saw one. Candy could probably name the salon it came from.

"Oh, excuse me. That sounds so stuffy." Meg's eyes crinkled. She bounced up and poured coffee from a silver carafe. "Can I tempt you with some?" She was polite, professional and perky. I suppressed a shudder: perky people give me a rash.

Arun Rao sat directly opposite her as if observing an informal pecking order. Despite his subdued manner, those lively dark eyes never missed a step.

"Our work here is complicated," Meg Cahill said, shrugging. "I'd be glad to give you a tour, but I'm sure your makeup company needs you."

I patted Candy's arm to calm her down. The good doctor was playing with fire by equating Sweet Nothings with the corner drugstore. I summoned my corporate smile and flipped open my notebook.

"Actually, we carved out a block of time just for this. I've read your corporate brochures, but they're rather vague. Understandable, of course. Competition is fierce these days in high tech."

Our new partners exchanged blank looks. Arun Rao was the first to recover. "Of course. We just assumed you would want to sell your shares. You know, reinvest the proceeds in your own company." He carefully distributed two vellum folders to us.

Resisting temptation, I folded my hands and waited. Candy's head jerked up. She had plenty of dreams for Sweet Nothings, and most of them required cold, hard cash. I caught her eye, giving her the steely glare reserved for competitors and tardy vendors. She followed my lead and did nothing.

Rao finally broke the silence. "Forgive me. Aren't you going to read it?" Some of the veneer had worn off his grin. He seemed twitchy and unsure.

Meg Cahill widened her smile. "Check it out," she said. "It's a very attractive offer. I had our attorney draw it up in case you wanted to sign today."

I ignored the spark of hope in Candy's eyes. Meg Cahill's rush to judgment made me shiver. Why the sudden sales job?

"I'm afraid we couldn't make that kind of decision so soon. Besides, I need to consult my own estate attorney. Trusts aren't my field of expertise."

Dr. Meg Cahill was a deft politician who knew when to punt. "Naturally," she said. "After you consider it, I'd be glad to answer any questions you might have. Forgive us for our haste. We never meant to be insensitive."

Arun Rao's frown broadcast a different message: angst, uncertainty, and a touch of anger. There was one sure antidote to that, my secret weapon, Candace Ott.

She got the message and targeted Rao. I stifled a grin, confident of what was to follow. Most men succumbed immediately to her feline grace and big-eyed stare. Rao was no exception.

"Help me out here," she said. "Can you explain what CYBER-MED does?"

Meg Cahill disguised a sigh with a sudden cough while Dr. Rao transformed from ninja to knight errant. He sprang up, grabbed a laser pointer and touched a convoluted wall chart. I recognized a process analysis diagram so beloved of technophiles. Within seconds, he launched into a spiel about outputs, capacities, bottlenecks, and performance measures. It was business school *redux*. I'd always loathed using techno-babble to obscure truth. For Candy it was sheer torture. Her eyes crossed immediately, and she held up her palm like a traffic cop.

"Please, Arun," she pleaded, "have mercy. Use plain English."

"Of course," Meg Cahill interjected. "I'm afraid Arun gets carried away sometimes. We all do around here." She poured more coffee and swiveled toward us. "Simply put, CYBER-MED is a watchdog. We monitor electronically implanted medical devices for physicians and hospitals. Think of us as a type of shield, protecting patients from malfunctions and intrusions that could cause them harm." She shrugged. "It's simple, actually. Simple but elegant."

Candy raised her eyebrows. "I don't get it. What kind of things are we talking about?"

Rao dropped his pointer and returned to his seat. He grinned at Candy and me, doing a cultured, scientific version of an 'aw shucks' routine. "Think of people you may know. How many have pacemakers or infusion pumps to control diabetes? How many lives have been saved by implanted defibrillators? These devices transmit health data directly to physicians through wireless connections. They can be monitored without ever stepping into their doctors' offices." He flashed that grin again. "Pretty cool, no?"

"I assume some risks are inherent in this process?"

He looked startled, as if he'd forgotten that I existed. Dr. Cahill nodded, giving me a brisk stamp of approval.

"Exactly, Mrs. Buckley," she said. "That's where we step in. If anything goes awry, CYBER-MED identifies the problem and its source. We immediately interface with both the patient and the physician."

Tommy's newspaper clippings sprang to mind. I decided to table that discussion until Meg Cahill left us. Her sharp, probing eyes saw way too much for my comfort level. Visions of an angry bird of prey sprang to mind, Meg the hawk, focused and deadly.

"We're set up like a regular security company with one big twist." Arun beamed like a proud papa. "Our shift supervisors are either physicians' assistants or nurse practitioners. They evaluate the problem and refer it immediately to our doctors."

"Ingenious," I said. "How big is the staff?"

"Fewer than fifty for now. We only service the immediate Boston area." Meg adjusted the jacket of her tailored red suit. "But we have plans for expansion, big plans. Once we prove ourselves, CYBER-MED can franchise its offices nation-wide."

No wonder Tommy had been so excited. With a modicum of luck, he was sitting on a veritable gold mine, an untapped field with tons of potential.

"Perhaps you can give us a tour," I suggested, ignoring Candy's yawn. "It's so fascinating. I'd love to learn more. This kind of startup reads like a business school case study."

"Naturally. Dr. Rao and I have a meeting we can't miss, but I'll leave you in the capable hands of my executive assistant, Rand Lindsay. He's just completing his PhD in computer science."

"Another MIT alum?" Candy asked. "The woods are thick with them around here."

"So true." Meg Cahill shrugged. "A mere cardiologist like myself gets left at the starting gate half the time."

We joined in a chorus of polite, disbelieving laughter. Dr. Meg was one of the nation's top specialists, a close friend of the wealthy and well positioned. She had leveraged the political connections of her husband, philanthropist Carter Cahill, to climb still higher.

She buzzed her secretary and issued brisk instructions. "One final thing, ladies. If you decide you've got too much on your plate, our offer to buy you out still stands. Right now we're a privately held corporation. We're prepared to offer you ten percent over the current share price. If we ever take CYBER-MED public, the value would escalate considerably." She pushed aside that dainty porcelain cup. "That won't happen for some time, if at all."

"I guess Betts and I are the new bosses around here," Candy giggled. "Pretty cool."

Meg flexed her fingers as if she longed for a scalpel. If she'd had one, Candy's tongue might have felt its sting. "Technically, I suppose that's true. Rao and I worked as a team with Thomas, so I assumed that would continue."

I leapt to the rescue. "Of course. We'll certainly consider your generous offer. Thank you for your time. I'll set up an appointment later to review your financials."

Dr. Cahill maintained a tight, minimally polite smile. "I forgot you're a lawyer, too, Mrs. Buckley. Thomas said you were his classmate at business school. Well, you're wise to be cautious. After all, CYBER-MED is his legacy to you. Both of you."

After a soft knock on the door, a large man with thinning brown hair and a million dollar smile entered. I liked him immediately. That's a bad habit of mine, although invariably, it serves me well. Rand Lindsay was older than I expected, in his mid-forties, I'd guess. His affable grin was the antithesis of the Cambridge computer culture. I would have pegged him for a sociologist if he worked anywhere else.

Rand immediately clasped our hands. "I'm so sorry about Tommy," he said. "He was a great guy. A wonderful boss, too. He made coming to work fun."

It happened again. My eyes filled, and I had to turn away. Candy had a similar reaction. The loss was too raw for us to do otherwise. I still expected Tommy to spring out from behind a sofa, announcing that the whole thing was a particularly tasteless joke.

Rand Lindsay patted my back. "Come on," he said. "I'll give you the grand tour." He nodded to Meg and Arun and led us from the conference room. "Would you like to see his office, or is it too soon?"

I dabbed my eyes with a monogrammed hanky Kai had given me. It was a beautiful square of Irish linen from County Cork, home turf of the Buckley clan.

No more nonsense. Focus, Lizzie Mae.

"Let's see it," Candy said. "I hope the cops haven't trashed everything."

"Nah, but they were pretty thorough." Rand chuckled. "Tommy was so neat, they didn't have to disturb much. That Sergeant Andrews, I think it was, rousted me out of bed to open up the place. Not that I was doing much at the time." He gave a rueful shake of his massive head. "My life is pretty boring. Work, study, pray."

"Pray?" Candy asked.

She earned another smile. "I pray that I can continue to work and study." Rand used an entry card to access Tommy's workspace. It was identical in size and décor to those of his partners, but he'd added his own Tommy touches. Framed Civil War era etchings and a soft green throw made the space less forbidding. A bronze Art Nouveau lamp warmed the sitting area. It was a signed piece. Kai had found it at the Paris Flea Market and given it to Tommy as an office gift.

Candy plopped down on the couch and buried herself in the throw. "I made this for him," she said, her voice wavering between grief and pride. "I thought he hated it."

I scanned the rest of the office, noting the framed photos of us with Della. They were family photos. We were Tommy's family. All four of us were only children whose parents had died young. Weird, when you think of it. Eerie.

"Let me ask you something," I said to Rand. "What risks are typical in your business?"

He answered cautiously, as if sifting through a minefield. "Two biggies: access to private information and interference with the devices. You know, monkeying with the programming."

Candy's eyes widened. "Wow. Have you ever had any trouble with that?"

"Not really. The technology is very new. Naturally, we stay alert. Eternal vigilance and all that stuff." Rand's cheeks grew rosy.

He was lying. I'd bet money on it. Time for some risk taking. Tommy's newspaper clippings came to mind and one name, Mary Alice Tate.

"Wasn't there some tabloid scandal? That socialite, what was her name, Candy? You know, your friend. The one who killed herself?"

"You mean Mary Alice Tate?" Candy caught on right away. "Tommy said she was your client." Sometimes Candy's ability to lie alarms me. Today, I applauded it.

Rand Lindsay's mouth opened. He gulped and got himself under control. "I'm surprised Tommy told you about that," he said. "Big scandal. Dr. Cahill cracked down on everybody after that." He lowered his voice. "We're still not sure how it happened. Rao swears that someone at her own doctor's office leaked it. Those scandal sheets pay pretty well, I hear. Mary Alice had a pacemaker, but there was no problem with that. We had an independent lab check it out."

Something about Rand Lindsay inspired trust. Maybe it was his guileless blue eyes or the innocence of his baby face. I had to show my cards.

"You know that Tommy was murdered, I presume?"

"You mean killed, don't you? Hit and run's a felony, but it's manslaughter, not murder." He spread his hands. "Not that I'm minimizing the crime, you understand."

Candy leaned toward him. "You don't get it. I thought the cops spoke with you."

Rand licked his lips. "They never said anything about murder. Sergeant Andrews is coming here this afternoon. I ..." He looked helplessly around the room.

"Here's my question. Did Tommy have any enemies here? I'm talking employees, vendors, clients, the works." I felt a mix of guilt tinged with pride. I was finally getting the hang of this bully stuff. I had to admit that it felt pretty good playing the heavy for a change. Kai had always sheltered me from life's vicissitudes, but those days were long gone.

I had another nature video moment. This time I was the spider, and Rand Lindsay the hapless fly caught in my web, awaiting extinction. He stayed silent for a moment.

"I don't know what to tell you, Mrs. Buckley. People liked Tommy. He never played God or screwed with them. That's mighty rare in the scientific community, let me tell you. Why would anyone from CYBER-MED want him dead?"

"When I know the answer to that, I'll rest easier. Come on." I beckoned to Candy. "Let's get on with our tour."

Five

We spent the next ninety minutes exploring the nerve center of CYBER-MED. Rand Lindsay fairly bounced along the corridors, exposing every nook and cranny of the organization he so obviously loved. He knew everyone and every aspect of their jobs and prodded us to ask the tough questions.

"What if one of those things malfunctions?" I asked. "Can you act fast enough?"

"Me, personally?" Rand laughed. "Ma'am, I don't do anything fast, but my teammates here sure do." He clapped a muscular Latino on the shoulder. "Meet Tony Torres. We call him Tornado. I mean, this guy has already saved three lives."

"Wow," Candy said checking out Tornado's manly form. "Are you a doctor or a computer whiz?" Her dimples deepened as she gave him the star treatment.

Torres flushed. "Neither. I'm a nurse practitioner. We were monitoring a patient with a defib, and the system went wild." He gave Candy a Chiclets grin. "See, all this stuff is encrypted when it comes to us. There's a radio frequency band just for that purpose. Anyhow, this patient didn't listen to his doctor. His kid had MP3 headphones, and they started screwing around together. Bam! Those things can interact, and our guy got a nasty shock." Torres shrugged. "Actually, it was no biggie. I buzzed his doctor and sent the paramedics. Our guys reprogrammed his gizmo, and all was well."

"He's being modest," Rand said. "The Tornado rules." He checked his watch. "Ready for lunch, ladies? There's much more to see."

Candy exhaled, and I took the hint.

"We'll take a rain check, if that's OK. You've given us an awful lot to digest."

Rand chuckled. "I know I get carried away, but CYBER-MED is just so cool. It's my dissertation topic, you know."

"Really? What are you focusing on?"

"Yeah," Candy said. "Any trade secrets flowing to MIT? After all, graduate school costs a fortune these days."

There was that flush again. "Ladies, I know you're playing with me, but I love it." Rand handed us his card. "You can call me directly, if you want, or go straight to the top. Dr. Cahill said you get access to everything."

We shook hands, nodded to Rob the receptionist, and spilled out to the sunshine of a beautiful Boston day.

~

"I thought you'd never leave," Candy groused. "My eyes crossed after the first ten minutes in that place. All those nerds staring at computer screens, creepy."

"It wasn't that bad. Anyhow, we're just scratching the surface. Expect more of the same the next time we're here."

She arched her back as if preparing for a feline hissy fit. "No way. Count me out. I say we sell those shares and move on with our lives."

I know my friend. Her mood is invariably bright, full of optimism and sunshine, until the weather changes. When clouds roll in, logic only inflames her.

"Well, we have plenty of time to decide that. Tommy's estate has to go through probate. That could take a while."

Candy whirled around, hands on hips, eyes narrowed. "OK, Elisabeth Mae Buckley, come clean. What are you up to?"

I flashed her the peace sign. How could I explain something I wasn't certain of myself? CYBER-MED was a respectable firm staffed by educated, highly trained professionals. Tommy had researched it before ever committing to the business. He'd even gotten Kai involved. No one was more rigorous than Kai when it came to research. Five generations of Buckleys made and kept their fortune through smart business decisions. What could I possibly add to that?

Candy hadn't moved an inch. She stood there, glowering. "You're no detective, Mrs. B. I can coax things out of people much better than you can. You're such a lawyer, all formal and stiff."

I forced myself to count way past ten. She was right. Candy scored higher on the charm chart than I could ever hope to. She had aced Hypocrisy 101 while I scraped through with a barely passing grade. Scores of vulnerable men swooned at her feet everywhere she went. Except Kai. He'd never looked at anyone else from the day we met. Neither had I.

I patted my friend's shoulder. "You're right. That's why I need your help. Come on." I played my hole card. "After all, it's for Tommy."

Her lips puckered in a pout. "Oh, for heaven's sake. Blackmail is against the law, isn't it?" She raised her arm and hailed a cab. "I'm heading back to Sweet Nothings. Today's new product day, in case you've forgotten. I hook up with my beauty bloggers at two sharp."

That was part of her genius. Candy identified and absorbed social media trends like a sponge. While larger firms ignored user groups, she heard them out. Beauty bloggers, a fiercely independent lot, became her staunchest allies, testing products, offering advice and spreading the gospel according to Sweet Nothings. Candy co-opted them for the price of free makeup and a sympathetic ear.

"See you later," I said. "I need a walk to clear my head." I trotted up Cambridge Street, heading for the subway. Candy hates public transportation, but I enjoy the T. It's a pretty good deal, offering a fast ride and free entertainment for a modest fee. My mind whirled with facts, figures and speculation. Tommy's murder and CYBER-MED might be totally unrelated. After all, he'd cut a swath through half the eligible female population of Boston. Occasionally, he'd included married women in the mix as well. Maybe a spurned lover or her angry spouse had run him down. He'd had a few scrapes before. *Maybe I should tell Andrews.*

I'm tall but ungainly. Kids taunted me about that throughout grade school, called me Giraffe. My mom chided me more than once for wandering around in a haze. I should have listened to Mom. Instead of staying alert, I followed the herd, stepping blindly off the curb into traffic. A horn blared, and I froze as a speeding truck bore down on me.

Is this how Kai felt on that mountain? Did Tommy die this way?

Before I could even scream, an arm yanked me back from perdition. The sleeve felt soft and comforting, but my savior's voice was harsh.

"What's wrong with you?" he growled. "Do you want to die?"

Good question. I scrambled to my feet and faced him. With his wild mane of hair and scruffy beard, he seemed more devil than angel. His blue-green eyes flashed like lightning.

"Thank you," I stuttered. "I …" My legs wobbled, defying gravity.

The man tugged me none too gently toward the side of a building and propped me up against the wall. "Are you injured?" he asked. "Shall I call an ambulance?"

"No, I ..." No one would call me glib, but syntax was the least of my worries. Something about this stranger both attracted and frightened me. His intensity flirted with madness.

"Good," he said. "We need to talk, Mrs. Buckley."

"You know me?"

"Not officially, no, but I met your late husband."

"Kai?" I was half mute, incapable of speech. "Who are you?"

He thrust his arm through mine, propelling me toward the nearest Starbucks. "Come with me. I will explain."

Despite the odds, we found an empty table. The stranger took my order, slipped into line and returned quickly with two Chai lattes. I sat silently sipping my tea, studying him. He didn't look homicidal. In fact, several women in the place were boldly eyeing him. That was a plus. On the other hand, Theodore Bundy, serial killer extraordinaire, was very well groomed and rather hot. So much for appearances.

"OK, what's this all about? I'm grateful to you, but that's it. How did you know my husband, and what do you want?"

That coaxed a grin from him. His sea blue eyes actually twinkled. "My name is Lucian Sand, Dr. Lucian Sand." He had the faint whisper of an accent. French, I think. Something about his sentence structure and phraseology suggested that English was an acquired language.

"Why were you following me?"

"Fortuitous, would you not agree? I wanted to meet you and your partner. Speak with you. As I mentioned, I had a discussion with your husband last year." He stopped and spoke softly. "His accident was a tragedy. Please accept my condolences."

I stifled a sob. Some day it wouldn't hurt so much. Some day when I was dead.

"I repeat. What do you want, Dr. Sand? I'm busy, and my partner, Ms. Ott, is unavailable right now."

Lucian Sand leaned forward. He was taller than Tommy by several inches and had the taut body of a dedicated gym rat. I pegged his age at about thirty-five.

"I am a scientist, Mrs. Buckley, a professor at Concord University."

"What's your field?" Something about him aroused my suspicions. Maybe it was his passion. Admittedly, I was out of practice, but he had the lamest pick up line I'd ever heard. Invoking the name of my dead husband didn't make me feel one bit amorous.

Another half-smile. He had perfect teeth, not the Chiclets variety like Tony the Tornado, but straight, white teeth that fit his face. Too bad he wore that scruffy beard. I really loathe beards.

"It is rather boring, I'm afraid. My field is computer modeling, building and analyzing threat models. My specialty is implanted medical devices."

The tea finally revived me. Now it all made sense. Lucian Sand was connected to CYBER-MED in some way. Why else would he lurk around the building, hiding in shadows?

My years at Harvard hadn't been wasted: I could analyze a case study in record time. I'd gotten better grades than either Tommy or Kai with only half the effort. This was child's play.

"Bottom line, Dr. Sand. What's your interest in us and CYBER-MED?"

He flushed. "You are very direct, Mrs. Buckley. I understand you and Ms. Ott are the new majority owners of the company. I have a proposition, strictly business, to make to you both."

I gathered my things and rose, switching into frigid lawyer mode. "I'm afraid we're not interested. Furthermore, until my friend's estate is settled, any financial discussions would be premature." I extended my hand.

Lucien Sand clutched my wrist. "Wait. You are playing a dangerous game. Look what happened to your friend." Lightning flashed again in his eyes. "I tried to warn him too."

I kept my voice calm. "Let me go, or I'll scream. If you have any information about Mr. Yancey's death, tell Sergeant Andrews of the Homicide division. Otherwise, leave me alone. Do you understand?"

He didn't even flinch. "This isn't over. Trust me on that." He thrust a manila envelope at me without saying a word.

I pulled away, sped out the door and hailed a cab. No public transit today.

Six

"What does he look like?" Trust Candy to focus on the big picture.

"Normal. OK, I guess." I hadn't really studied him except for those eyes. Men didn't interest me that way anymore. Probably never would again.

"Good body, I bet. Or is he doughy? So many of those computer nerds go steady with a bag of Cheetos. I mean, Rand is a great guy, but really ..."

"He wasn't fat. Kind of athletic looking. But unhinged, definitely unhinged. Avoid him at all costs. If he bothers us, I'll call the cops."

Candy pranced around her desk and slouched on the sofa. She was definitely hiding something. Probably some business coup.

"I'm no Shakespeare scholar, Betts, but isn't there something about a lady protesting too much? Lucian Sand sounds promising."

"Forget about all that, it's not important. You're hiding something. Come on, out with it. You're dying to tell me."

"Guess who has a date tonight," she purred, "with a new man?"

Time for a big, heaving sigh. "Well, I know I'm not the lucky girl. Who is he?"

Her cat eyes sparkled. "You met him today, Betts."

"The Tornado?" I asked. "Kind of downscale for you, isn't he?"

"Don't be absurd. Arun Rao called this afternoon. We're meeting for drinks at the Four Seasons." She checked the delicate Patek Philippe watch on her wrist. She'd ditched her father's gift for something much more elegant.

"Oops, gotta run. Lucky thing I keep fresh clothes in here."

I should have kept my mouth shut, but everything connected with CYBER-MED seemed odd. Now one of our partners was nosing around my friend.

"Candy, do you think that's wise, getting involved with a business associate?"

"Involved? Whatever do you mean? Dating isn't a felony, you know. I never took vows of celibacy. That's your thing, Betts."

Her blistering glare seared me as she swept out the door. Candy was right. I'd become a nudge, a perpetual scold, inflicting my misery on everyone else. Even in college I'd never dated much. Way too shy. When Kai found me, my world opened up. I couldn't believe that a man like him would even notice me. Afterwards, every day was electric until death pulled the plug.

~

I couldn't relax that night. Damn Lucian Sand! His accusations consumed me, rattling around my brain like a slippery screw. Twice I reached for a Xanax but thought better of it. How easily I could descend into oblivion, becoming a pill-popping, wine-swilling zombie. No, thanks. Alcohol didn't really interest me. That was Kai's thing. He was an oenophile, a true connoisseur who knew all the buzzwords and had a refined palate. I just went along for the ride. Sometimes sipping a glass of his favorite vintage comforted me, made me feel closer to him. It was tempting but terrifying to tiptoe down that slippery slope.

The envelope stayed there, an uninvited guest decorating the center of my Chinoiserie commode. I'm cautious by nature, prone to overthinking things. Not Tommy. He was intrepid, plunging into things without considering the downside. That's what happened on Mount Washington. That's what killed my husband.

A tide of loneliness swamped me. In all my life I'd had only three friends I could count on. Two were gone forever, and Candy was currently incommunicado. I cursed the shyness that had stunted my life.

For Christ's sake, Lizzie Mae, buck up! Open the damned thing, and get it over with.

Damn! Lucian Sand was nothing but trouble. Maybe the whole thing was some sort of bizarre joke. I picked up Della's brush and groomed her silky coat. Even if he was the Nutty Professor, I couldn't discount Lucian Sand's information. My best friend's murder was a reality, not a joke. Maybe a change of surroundings would clarify my thoughts.

Before heading to Sweet Nothings, I reached out to the law. Mark Andrews was still at work despite the late hour. I'd counted on that. He didn't look like the type to cut out early for a hot date.

"Mrs. Buckley," he drawled, "this is a surprise. What can I do for you?"

I decided to play it cool.

"Just checking in. Any developments on my friend's murder?" After a long pause I stuttered, "Thomas Yancey, I mean. That's his name."

"Thanks for jogging my memory." Sarcasm stung me like a whip's lash. "Still there, Mrs. Buckley?" he asked after a while. "Do you have anything to report?"

"Not really. I hoped you'd found some leads. You know, the crucial first forty-eight hours after a murder …"

Scorn wafted out of the telephone. Andrews was probably enjoying this. "You've been busy, haven't you?" he asked. "You and Ms. Ott couldn't wait to hotfoot it down to CYBER-MED. Beat me to it."

"Now just a minute." By an act of sheer will, I stopped talking. I refused to justify my actions to this cop. Our trip to CYBER-MED had been strictly business. "Back to my first question, Sergeant. Where are we on Tommy's case?"

Andrews didn't soften the blow. "*We* are nowhere, Mrs. Buckley. *I*, on the other hand, have made progress. The impound lot has the car used in the murder, a black Mercedes stolen that very night."

I gasped when he said that word. Murder is a cruel, hard word, but Tommy wore a constant grin that crinkled his eyes. He loved animals and specialized in practical jokes, couldn't wait to spring them on you. Nothing about him was cruel or hard.

"He'd hate that," I said. "Tommy despised Mercedes, called them Nazi cars."

"I'm sure his thoughts were elsewhere that night. Anything else I can help you with?"

"Motive. What was the motive?"

Andrews had exhausted his small store of charm. "When I learn that, I'll make an arrest, unless you and Ms. Ott beat me to it. Now, if there's nothing else …"

I cleared my throat. Andrews is a public servant, and I am one of the public.

"Who owned the car? The one that killed Tommy?"

His sigh was audible. "It belonged to a little old widow from Wellesley who had pasted photos of her Yorkie all over the dashboard and didn't even know it was gone. And before you ask, she's half blind and has no children, nephews or friends connected to Thomas Yancey or CYBER-MED. It's a dead end."

I should have told him about the clippings. Probably should have mentioned Lucian Sand, too, or hinted about Tommy's love life. Something deterred me, something I could never explain. Andrews would sneer at anything I offered now. I didn't have proof. There was plenty of time for that.

~

Sweet Nothings occupied the third floor of a Beaux-Arts building in the shadow of Prudential Center. Its renovation — paint, hardwoods and art — focused more on style than substance. Like Sweet Nothings itself, everything looked young, bright and bursting with optimism.

After a quick nod to Otto, the guard, I strode toward the elevator. The mysterious Lucian Sand had probably sent me on a fool's errand. Something about that man irritated the hell out of me.

The hallway swelled with a cacophony of work noises blended seamlessly with a dash of salsa music and banter. We'd pulled plenty of all-nighters here. Those were good times, filled with hard work, shared purpose and mutual affection. Candy, Kai, Tommy and I had breathed life into a concept and watched it thrive, almost like giving birth. I gulped. No time to dwell on that.

Our conference room is the makeup equivalent of Ali Baba's cave. Every manner of pencil, shadow, lip gloss and foundation is on display, accompanied by a neatly printed card and plenty of mirrors. I shivered at the contrast between this joyous space and my grisly task. Tommy had spent many hours here, planning, arguing and kibitzing. Now I was here pondering his murder.

There are no brick and mortar stores at Sweet Nothings. Our business plan mandates an Internet-only presence. Candy's mission involves scheduling live e-chats to promote new products and answering questions. She's a genius, a natural saleswoman with a pinch of larceny. Employees revere her commitment to quality and her willingness to improve everything. Products are handmade in small batches by local workers, most of whom are holistic zealots.

Before leaving home, I'd done a quick check of Lucian Sand on the Concord University website. His CV was typical of the Northeast intelligentsia, Exeter and MIT, with one glaring exception. His original academic discipline was philosophy, of all things. He had gotten a PhD at the Sorbonne. That explained the whisper of French in his voice. Nothing explained or excused his brusqueness.

The palms of my hands moistened with fear. *Time's up, Lizzie Mae, no more stalling.* I placed the envelope face down on the conference table alongside a bottle of Pellegrino. A tall crystal goblet winked at me as I slowly sipped the bubbly water. Ritual was useful. It distanced me from whatever was to come. Candy is normally the fanciful one; I'm the pragmatist of our duo. Not tonight.

Get on with it, I scolded. *You've waited long enough.* Was someone cooking the books? Tommy had six months to suss it out, and he'd be onto a financial scam faster than a flesh-eating virus. We'd always competed with each other tooth and nail to find the right answer, but Kai laughed at both of us. He had no need to prove himself.

What was Lucian Sand saying? Had someone murdered Tommy to cover up hanky-panky? CYBER-MED was privately held. If the company went public, a mandatory audit of the books would kick in, awkward if someone's fingers were in the financial pie. On the other hand, Tommy's death could also trigger an audit. How else to value his estate properly? I got a sudden mind meld from Estate Law 101. If the parties in a privately held entity agreed, the estate would be valued at fair market value of the shares. No audit. That slick Meg Cahill couldn't wait to buy us out. She and lover boy Rao were shocked when we declined. She had addressed taking CYBER-MED public, too. Said it wouldn't happen for a while, if ever.

I closed my eyes and took a deep, cleansing breath. Mark Andrews would love hearing that theory, especially when I mentioned that Lucian Sand had also made an offer. It proved only that CYBER-MED was an attractive company with savvy investors.

The disc beckoned to me like Circe. After fumbling with the computer, I finally faced it. Sound quality was very poor, but I recognized Tommy's voice instantly. He wasn't his normal jovial self. My stomach flip-flopped as my friend spoke in slow, measured tones.

"You knew I'd find out, didn't you? Don't deny it. Why would you do this? Money? You have no need for blood money."

The reply was inaudible, disembodied. Impossible to tell if it were male or female.

"Fun! Are you insane? People died because of you. I'll find proof just you wait and see. Bastard! You're not so smart."

The tape ended with a raucous laugh.

My heartbeat zoomed. I felt weak and disoriented, unable to breathe. My leg muscles twitched. *Is this it? A heart attack. No one will find me until it's too late.*

Oddly enough, that calmed me. I didn't fear death. Oh, no. The abundance of death enticed me, lured me into the hereafter. I knew that Kai waited there for me. Maybe Tommy was with him, too. I stretched my leg, lessening the muscle cramps.

Hyperventilating again, Lizzie Mae. That refrain had become my constant companion of late.

Candy was home this time, her voice vibrant, bordering on smug. "Where are you, Betts?"

"I'm just leaving Sweet Nothings. Are you alone?"

I heard a masculine rumble and Candy's distinctive laugh. During their numerous quarrels, Tommy swore she brayed like a donkey.

"Arun's just leaving. It's raining outside."

"Stay there. I'll be right over." I scooped my things into a tote and grabbed my umbrella.

The elevator took forever. Old buildings are charming but quirky. Otto was still on guard, peering out into the darkness like a furrowed sentry.

"Want I should get you a cab, Mrs. B.? It's a bitch out there." Political correctness eluded Otto. He was still plowing through the mysteries of the twentieth century, forget about the twenty-first.

Getting a cab on a rainy Boston night was a quest that would flatten Don Quixote. Candy lived only two blocks away. I'd be there before Otto found me a cab.

"Thanks, Otto. I'll walk. I won't melt."

"I don't know, Mrs. B. You're awful sweet." Otto had passed retirement age long ago. He'd earned a few idiosyncrasies.

"Wish me luck." I unfurled my brolly and headed out. It was a sturdy Burberry model we'd found in England. The Brits know all about rain.

I plunged eastward into a web of deserted streets. Before long I heard the distinctive slap of footsteps on the pavement directly behind me. Too close, really. Out of the corner of my eye, I saw a dark figure clad in rain gear.

Another idiot like me without a life.

I quickened my pace. My shadow did, too. A thin finger of fear raced through me as I considered my options. Two blocks, two long city blocks. Was I overreacting, being a fool? Could I outrun whoever it was?

My iPhone nestled somewhere in my tote bag. Close, yet impossibly far. I dared not stop to find it. Why, oh why had I worn high heels tonight? They hobbled me, giving any mugger an incalculable advantage.

The rain slowly subsided, and street lights painted ghostly grins on the sidewalks. I clutched my umbrella, comforted by its hardy ribs, sturdy shaft and sharp ferrule. Fragments from a long ago self-defense course burbled up. Hug the curb; move briskly; show confidence. Those tidbits made more sense in a warm dry classroom with Kai sitting next to me. Tonight they sounded absurdly optimistic.

My pulse reached stratospheric levels as I made a choice. Those well-mannered black pumps flew behind me like grenades. I felt liberated despite my sopping hosiery and aching feet. It was now or never time, possibly do or die. I chose the only path open to me. I ran.

Seven

I ran faster than I ever had, faster than seemed humanly possible. I wouldn't last long running barefoot on the bruised and broken Boston pavement. Some stranger, someone right behind me, wanted me dead. I knew that with a certainty that astounded me.

The adrenaline high was wearing off, leaving me with sharp pains and ragged shreds of breath. One more block, a short one this time. I saw the roof of Candy's building in the distance. Thank God I'd kept my tote. Louis Vuitton doesn't grow on trees, and that thick-coated canvas might stop a bullet if it had to. Stubborn. Stupid even. I should have waited, found a cab.

A slate grey sports car pulled up to the curb, gunning its engine. Porsche Cayenne, I think that's what it was. Kai priced one just like it before he died. Family friendly, he'd said.

Maybe that stabbing pain I felt was just heartbreak. Since Kai died, nothing mattered much anyway. I wanted to look back, confront my pursuer, but that was dumb, a loser's play. What defensive skills did I have other than an agile mind and a powerful set of lungs? A razor sharp tongue doesn't count. Good grades don't cut it on the mean streets. The only test that counts is survival, and I might fail the course.

The engine's roar intensified as someone called my name. A car window rolled down, magnifying the volume. The driver flung the side door open wide.

"Hurry." The voice was unmistakable.

I saw his face, made a choice, and jumped in.

Lucian Sand saved my life.

At first I couldn't speak. Fear, misery or something like it robbed me of my voice. He floored the Porsche, aiming it toward Candy's building.

"How'd you find me?" I croaked.

He calmly shifted into second gear, harnessing the machine's five hundred horses. "What, no thank you?" he asked with a grin, "after I just saved your life?"

"You don't know that. I was running to avoid the rain."

His smile was charming. Cocky, but charming. "You always run barefoot on the streets, Mrs. Buckley? Hard on the toes, no?"

The man was impossible.

"OK, you're right. Did you see who was following me? Was it a man or a woman?"

He swung into the underground garage adjoining Candy's building and found a spot.

"Couldn't tell. Someone fairly tall, though. Could be male or female."

Lucian Sand was no help at all. I unsnapped my seatbelt and opened the door. "Thanks for the ride," I said. "I'll be in touch."

"Hold on." He jumped out and locked his car.

"Where are you going?"

"With you." He steadied me as I limped toward the elevator. "Ms. Ott invited me. Unless you object, of course. That's where I was going when I ran into you."

I swallowed my pride and leaned on him as we entered the lobby. It felt good, leaning on someone else for a change. Candy lived on the penthouse floor, a perk that required a special access key. Her doorman recognized me and waved. "Go right on up, Mrs. Buckley. She's expecting you."

Lucian and I retired to opposite ends of the elevator, each of us maintaining a stony silence. Suspicion hitched a ride with us, too. I don't believe in coincidence, and Professor Sand's sudden appearance was a big one. Perhaps he had engineered the whole thing. What better way to earn my trust and gratitude?

"You never answered my question," I said. "How did you find me?"

He gave one of those elegant Gallic shrugs accompanied by a raised eyebrow. Like most Americans, I'd never mastered that trick. Tommy looked like Quasimodo when he tried it. Candy never even bothered. Only Kai was up to the task. He'd been the ultimate Francophile, honing his language skills and perfecting that shrug.

"Never mind," I said as the door opened.

Candy was waiting for us, bouncing from one foot to another. She stopped short when she saw me. "Oh, my God! What happened, Betts?" She flung her arms around me in a stranglehold. "You're wet! And what happened to your shoes?"

It took her only an instant to size up Lucian Sand. "You must be the professor," she said, eyes twinkling. "Perhaps I should call you Sir Galahad, since you saved my friend from drowning."

He bowed. "At your service, Mademoiselle.

"That's not all," I said. "Someone was following me, I think, until Dr. Sand appeared."

Candy blanched. "Oh, no. This is too weird. When you called, I told Rao ..."

Rao! Where was Arun Rao when I left Sweet Nothings? Candy's building was so close, only two blocks. Maybe he had decided to surprise me. Thrill me to death.

"Where are my manners?" Candy said. "Come in. Have a drink." She herded us into her parlor with a skill reminiscent of Della.

"Give me some hot tea, if you've got it. No caffeine, or I'll never sleep tonight."

Candy grinned at Lucian Sand. "How about you? Tea or something stronger?"

He turned bright azure eyes on her. "Both, if you please."

After lighting the gas fire, Candy bustled off to the kitchen to play hostess while I snuggled under her velvet throw and watched him. Impossibly handsome men have always intimidated me, even Kai. I feel so inadequate next to them.

Lucian Sand was straight from central casting, movie star perfect right down to the ponytail, French accent and awesome abs. His manners could stand improvement, of course. He was probably used to coeds who bowed and scraped to his every whim. That wouldn't happen with me. Unlike most women, I was bulletproof, armor-plated, too numbed by loss to react to mere flesh and blood.

"Did you listen to it?" he asked.

I nodded, not trusting my voice.

"Listen to what?" Candy asked, sweeping into the room with tea and fancy snacks.

That did it. If I ignored her, Candy wouldn't rest until she'd wormed the information out of me. Better to fess up and seize control of the situation.

I fished the disk from my tote. "Here. Dr. Sand shared this with me. See what you think."

Candy is no Einstein, but her survival instincts are first rate She flipped open her laptop, inserting Lucian Sand's prize package. I tried not to listen. It was painful hearing Tommy's solemn voice speaking with his murderer. Candy handled it remarkably well. She switched off the machine and sat quietly, hands folded like a chastened schoolgirl.

Finally, she glanced up and cleared her throat. "OK. What does all this mean?"

"We wondered what got Tommy killed," I said. "There it is. Part of it anyway." I turned toward Lucian. "Unless there's more. I doubt that fudging figures would lead to murder. It would have to be one hell of a scam. You know Tommy. No way could he keep from spilling the beans to us."

Candy bit her lip. That's never good news, especially since she constantly slathers lip gloss on her mouth to keep it moist.

"He tried to, Betts. Tommy, I mean. Remember that last week when he tried to contact you? I spoke with him instead."

"You? What did he want?"

"That's just it. He wouldn't tell me, just said to make you call him. I'm sorry."

I kept my face statue still. Betraying Tommy was bad enough, but I'd be damned if I'd let an arrogant stranger see me cry.

"Now you understand," Lucian said. "The situation is dangerous. I repeat my offer. Sell your shares to me, and stay safe."

Candy cocked her head. "What offer? Don't tell me you want our shares, too?"

"Do the police have this?" I watched him closely.

He gave that stupid shrug again. "Nope. They won't get it either. Not right now. They'll march through CYBER-MED and destroy everything. High tech is precarious. One whisper of scandal, and investors get very squeamish. That company could be worth a fortune some day, and I will not risk it."

My head swam with facts, figures and fears. Sleep was no luxury; it was a necessity.

I patted Candy's back. "I'm going home. Tomorrow, after I've had some sleep, we'll discuss this."

"Stay here, Betts. Your place might not be safe." Candy's lip quivered as if tears weren't far away.

"I can't leave Della alone. Don't worry. I promise to take a cab." I hugged my friend and started for the door. Lucian Sand was right behind me.

"Don't be absurd. My car is right here." He kissed Candy's hand and gave her a half bow. "I will take Mrs. Buckley to her door, I promise."

Exhaustion claimed me, making me pliable for a change. I meekly followed him to his Porsche and climbed in. My eyes closed for just a second. When they opened we were parked outside my home on Commonwealth Avenue.

"How do you know where I live?"

He opened the car door and helped me out. "I know more about you than you'd ever believe." He squeezed my hand as if he had a right to and guided me up the stairs to Della.

"I'll take that disc now," he said.

The man infuriated me. How dare he intrude on my life? Intrude? That's way too mild. He had stomped into my life, demanding things I could never give. He had no right to do that, not when Kai's memory was alive. I didn't want or need a flesh-and-blood man. My husband's spirit was enough.

Lucian stared at me with those mesmerizing orbs of his, blue green, how ridiculous was that? Cold, imperious eyes that froze out anyone who defied him. His accent deepened whenever things annoyed him. Just a touch of France peeked through.

"I need that information," he said. "I mean it, Mrs. Buckley. It's important."

He blocked my path and stood there like a stone pillar. Admittedly, images of Michelangelo's *David* flashed before my eyes, but that didn't change anything. He really was a statue — cold, unyielding marble.

"Forget it," I spat, reaching for my keys. "I'm not giving you anything."

He moved slowly, ineluctably toward me. His eyes had changed. They were closer to mountain rain than glacial pools now. Soft, gentle rain. His fingers moved slowly down my arm, inflaming every nerve.

"So lovely," he whispered. "In France your name would be *Elisa*. Much softer, no? I think I will call you Elisa from now on, if you will permit me."

I gulped, more than once. Sensation was foreign to me. I'd been numbed by grief for so long, unable to react or feel anything but Kai's memory.

This can't be happening. It isn't real.

His lips brushed against my hair like the kiss of a sea breeze. Now I shivered.

"Don't fear me," he said.

The man was so damn cocky!

I tried to move away. Tried and failed. "Leave me alone. You don't scare me. I'm not afraid of anyone."

He tilted my chin toward him, watching me for a second. I was mesmerized, unable to look away.

"You were very brave tonight, *ma petite*. You fought so hard to live." He drew me to him. "Only the living can give you what you need. The dead can't hold you when you feel afraid." His kiss was a gentle promise of much more. For a moment I forgot everything else and floated in a sensual sea of pleasure.

"Stop worshiping ghosts," he whispered. "I'll never leave you alone, my Elisa. That's a promise." Lucian Sand whirled around and vanished down the stairs.

~

"Tell me everything," Candy said. "Come on. Don't be shy, Betts."

She'd called me as soon as I got home, eager to dish the dirt. I'd never admit what happened with Lucian Sand even to Candy, especially to Candy. My feelings were a tangled mass of guilt and rapture, utter folly for a married woman. My eyes stung.

That's the problem, Lizzie Mae. You're not married anymore. Kai's gone, sacrificed to Pan the mountain god.

I felt the flush of deep emotion. Not the sorrow I'd made peace with, but anger, pure, unadulterated anger at the man who had betrayed me by trading our whole life for cheap thrills. For the first time it hit me: I really was alone.

"Oh, my God, is he still there?" Candy's voice was full of hope. "I get it. Don't say a word."

"Of course he's not here. You're the one who has something to tell, Ms. Ott. Dr. Rao made a house call, after all."

I heard her sigh over the phone line. Not a good sign.

"He was a perfect gentleman," Candy said. "Damn it to hell. I think he was tempted, though. Don't you just hate a man with scruples?"

"Hmm. Did he mention anything about Tommy or CYBER-MED, anything that might be useful?"

It took her a moment to respond. I knew she was carefully editing everything that happened that night, sifting through minutiae.

"He asked a lot of questions, mostly about my work at Sweet Nothings. Quite a few about you, too, Betts. He seemed fascinated by our friendship, you know, how the four of us got together and stuff."

"What about Tommy? Any clues about what was bothering him?"

"Nada. Arun's quite a fox, but pretty boring, too. Sang the praises of Dr. Cahill like a church choir, how brilliant she is, what an innovator, blah, blah, blah. If she weren't so old, I'd suspect something was going on between them."

"Hmm. Don't count her out. I'll bet she has a lot of life in her." Time to change the subject. "Arun isn't married, is he? You don't want to become a home wrecker."

"He never mentioned a wife. In fact, he said all he did was work. You know how it is with a startup, sheer drudgery."

I remembered our first year at Sweet Nothings. It had been the best time of my life.

"Betts! You're not listening again."

"I'm exhausted. No more talk until tomorrow. See you then."

I walked Della, undressed, and hit the bed like a granite slab.

~

The next day Sergeant Mark Andrews appeared at Sweet Nothings without an appointment. Judging by his snarls, the aggressively female surroundings brought out the beast in him. No Francie Cohen to act as spirit guide this time; Andrews had to tough it out alone. I normally brush off casual visitors, but one look at his face convinced me that there was nothing casual about this.

"You've been holding out on me, Mrs. Buckley." He remained standing with his bony arms protruding from his pockets. "I thought you cared about your friend."

Today was Della's day to visit the office. She glided up to Andrews, tail wagging, and licked his arm. The cop jumped a mile, then relaxed when he recognized her.

"I like dogs," he admitted as if it were a character flaw. "Wish I could have one."

My feminine wiles are rather rusty. That's Candy's department. I pasted a perplexed smile on my face and said nothing. Fortunately, Candy slithered into the conference room, oozing genteel charm.

"Sergeant? How nice to see you." She motioned to her assistant, who placed a steaming latte and a fruit plate in front of Andrews. "Help yourself. I know policemen never get time for decent meals."

He grunted, torn between hunger and control. Hunger won out. "Very kind of you, Ms. Ott. I got an early start today."

My partner wore a pink silk shirtdress that suited her perfectly. Tommy had dubbed it her "cotton Candy ensemble," a deliberate fashion choice that dazzled onlookers. Candy used wardrobe strategically in a cynical play for control. Most men succumbed, but it had absolutely no effect on Andrews. He was far too busy wolfing down mango slices to care or notice.

"You were saying, Sergeant?" I glanced pointedly at my watch.

He brushed the corners of his mouth with a napkin. The gesture was surprisingly dainty. "Why didn't you tell me about Lucian Sand?"

"Dr. Sand? What about him?" I closed my laptop, uncomfortably aware that my recent research was still displayed on its screen. I'd spent the past hour scanning the tedious academic treatises authored by Lucian Sand. At least he wasn't a total fraud. He had won a slew of national awards and foundation grants. I sensed that something catastrophic had turned him from a brilliant computer nerd to a zealot obsessed by the security of implantable medical devices. The hot doc was prolific: he'd authored numerous articles on the topic and served as Director of LIPS, the Laboratory for Implant Patients' Security. Was CYBER-MED really a rogue operation or one man's warped crusade? Hard to tell.

"He's a wacko, that's what." Andrews' cheeks turned pink. "Complained to the Commissioner about my investigation. Guess whose name came up, Mrs. Buckley?"

I've never been a good guesser. That's why I refuse to play those games. I gave him that blank look you learn in Introduction to Advocacy. "Let's deal with certainty, not speculation, Sergeant. What about my friend's murder? Any progress?"

Candy plowed right in. "Yes, Sergeant. Is there anything we can do to help?"

Andrews bared slightly crooked teeth in a grin. "Tell me about Mr. Yancey's personal life. Any ex-wives, girlfriends, or significant others?" He cocked his head. "Oops. Forgot this is Massachusetts. Any life partners?"

"Certainly not." Candy, that most liberal of souls, bristled. "Tommy was into women in every possible way."

Andrews leaned forward. "Really? Does that include his partner, Dr. Meg Cahill? I'm told she and your friend were exceptionally close."

I forced myself to power down. Tommy and that ... that perky cougar? Impossible.

"Mr. Yancey would have mentioned it. We shared everything."

"Then you knew about the insurance?" Andrews looked smug.

"You're not making sense, Sergeant. Stop hinting around. Just tell us." Candy folded her arms and glowered like a bubble gum goblin.

He tented his hands. "You're right. I apologize. Mr. Yancey's life was insured for a considerable sum, five million dollars payable to CYBER-MED."

Candy's eyes bugged, but I wasn't surprised. "That's a lot, but it's not exceptional, you know. Businesses usually have a key person policy."

"Oh, yeah," Candy said. "Why we had one here when ..."

She looked guiltily at me, knowing the outcome. Kai had been one of the key partners in our business. When he died, Sweet Nothings collected two million dollars, a pittance compared with the enormity of our loss. My loss.

Andrews was a bulldog, I'd give him that. He plunged on, heedless of the consequences. "Look, ladies," he said. "I'm not trying to be a hard ass here. Just tell me this. What made Mr. Yancey worth five million bucks to CYBER-MED?"

I took a deep breath. Where to begin? Would a solid, meat and potatoes guy like Andrews ever understand Tommy? His enthusiasm and impish sense of humor? Rand Lindsay got it perfectly. Tommy inspired his coworkers. He made work fun.

"Startups are unique businesses," I said. "No track record or hoary traditions. You sort of make it up as you go along. Tommy had a rare quality. He was a catalyst who inspired creativity. People loved him."

Somehow I got through that speech without choking up. Everything about Thomas Yancey, his quirky humor, sloppy clothes, and piercing intelligence surfaced in a seismic wave that swamped me.

"Yeah. Sounds nice," Andrews said, "but since when is nice worth five million bucks? Maybe someone decided to cash in."

That annoyed me. I toyed with smashing his bony face but settled instead for reason.

"Tommy did much more than that. He was their CFO, the numbers guy. Not the mundane stuff that accountants drool over. His specialty was strategic finance. There was no one better at it."

Andrews played dumb. At least, I hope he was pretending. Otherwise, law enforcement in Boston is doomed.

"What does that mean, Mrs. Buckley, strategic finance?" He kept his pen poised over a shabby notebook, ready to capture every pearl of wisdom.

Candy threw up her hands. "These MBAs! Always dropping terms like that. They did it at Sweet Nothings, too, in the old days. Tommy, Betts and Kai had their own language. Me, I just dreamed up products and found customers."

She earned a look of gratitude from Andrews, as if he'd found a friend in a foreign world. Like most of her stunts, it was a calculated move designed to snare an ally.

"It's fairly simple," I said. "Tommy plotted directions, strategies and ways to get financing. He had a talent — a gift actually — for making the right financial move at the right time. He was a genius. A star."

"Hmm," Andrews said. "You sound just like Dr. Cahill. Could be reading from the same script." He gave me a steely glare as if expecting an immediate meltdown and confession. That routine came from a playbook too, every bad cop show of the past fifty years.

After a lengthy silence, Andrews continued. "You never answered my first question. What do you know about this Dr. Lucian Sand? Your new colleagues certainly know him."

"He's mega-hot," Candy said. "Smokin'."

Andrews threw up his hands. "That's not quite what I meant, Ms. Ott. I'm interested in this professor's motives. He was banned from CYBER-MED, you know? Caused all kinds of trouble. I even heard that he clashed with Mr. Yancey."

"Tommy?" My surprise was genuine. No need to pretend.

"Yes, Tommy. Dr. Sand got into a shouting match with him last month. Witnesses swear to it. This guy's got quite a temper." Andrews leaned forward. "Might make him lose control."

Candy's face got a greenish tinge that no makeup could eradicate. I knew she was picturing our friend's final moments as he fought for his life. I poured her some Pellegrino and slid it down the table. She's a fainter, hits the deck on a regular basis. Fortunately, I'm not the fragile type. I've only fainted one time in my life. Under the circumstances, most people would understand.

"Is that all, Sergeant? We have several appointments this afternoon." I rose and guided Andrews toward the door. "We'd like to make arrangements for a memorial service. Any problem with that?"

Ichabod Crane Andrews gave his cadaverous grin. Maybe it worked in Sleepy Hollow. In Boston, it was a nonstarter.

"In due time, Mrs. Buckley. We're not ready to release Mr. Yancey's body yet."

Candy gave a strangled cry. That was all the encouragement Andrews needed to get out of Dodge. As he grabbed his folder and slipped through the conference room door, he fired one final shot.

"Remember what I said, Mrs. Buckley. Stop screwing around."

Eight

Candy clutched the stem of her water goblet in a death grip. She looked wan, drained of her usual vitality. Luckily today was her product-sampling day. She assembled enthusiastic focus groups twice a month. These women — and a few men — vied to spend two hours with the legendary Candace Ott. They willingly slathered creams, conditioners and scrubs on their bodies in return for personalized advice and fantastic goody baskets filled with Sweet Nothings products. Volunteers signed up months in advance via Candy's blog. It was what we business school types call "a win-win."

I never participated. Because of my job I wore makeup, used hair products, the whole nine yards. *Noblesse oblige* and all that. I endured it but never loved it like Candy and her minions. Modeling products was an integral part of our business strategy. Both Tommy and Kai had used our men's line. Kai fluffed his luscious locks with a hint of gel, while Tommy stuck to pomade. They had been a toothsome duo, those two. My heart ached.

Andrews had done me a favor. It was strictly inadvertent, but there it was. I'd almost forgotten about those clippings Tommy had sent. Since Rand blabbed about Mary Alice Tate, I knew she was a client. My task was to determine if Judge Jacob Arthur, Ian Cotter or Richard Chernikova were clients of CYBER-MED. Tommy was never fanciful. He had sent those unadorned clippings for some reason. I thought about the disk. It was someone he knew, someone capable of murder. Probably affiliated with CYBER-MED but maybe not. After all, he'd made plenty of contacts at Sweet Nothings and elsewhere.

I checked the listings in my iPhone and phoned Meg Cahill's private line. She answered on the first ring, sprightly as ever. We exchanged social niceties, then got down to business. There was much to admire about her, but I knew we could never become friends. That veneer of sticky pseudo-sweetness was a big turnoff. Kai always said my major liability as a lawyer was that I had no talent for duplicity. Nevertheless, I simpered a few bits of nonsense before closing the conversational gap.

"Listen, Meg, I'll get right to the point. I know how important Tommy was to CYBER-MED."

Wariness crept into her voice. "You're so right. Rao and I contacted an executive search firm only today. Perhaps you can join us when we interview candidates, Elisabeth."

"Excellent. Until then, you can make use of my services. Tommy and I had the same academic training, and we shared the financial duties at Sweet Nothings. Ms. Ott and I have already discussed it, and I can handle both positions with no problem."

Meg Cahill gulped. She covered it with a weak cough, but I got the message. For once in her life this pillar of rectitude was speechless. Dare she risk offending the majority partners? Probably not. I sweetened the deal by dangling some bait in front of her.

"I'll only be available on a temporary basis, of course. Assessing the business will really be useful." I lowered my voice. "Confidentially, my partner is inclined to sell her shares once Tommy's estate is probated, but she wants a fair settlement. I'm still undecided."

Meg clucked sympathetically. "I understand entirely."

"So. How does that sound?"

"Exciting, Elisabeth. Why don't we meet tomorrow to discuss it? Rao is gone for the day, or I'd conference him in right now."

"Great. I'll be there at nine with Ms. Ott."

~

"Are you crazy?" Candy asked. "What are you trying to prove?" She was working up to a major fit of pique. All the signs were there: wringing hands, mascara tracks, trembling lips. I'd seen it all before, and I knew how to handle her. I channeled my inner cherub.

"It's not about me, Candy. Tommy sent me a message, and I plan to decipher it. Staying at Sweet Nothings won't help one bit." I patted her shoulder. "I won't let him down again or you either."

She closed her eyes and started chanting. Whatever mantra she used, it worked.

"OK. I get it, but that place might be dangerous." She threw her arms around me and squeezed. "Oh, Betts. If something happens to you, I'll die. I can't stand any more loss."

Loss. I was an expert on that topic. Without Kai, I'd spent the past year only half alive, a zombie. Now after twelve months of wandering aimlessly, I was finally focused. CYBER-MED might be my destruction or salvation. Either way, it was put up or shut up time. I almost convinced myself that it had nothing at all to do with Lucian Sand.

Della curled at my feet while I spent the afternoon researching. There was a ton of material about Judge Jacob Arthur. Some of it was the society fluff endemic to the fabulously wealthy. His family owned one of the largest private banks in the nation, and Arthur dabbled in philanthropy. It shocked me to realize that I'd actually met the man several times. Kai was a major booster of Angel Memorial Animal Hospital, and a few weeks before he died we'd taken Della to their Furry Affair fundraiser. Jacob Arthur had been the enthusiastic, somewhat pompous master of ceremonies, presiding over the auction with a firm bang of his judicial gavel. Funny, I'd totally forgotten him in the filmy haze of that special night. I'd just learned that I was pregnant. Kai was so ecstatic that he couldn't keep his hands off me. We had toasted with Pellegrino instead of Cristal and danced the night away. One month later Kai was gone and so was our son.

Focus, Lizzie Mae. Focus. Bury the past.

When Candy poked her head in the door an hour later, she caught me dozing at my desk. No energy crisis for her. She'd adjusted her attitude and banished her tears. I could tell by the flawless makeup that adorned her face. Experience told me that any attempt to ignore her was doomed. In her manic state, Candy's impervious to snubs and slights. She leaned over my computer and pointed.

"Well, what do you know? Look at the couple of the year."

I zoomed in on the images section and gasped. There, bigger than life, was a photo of the late Judge embracing none other than Dr. Meg Cahill. What followed was a short blurb on implanted medical devices, which were hailed as a huge breakthrough in quality care. Lots of kudos to the medical community, especially cardiologist Margaret Cahill. According to her patient, Jacob Arthur, his pacemaker had saved his life more than once. The article coincided with the startup of CYBER-MED, a company designed to monitor such devices.

"My God, Betts, we're two for two so far. Arthur and Mary Alice." Candy shivered. "I'll bet you'll find that Ian character was involved too. Every woman I knew either trained with him or wanted to." She winked. "They said he exercised every muscle in your body, even ones your husband hadn't worked in years, if you get my drift." She hugged herself. "It's … it's not really funny. I'm scared."

"Hold on. Let's analyze this thing calmly. After all, people with medical problems die all the time no matter how closely they're monitored. Even if CYBER-MED had all of them as clients, the worst case would be negligence. That keeps lawyers like me in business. You know how cautious Tommy was. He was paranoid about lawsuits and probably wanted to run that stuff by me."

Candy pointed an accusing finger at me. "What did Dr. Dreamy say about that? Something about dangerous short-cuts, right?"

"I didn't really listen to him. He's a fanatic. I told you that." I turned my face toward the window to avoid her gimlet eye. Why did I bother?

"Elisabeth Mae Buckley, you're blushing." Candy forgot her night terrors and spun me around. "What really happened last night with Luc? Come on, spill."

"Nothing." I bent over my briefcase and grabbed a pen.

"I know. He made love to you, didn't he? Frenchmen are so passionate."

"Certainly not! He only kissed me." Oops. I was out of practice keeping secrets.

Those cat eyes glowed with excitement. Candy was more turned on than I was.

"Kissed you? Tell me everything." She sat on the corner of my desk.

"It was a mistake. You know I'm not interested in men. I'm still with Kai."

Her sigh filled the room. "Honey, I loved Kai too. He was special, but you can't spend your life in mourning. You'll be mummified like a museum relic. You're young. You need a flesh and blood man, one who can give you babies."

Aristotle called friendship a single soul dwelling in two bodies. Ari never met Candace Ott. Her rapacious soul trampled my tender feelings without a scintilla of guilt. Still, I couldn't lash out. She was all I had.

"I'll verify this tomorrow once I get settled at CYBER-MED. I'm sure it's something innocuous."

She fingered my silver letter opener. "Tommy's dead. Murdered. That's not innocuous. And what about that tape?"

"Forget about that stuff. I'll start with the financials tomorrow and see where that leads." This time I was the one pointing a finger. "And you butt out. No more matchmaking or mooning over Lucian Sand unless you want him for yourself. Agreed?"

Candy gave a little half smile and nodded. "Dr. Dreamy doesn't want me anyhow. Must have a thing for redheads." She twirled a ringlet around her pinky. "Besides, I have a date tonight. Arun is taking me to L'Espalier. I'm so psyched."

"Wow, you must have made quite an impression. That's pretty pricey." L'Espalier, the pride of Boylston Street, was one of Boston's best restaurants. I hadn't been back there in some time.

"What about you? Want to tag along?"

I chuckled at that one. "Yeah, it's my dream to chaperone you. Go along and have fun. Della and I have some things to do here. And don't worry. I'll be very careful."

~

There were plenty of items about Secretary of State Richard Chernikova, but none of them mentioned IMDs or CYBER-MED. I felt reasonably certain that he had an insulin pump and positive that his medical business would remain his own. Chernikova was a polarizing figure around the world, accused of being a Zionist or a cowboy, depending on the political bent of his enemy. Personally, I admired his blunt pragmatism. He had been a rousing commencement speaker at our law school graduation. Kai's family had once owned a summer home near the Chernikovas, and he'd described them as solid people with a bent for public service. His endorsement was good enough for me.

At six-thirty Della gave me the eye. Herding dogs are masters of that. It helps them control the sheep and move the flock. Being a docile ewe, I gathered my things, preparing to leave for the day. Then the phone rang.

I stared at the receiver like a mesmerized cobra. I knew who it was, even before I saw Concord University on the caller ID. *No need to be a fool. Answer the damn thing, Lizzie Mae. Stop playing the ingénue.*

"Mrs. Buckley," I said firmly.

He paused. "I've been thinking of you, Elisa."

Naturally, with that whisper of French it sounded so damn sexy. I tried desperately to regroup.

"Dr. Sand? How may I help you?"

He laughed. A guffaw, really. Deep and masculine. "We don't have to discuss that now. Are you ready for dinner?"

"Dinner?" I sounded like a rube unaccustomed to the ways of society. "Actually, I was just getting ready to go home. Della's with me."

"Wonderful. I'm right outside your building." Lucian Sand was conceited. Quite boorish. My heart started thudding like a bongo.

"I … I can't go out tonight. Tomorrow's a big day for me."

"I'm an excellent cook," he said. "Frenchmen always are."

"I haven't shopped. I have nothing at home. I don't cook much anymore."

Why be defensive about the contents of my refrigerator? I patted my hair. There was just too much of it springing around my head in an auburn blaze. I grabbed a mirror. At least I had some makeup on. Enough to pass for human, anyway.

"Dr. Sand ..."

"Lucian, remember? You can't starve a man who's kissed you. It's against the Geneva Convention."

That made me laugh. "OK. Della and I will be out in five minutes, but I can't stay up late."

"Understood. I'll be waiting."

As I locked my office, it suddenly dawned on me. My phone's unlisted. How in the hell did Lucian Sand get a private number?

I discovered a bit later that he didn't lie. If anything, he'd been modest. To the strains of cool jazz, Lucian Sand whipped up a feast fit for the gods. It was thoroughly French, *coq au vin,* and incredibly luscious. He was more at home in my own kitchen than I was.

While he did the dishes, I stretched out on the sofa, thinking about the last time a man had cooked for me. Six months ago Tommy had arrived uninvited, wearing a chef's toque. Despite my protests he had prepared the only dish he knew, *huevos rancheros.* Then he'd poured us both a flute of Cristal and proposed a toast to Kai.

"He was my best friend," Tommy said. "Because of me, because of my clumsiness, he died. I'm sorry, Betts, so sorry I took Kai from you."

We'd talked a little, cried a lot, and held each other. Afterward, Tommy sacked out in the guest room while I led Della to bed, feeling emptier than before.

"Tired?" Lucian asked. "Don't move. It's OK."

I bolted upright, shocked to find my head nestled in his lap. I felt embarrassed, mortified and so good.

"I'm sorry, Lucian. I didn't mean to doze off. You must think I'm a horrible hostess."

He leaned forward, brushing my forehead with his lips. "I think that you are way too hard on yourself. In France a little nap after dinner is a compliment to the cook." He unbuttoned my suit jacket and gently ran his fingers over my collarbone, making my whole body shudder. I bit my lip to keep from crying out.

"You're very beautiful, Elisabeth. Do you know that?" He stroked my hair, savoring each silky strand. "Too beautiful to be lonely."

I hauled myself up and faced him. "Alone isn't the same as lonely. I have Della and my work."

"Work can't keep you warm at night," Lucian said. "I know that better than most." He massaged the tense muscles of my neck with strong, deliberate strokes. When "Angel Eyes" started playing, he pulled me to my feet. "Dance with me," he whispered.

He was taller than me by several inches. Shorter than Kai, but still tall and well muscled. Lucian held me so tightly I thought I might faint. His hand moved slowly down my back, caressing every inch of me while his lips planted soft kisses on my neck. When the song finished we broke apart and stood watching each other warily in the dim light. I felt feverish, ready to melt. Yearning that I hadn't felt in months stirred in me, followed immediately by overwhelming guilt. I turned away and almost wept.

"You're not ready yet, are you?" he asked. "Things have to be just right for us."

"Everything's confused. I need your help," I told him. "There's something I must do for Tommy and for myself."

~

I was taking a big risk. What did I really know about Lucian Sand? He was a gorgeous hunk of man with the power to shake my soul. Check. But I knew nothing about his motives. Why burrow into my heart? Perhaps my shares of CYBER-MED were the attraction, not me. Every childhood insecurity welled up in me. I was a wealthy woman who might seem like easy pickings. Just because Kai loved me, it didn't mean I was irresistible. Far from it. I had eyes and a mirror. I knew better. Still, Tommy counted on me to make things right. I had to trust someone.

"Your plan might be dangerous," Lucian said after I'd sketched the broad outlines for him. "You have no idea who was on that recording. Odds are it was someone at CYBER-MED. Someone who murdered your friend. Someone who followed you last week."

He was absolutely right. For all I knew the mystery voice might even be Dr. Lucian Sand playing a treacherous double game with a needy, credulous woman. I banished that thought and the self-doubt that accompanied it.

"No one at CYBER-MED will take me seriously," I said. "Not as a threat. To them I'm just a nerdy lawyer checking out their books and asking money questions. It would be more suspicious if I didn't poke around. Candy and I are the majority partners, after all."

He grumbled for a moment, then took my hand. "How can I help you?"

"Tell me why you left CYBER-MED. Sergeant Andrews thinks you're a lunatic."

His full lips twisted in a smile. "And you, what do you think, Elisa?"

I matched his smile and upped the wattage. "I'm undecided."

"Fair enough. I was hired as a consultant to CYBER-MED. You know I'm the president of LIPS, I guess. We do a lot of work on cyber-safety, especially when patient information's involved. Anyway, Arun Rao knew me from the high tech circuit. We'd been on a few panels together. He offered me a consulting contract, and I accepted."

I poured each of us a glass of wine. Don't ask about the vintage. It was a bottle of red from Kai's stock, so it had to be good. I felt comfortable puttering around, performing housekeeping chores. They spared me from meeting Lucian Sand's liquid gaze. Those eyes disturbed me, mesmerized me. His name should be Rasputin, for God's sake.

"Things went well at first," he said. "Most of the staff at CYBER-MED are quite competent. Lots of MIT people. Then I noticed things, small things at first, that troubled me."

He took my hand and kissed it. Damn! How could I concentrate with those azure orbs watching everything? I used Della as a distraction. Anything to regain my senses.

"What kind of things bothered you? Safety violations or procedural things?"

"Both. When lives are involved, even procedures are important. I told them that both the patient information and security of those devices were at risk. I demonstrated how easy it would be to compromise them."

"What?" Dr. Dreamy sounded more like Dr. Death at this point. Della's head shot up, and she gave both of us a reproving look.

"Not on a real patient. I got some things from Radio Shack and did a simulation, showed them how easily I could activate one of their defibrillators. Rand Lindsay helped me. Poor guy. He almost lost his job over that."

"So who went ballistic? And what did Tommy think?"

Lucian hesitated. "Your friend was cautious. Concerned about finances. Truthfully, I think he wanted to do a cost/benefit analysis first. My proposal would have hurt the bottom line in the short run. Long term, it was the only viable solution."

That sounded just like Tommy. He was generous to a fault with his own money but wary with the corporate purse. Something must have spooked him. Otherwise, he would never have sent me those clippings. We had often used each other as sounding boards back in the days when I was a whole person instead of a wraith. Tommy had reached out to his old partner, the sprightly Betts who loved to banter with him, hoping for a miracle. I winced, thinking how tedious it must have been dealing with me.

"How did the others react, Dr. Cahill and Arun Rao?"

Lucian frowned. "Dr. Cahill listened calmly to me, left the room and never spoke with me again. Arun was the hatchet man. He swore if I ever came back to CYBER-MED or shared my concerns, they would destroy my reputation." That memory made him chuckle. "He wasn't kidding either. Meg has the connections to do just that. Her husband is a big donor to Concord University, and his word carries weight."

Arun Rao's name kept popping up everywhere I went. He didn't frighten me, but I was concerned for Candy. What if he abused her or broke her heart? She was naïve, almost child-like when it came to romance. I knew she was already sizing Arun up for the role of Prince Charming.

"Tell me something," I asked. What kind of guy is this Rao? He's been hanging around acting very interested in my partner. Tonight he's even taking her to L'Espalier. Most men expect something when they lay out that kind of money."

That amused Lucian, transforming him with a sudden smile that caught me unaware. "Is that your experience, Mrs. Buckley? Men still want their dates to put out?"

I could feel the slow blush of shame burning my cheeks. "Well, no. That is, I'm out of the dating game, but I understand that things haven't changed much. So answer me. Is he a predator, a married man who woos unsuspecting females?"

Some men have perfect profiles. Lucian Sand's should have been on a coin or in the Louvre. I hoped it wouldn't end up on a police blotter.

"You really know how to turn a phrase, you know that?" There was that sexy smile again. "The French have better words for it. Roue, rake. Take your pick."

He had a talent for making me feel like a schoolgirl. It was also a strategy for deflecting questions too awkward to answer.

"You're making fun of me again," I said. "I'm serious. Candy means a lot to me."

Relax," he said. "As far as I know, Arun isn't married or a predator. He is somewhat of an opportunist, though. He and Meg are as thick as thieves when it comes to CYBER-MED. Arun didn't even flinch when he threatened me."

He raked his mop of sun-streaked hair with strong, probing fingers. A man with great hair is such a turn-on. I caught myself before my silent comparison of Kai and Lucian took root. Both had major league locks.

"Weren't you worried?" I asked. "What about your career?"

Something about him made me wonder. The blasé attitude, expensive car and designer duds weren't typical of a professor living on a monthly stipend. Might have been family money, of course. Kai's life had been cushioned by that. Another less attractive option reared its ugly head. The money trail might lead to something illegal. I had only his word about Tommy, and Lucian Sand was still a stranger.

He dismissed my concerns with a wave of his hand. "I'm not ambitious. Position and jobs are not things that concern me." He squeezed my arm. "I'm not driven like you."

Those words stung me like a Sea Wasp's spine. All my life I'd studied, worried, competed to be the best. Tommy and I had enjoyed matching wits, making each other achieve successively higher goals. Candy and Kai were different. She had opted out of the academic grind, focusing on the creative things that she did best. Kai was the most self-confident man I'd ever met. His effortless brilliance dazzled me as much as his physical perfection. We were an odd quartet with a strangely symbiotic relationship that made Sweet Nothings hum. Those days were gone now, recaptured only in my dreams.

"Did you hear me, Elisa?" Lucian touched my arm again. "I meant no disrespect. A woman with fire, she is irresistible. You draw me like a flame." His eyes crinkled. "And I am the poor moth, doomed to burn."

I dismissed his flowery speech and focused on my task. "You never explained how you got that disk or my unlisted phone number."

He sipped his wine, pensive now. "Let's say a friend gave them to me. I still have some contacts at CYBER-MED. Things are difficult there." Lucian gave me a long, cool look. "You're the MBA. Who better than you to decipher your friend's records?"

His arrogance was as sobering as a splash of ice water. I was finally in control of my body, able to resist any overtures this professor might make. Once again, I used Della as my backup.

"You'll have to excuse me, Lucian. Della needs her bedtime walk."

He uncoiled his sinewy frame with spectacular grace. There was something almost feline about his movements.

"I could use some exercise," he said snapping his fingers at Della. "I'll go with you. Besides, you need someone to watch your back."

Lucian had an almost fey sense about him. Della strained to reach him, dropping down at his feet.

"Tell me how you met my husband," I said. "How did you know Kai?"

"I met him once right before he died. Can't say that I really knew him. Mr. Yancey introduced him as his lawyer. We had a beer and discussed CYBER-MED. Several beers, as it turned out."

"That makes sense. Tommy respected Kai's judgment. What happened?"

"They were troubled by something. Both of them. Your husband quizzed me about my suspicions, wanted proof, a typical lawyer." Lucian laughed and took my hand. "I liked him, Elisabeth. He was the kind of man I could admire and perhaps be friends with."

I gulped and bit my lip. "Most people reacted that way. Kai had a presence. Even now I can feel it."

Lucian moved closer, putting his arms around me. For a moment I thought … surely he wasn't wearing Creed? It couldn't be.

He gave me a gentle squeeze. "My beautiful Elisa, you need more than memories. Some day, I will make new ones with you."

His certainty confused me. This man was a stranger, yet his actions were so intimate.

"How can you say that? You don't even know me."

"You're wrong," Lucian whispered. "I've known you forever."

Nine

Sleep eluded me that night. Lucian planted a chaste kiss on my forehead, patted Della, and disappeared from everywhere but my thoughts. After tossing and turning, I slipped into a troubled sleep that left me restless. As usual in times of stress, Kai crept into my dreams like a sneak thief. I felt his strong arms holding me, thrilled to the feel of his lips brushing gently across my skin. As his fingers kneaded the sensitive spots on my body, he softly murmured my name. Suddenly I pulled away. Something was wrong. Kai didn't sound like that. In slow motion, he turned his face toward me. Instead of my husband, I saw sun-streaked hair and sea blue eyes. He'd morphed into Lucian Sand.

I leapt up, feeling shaken and ashamed. *You're pathetic, Lizzie Mae, fantasizing about a stranger.* Kai would have teased me mercilessly; Tommy would have crowed like a rooster.

Not an auspicious start to my first official day at CYBER-MED. Fortunately, wardrobe was no problem. Candy had already sent me an e-mail mapping out each detail from lingerie to pumps. I deleted her message. This was a business venture, not a fashion show. I'd adapt to CYBER-MED's corporate culture by wearing something dull and unremarkable, a navy suit and Ferragamos that spelled serious and sensible. My goal was to blend in, not stand out like a parrot in a henhouse.

After feeding Della, I wound my hair into a knot, donned a pair of heavy, black-framed glasses and strolled out the door. For the first time in ages there was a spring in my step, a feeling of anticipation. Those months of passivity were an ill-fitting garment sloughed off and replaced with a growing sense of purpose. Maybe my quest was futile, even dangerous. No matter. The old Elisabeth Buckley, lively and intellectually tough, was slowly reasserting herself.

A badge and access card awaited me at the front desk of CYBER-MED. High marks to someone for efficiency, probably Rand Lindsay. I couldn't imagine Dr. Cahill doing such mundane chores. The divine Arun Rao was another matter. According to Candy's most recent report, his talents were limitless.

I settled into Tommy's old office, comforted by his lingering presence. Inside the top desk drawer I found his usual assortment of topless pens and markers. That man could not remember tops or caps to save his otherwise tidy life. The side drawer yielded something more personal: his iPod, loaded with many of the tunes we had all adored. Some of them were real oldies: "Light My Fire," "My Girl," and his special favorite, "The Gambler." I closed my eyes, revisiting the nights we'd danced, smoked a bit and sung those songs. Others might call it morose, but those happy memories strengthened me. Just as Tommy was with me now, Kai's spirit had never left me. It never would.

"Getting settled, Mrs. Buckley?" Meg Cahill's sprightly voice bolted me out of the chair. "Oh, excuse me. Did I startle you?"

Gritting my teeth might come in handy at CYBER-MED. It's a gift.

I waved her into the corner chair. "No problem. I was just thinking of Tommy. He was part of my life for a long time, longer even than my husband."

Physicians are used to maudlin ramblings. Dr. Cahill gave me a neutral, professional smile that never quite reached her eyes. "Of course. We can find you other space if this is too painful for you."

I shook my head. "Oh, no. I'm very comfortable here." The next move was hers, so I stayed silent.

Meg crossed her legs, giving me a peek of a surprisingly sexy chemise. "I have to ask you this. Have the police shared any theories with you? Have they speculated why Thomas ... why he died?"

I responded like a lawyer by saying very little. "What did Sergeant Andrews tell you about Tommy's murder?"

She flinched at the word murder. That's why I'd used it. People longed to sanitize things, to pretend my friend's death was routine. A crime like murder didn't intrude into the tidy, prosperous world of Meg Cahill and Arun Rao. It ravaged lesser beings.

"He said it was deliberate." Meg flexed her hands. "I find that hard to believe."

To my surprise, the perfect manicure of yesterday was gone. Polish on her right thumb and forefinger had chipped off leaving a crazy quilt pattern of mauve. I'd done things like that myself when I was worried or angry. What was Meg Cahill's story?

"Tommy was incredibly fit," I said, "a natural athlete. He could have escaped almost anything." I gulped. "A car isn't your normal adversary."

"You believe that policeman?" Meg asked. There was a trace of asperity in her voice now.

Before I could digest that, Arun Rao rapped lightly on the glass and stuck his head in. "Hey, Elisabeth. Welcome. I'll send in Tommy's assistant to get you settled." His arms were filled with file boxes. "Naturally, everything we have is on disk. We're a virtually paperless office." He bared those perfect teeth. "Still, you know how it is."

"Were there any sensitive cases that involved Tommy? You know, pending or threatened litigation, anything that might impact on CYBER-MED?" I had nothing to lose by taking a risk.

"I don't understand," Meg said. "Aren't you interested in our fiscal picture?"

"Of course." I reached for my Mont Blanc. "Risk assessment is all part of it, as I'm sure you know. Tommy and I both specialized in strategic finance. Damage to CYBER-MED's reputation would cause waves and lower share value."

Arun played for time by shifting the boxes in his arms. "I can't think of anything. Rivalries exist, of course. That's pretty routine in any business." He flashed his grin. "Even cosmetics, I'll bet."

"No one ever died from using lip gloss," I said with my sweetest smile. "What can you tell me about Ian Cotter? Tommy had a file on him at home."

Meg Cahill leapt to the edge of her seat. "Oh, my God! He kept files at home?"

She clasped her hands into a knot. "That's a serious violation of CYBER-MED policy. There are privacy implications. You're a lawyer. You should know that."

Rao read the signals. He sped over to Meg's chair and put his arm on her shoulder.

"Steady, Meg. After all, Mrs. Buckley is part of CYBER-MED now. I'm sure she appreciates the confidentiality clause in our contracts."

Their eyes met in a gesture of shared intimacy. Lucian was right. Those two were closer than mere colleagues should be. I'd bet Arun was responsible for the sparkle in Meg's eyes. Poor Candy.

I flashed the bland corporate smile that covered a million sins. "Now, where were we? Oh, yes, Ian Cotter."

Meg's angst vanished, replaced by the media savvy Dr. Cahill who never cracked. "Ian Cotter was one of our clients. He'd had a defibrillator implanted by one of Boston's top surgeons. The whole procedure went fine. No incidents."

I watched as she slowly peeled off more of that mauve polish. "CYBER-MED monitored the pump. All indicators were normal; every fail-safe was in place." She motioned to Rao.

His handsome face set in grim lines as he recounted the story. "Ian was a good guy, lots of fun. I trained with him myself. Anyhow, we followed his surgeon's instructions and set up a 24-7 continuous monitor on that pump."

It wasn't easy keeping myself in the neutral zone. I longed to shake Candy's dreamboat like a terrier with a rat. The man was unbearably tedious. *Get on with it.*

"The theory was simple: if his heartbeat got erratic, the defib would stabilize him, alert our center, and we'd communicate directly with his doctor. Those things work like a charm."

"Except when they don't." I scoured any trace of blame from my voice.

Meg Cahill nodded. "Ian was a ladies' man, a Don Juan, actually. But charming, very charming. You must have read about it. They found him in the bed of a married woman. She said he hadn't complained about anything, except being … aroused."

Arun Rao picked up where she left off. "Something happened. The device activated and shocked him into eternity." His mouth was set in a thin, hard line. "CYBER-MED had no liability whatsoever. The maker of the device settled up with his family."

"Really? Ian was married?"

Meg's reply was an arctic blast. "Yes, although I don't see what that has to do with anything. His wife was devoted to him. She understood that Ian was … hypersexual, I guess you'd call it. He loved her, and she knew it."

"Surely you were monitoring his condition," I said. "What went wrong?"

"Nothing. I just told you that." Rao quickly lowered his voice. "Forgive me, Mrs. Buckley. It's just so frustrating. Our technician saw the screen and immediately called his physician and paramedics, but it was too late. Tony Torres is our finest operative. He would have noticed if anything went wrong."

Meg Cahill gave a hard, dry laugh. "Our procedures were perfect, but the patient died. Apparently, the device believed that Ian was flatlining and took action." She shivered even though the temperature was anything but cold. "It's so bizarre, like something from a science fiction movie. It killed a perfectly healthy man, my patient." She saw the look of shock on my face. "Oh, not recently. When I was in practice, Ian Cotter was my favorite patient. He was my trainer, too."

"I'm sorry, Meg. Isn't there some kind of fail-safe, you know, where CYBER-MED makes sure things are OK?"

"Impossible. The chances of a defibrillator running rogue are a million to one. This isn't the Twilight Zone, Mrs. Buckley. There are thousands of lines of code involved."

I kept my smile in place. "Call me Elisabeth, please. It's a lot friendlier."

"OK, Elisabeth. Jesus, you sound just like Tommy. He was obsessed with this Ian Cotter thing. Wouldn't let it go."

Opportunity knocked, and I put out the welcome mat.

"Any other skeletons in the corporate closet?" I flushed. "I'm sorry. That's a terrible metaphor. I know you have many prominent clients. Judges, politicians."

Meg slowly rose to her feet. "We've gained the trust of the medical community. Forgive me for overreacting, but in this business, reputation is everything. One casual slur or loose comment, and CYBER-MED is finished."

"I met Dr. Lucian Sand yesterday. Want to tell me about him?"

Rao lit up like a traffic light. "Him! That bastard used us, gained our trust and tried to ruin CYBER-MED. When I think that I was the one who endorsed him ..."

This time Dr. Cahill played peacemaker. "I don't understand, Elisabeth. What's your connection with Lucian Sand?" Her lips twisted in a faint smirk. "Oh, he's handsome enough, I'll grant him that. But I must warn you, stay away from him. Sand is nothing less than an extortionist. Thomas knew all about him."

Tommy again. He was in the room as surely as if he'd called the meeting. Whatever caused his murder was here at CYBER-MED, too. I was sure of it.

"Dr. Sand says you take dangerous shortcuts to conserve costs. True or false?"

Meg straightened her charcoal suit skirt, brushing off imaginary lint. "Look. Lucian is very talented, but like many scientists, he's a zealot with no head for business. If we employed every safeguard he proposed, we'd be bankrupt in six months." She beckoned to Rao and headed out the door. "You check the financials. Our profit margin is razor thin right now. We're doing a hell of a job balancing patient care with fiscal prudence. That's a tribute to your friend Thomas. The man was amazing."

When I glanced up, the office was empty except for me and the spirit of the man who inhabited it. Meg was right. Tommy was amazing. A wave of grief washed over me like a tsunami. How would I ever survive without Tommy and Kai? Did I want to survive without them? Lucian's words echoed in my brain. How come the man felt so familiar to me? I resolved to avoid him until this business with CYBER-MED was over. If only Kai were here, we would analyze the situation point by point and come to a conclusion. Feeling alone and hopelessly inadequate, I sat down at Tommy's desk. For some weird reason, Andrews and company hadn't taken his computer. Cahill and Rao had probably threatened him with a slew of injunctions. I tapped the Enter key, knowing that the password protection would defeat me. The computer was denuded of all traces of CYBER-MED. That information was probably contained in the disks Rao left for me.

I spent ten minutes idly trying a variety of passwords. Della, nope. Sweet Nothings, no luck. Then I recalled a conversation about childhood nicknames. He had whooped about mine, realizing that he'd hit a sensitive spot. Giraffe was something I'd rather forget. Candy's had been Sugar Plum. Leave it to her to have a sweet, sexy moniker. Kai's was another great one: Pan, the same mountain god who took him away. Tears stung me as I thought about that one. Then I recalled Tommy's childhood nickname, Topper. It was an allusion to a character in an old television series and his annoying habit of losing tops and lids. I input the word and waited. Suddenly, I was in. Tommy's directory lit up, giving me access to his private world.

Ten

His personal things were stored in files with vanilla, non-threatening names. I opened one entitled Black Book and quickly scanned the list. My God, Tommy was a veritable satyr. Next to each woman's name and address was a list of preferences, sexual and material, as well as any editorial comments he cared to add. None registered with me until I hit the letter C. Dear Lord, Candy was right. He'd done his perky partner Meg in ways I didn't even want to consider. According to this, Dr. Cahill was a woman with lusty, unconventional tastes in apparel and sexual positions. Ugh.

A knock at the door spared me. I quickly saved the file and exited from the computer before Rand Lindsay came wandering in.

"Hey, Ms. Buckley," he said in his soft Alabama drawl. "Here I am, ready to help again." He pointed to the sofa. "May I? I've been chasing around half the night. Midterms, you know." He lowered his bulk into the soft, yielding furniture and exhaled. "Well. I see you've survived the first day of the inquisition. Whatever you told them, it must have been a doozy. Rao was spitting nails, and Dr. M. had that fire-breathing dragon stare on her face." He rubbed his palms together. "Not so bad for day one."

I liked this guy. If only I knew enough about him to trust him with my concerns. Caution won over neediness. I summoned my inner waif and shrugged.

"I hope I wasn't too blunt. After all, it wasn't a client meeting. They're my partners."

Rand waved his meaty arm. "Ah, don't sweat it. They'll get over it. Just for fun, tell me what you asked."

His baby blues weren't quite so guileless anymore. Rand was an old soul, full of wisdom and a healthy dose of mischief.

"OK," I said. "I asked about Ian Cotter."

He spilled a slug of Coke on his shirt, coughing. "Holy Cow! Dr. Cahill never talks about Ian. I mean never. I'm surprised you even know about him, his connection with us, I mean."

"I saw a picture of him with Dr. Cahill on the Internet. Funny that the *Globe* never made the connection."

Rand wagged his finger at me. "Not so surprising when you figure that Carter Cahill is one of its major advertisers. He put big-time pressure on them not to mention us."

That made sense. Why have a bulging bank account if you never flex the wealth muscle? I wondered what other things Carter Cahill had swept under his Sarouk.

"Meg said he had a family. Ian, I mean. His poor wife. Bad enough to lose your husband, but finding him in some other woman's bed would be devastating."

Rand lurched up and closed the door. He lowered his voice to a near whisper. "You know what was really bad? Guess whose bed he died in?"

I shrugged. Candy knew everything in the society pages, but I was clueless. Fortunately, Rand was dying to spill the beans. His genial face split into a jack-o-lantern grin.

"Tatania Lake. You know, the fashion designer." He edged closer. "Ah, come on, Mrs. B. She's married to the most famous athlete in Boston, Todd Brantley."

"How come I never heard that either? I must be hopelessly out of the loop."

His meaty paw patted my shoulder. "You focus on important stuff, not tabloid fodder. But I can tell you it was a big damn deal with cops buzzing around, the sports media digging up dirt." Rand lowered his voice to a whisper. "Supposedly, Todd Brantley is connected." He touched the tip of his nose. "Everyone swore it was a hit. Either one of the aggrieved spouses had motive."

"Really?" Ian Cotter had died within days of Kai's accident. I'd been too absorbed in my own loss to process other people's tragedies. Didn't touch a newspaper for weeks.

"Yeah," Rand grinned. "You know how it is when all the conspiracy nuts get going. Nonsense, of course. Somehow that device went rogue, and Ian Cotter paid the price." He paused. "I'm taking a risk even talking about it. Dr. Meg would have my hide."

I remembered what Lucian Sand had told me. "You don't mind risk taking, do you Rand? Dr. Sand told me about that experiment you helped him with."

Rand slapped his forehead in mock horror. "Good Lord. You know Lucian Sand? You do get around, Mrs. B." His eyes twinkled. "Luc is a hell of a guy. Kind of prickly, but fearless."

"Cahill and Rao went ballistic when I mentioned his name. It sounded more personal than professional."

"God, I hope this room isn't bugged." Rand pulled out his handkerchief and dabbed the corners of his mouth. "You see, Dr. Cahill wanted things with Luc to be personal." He raised his brows suggestively. "Luc wasn't buying whatever she was selling. His only interest was business."

Gossiping with employees is a poor business practice that erodes a manager's moral authority. So what? I'd gladly barter that for the lowdown on Lucian Sand. I continued our tête-à-tête. "I suppose Lucian's wife was upset, too."

Rand cocked his head to one side. "Wife? Luc doesn't have a wife."

"He's gay?" I asked. That stab of disappointment probably meant nothing. Lots of phenomenal guys were either bi or gay. It was none of my concern.

Rand's hearty laugh startled me. "Gay? Luc? Don't I wish. No, my dear Mrs. B., Dr. Lucian Sand is disgustingly heterosexual. He was focused on a mission. No time for dallying with an office siren."

The information dump overwhelmed me. "Meg Cahill, a *siren?*" It didn't compute until I recalled Tommy's black book. Rand was the purveyor of more gossip than I dared hope. Might as well prime the pump.

For a moment Rand hesitated. He seemed torn between his loyalty to Lucian Sand and a natural propensity to dish. I placed a mental bet on the latter.

"He's very motivated."

I flipped to the interrogation page in my memory and said nothing.

Rand crumbled faster than a day old roll. "Don't ever tell him I told you about this. Luc is intensely private. His brother, his identical twin, actually, died tragically after some dufus screwed up his pacemaker. Marcus, that was his name. The brother, not the dufus. Anyhow, he had rheumatic fever as a kid and got a weak heart. Something about an untreated strep infection."

That explained Lucian Sand's fervor, but it didn't explain his attraction to me. I certainly understood the pain of losing someone you loved, someone who was part of you like a twin or Kai. But why put the heavy moves on a dull, dispirited widow who begged to be left alone?

"Why the interest in our Dr. Sand? Don't tell me you're attracted to him." Rand got that rakish look on his face. "Don't worry. I totally understand. He is hot, hot, hot. Great body. That man spends more time at the gym than ..."

The look on my face dampened his enthusiasm. "I'm sorry, Mrs. B. Ready to do those financials?"

~

When we met for dinner that night Candace Ott was wired. We ordered cocktails, perused the menu and got down to business. Whenever Candy has something to share, her eyes narrow, and she twists a clump of hair into a braid. She wonders why I always skewer her at poker.

"I've got news," she chirped, "but you go first."

"Hey, I wouldn't dream of it." I waved her on.

"OK. Get this. I chatted up a few clients and got some great scoop."

Torture isn't sanctioned by the ABA, but it sure is fun. I said nothing, showing Candy my stone face.

"Betts, aren't you curious?" Her cat eyes looked feverish.

By the time the waiter appeared, took our order with a flourish and glided toward the kitchen, Candy's patience was exhausted. She did a quick check of the area and took the plunge.

"OK. Both of my clients knew Ian Cotter. Very well. Her eye roll was a thing of beauty. "Apparently, he provided those extra services to virtually every woman he met, not just Tatiana and her ilk. Several husbands found out, and one actually duked it out with him."

I rewarded Candy with a nod of approval. When I spilled my tale about Meg Cahill, she squealed.

We sat silently while our waiter presented my cucumber and apple soup and her Salade Niçoise. Radius kept its temperature at a perfect sixty-eight degrees, but that didn't stop me from shivering. Tommy had connected these dots months ago. He was troubled, and he had tried to use me as a sounding board. I'd failed him.

"Oh, Betts, what are we going to do?"

Candy whined like a spoiled schoolgirl. I had no one to cling to anymore, and her dependency grated on me. Why must I always be the strong one?

"Calm down. Let's take this step by step. Did you learn anything new about Mary Alice Tate?"

She shrugged. "What's to learn? She offed herself. Everyone knows that."

"Focus, Candy, focus. We know she had heart trouble. Right? She had an IMD."

"IMD? Isn't that one of those explosive things they use in Iraq? What's that got to do with anything?" She was losing interest. Immediacy was the key to keeping the mercurial Candace Ott engaged.

"Implantable Medical Device, IMD, get it? Back to Mary Alice. In her case someone leaked confidential information. I don't understand the area enough to gauge the link to CYBER-MED, and I've pumped Rand Lindsay to the limit."

Candy's eyes sparkled. "How about pumping Lucian Sand? That would be something worth doing."

Deep breathing exercises didn't work. To Candy's delight, I blushed like a Cape Cod sunset. Sensing my vulnerability, she immediately pounced.

"Aha! You have been thinking of him, haven't you, Betts? Come clean. I hear that no one makes love like a Frenchman."

"Stop that right now, although I admit Lucian is attractive."

"Attractive? Honey, he's downright gorgeous and very into you. I can always tell."

A good offense always works with Candy, plus it sidetracks her immediately.

"I saw your sweetie, Arun Rao, today. Aren't you the least bit curious?"

We spent the next half-hour reviewing my day at CYBER-MED with special emphasis on Arun Rao.

"He's very intense, Betts. You know the type. Starts at your forehead and doesn't miss anything." She heaved a big sigh. "Not that I couldn't up his game a bit. More polish and a little finesse, if you get my drift. I got the teensiest hint that he was completing a mental checklist."

I got it, all right. Arun Rao was robotic, making love by rote. I prayed he wasn't using my friend, just as I hoped Lucian Sand wasn't deceiving me.

I patted Candy's hand. "Just be careful. Remember, someone at CYBER-MET may be a murderer. Arun has motive, opportunity and the right skill set."

Candy batted her lashes and switched back to Tommy. "So, our boy was doing Tinkerbell and anyone else he could get. I'm not surprised."

"Tinkerbell?"

"You know, Meg Cahill. I expect her to sprinkle fairy dust in the air some day and fly around the room. It's all an act, of course. That woman's a calculating bitch."

"Hmm. I didn't have a chance to open all Tommy's files. I'll do that tomorrow. Meantime, I spent three boring hours on their financial statements, quarterly projections, and accounts receivable. Frankly, it was underwhelming."

"How so?" She was humoring me. I knew Candy had zero interest in anything but the bottom line.

"Don't spend your inheritance just yet. From what I could see, CYBER-MED barely breaks even. I'm sure they're counting on getting more customers or a leveraged buyout. All that depends on maintaining a spotless reputation. It argues against cutting any corners. Too risky."

Sometimes Candy surprises me. This was one of those times. She tossed her head back and got that steely look.

"Tommy wouldn't allow shortcuts, not ones that jeopardized someone's life. He was too ethical and too smart."

"He did something that made him a target. Maybe I'll find it in those private files."

We shared dessert, spending several delicious minutes inhaling calories. Before we parted I gave Candy her assignment.

"OK, Lois Lane, here's your task. Chat up anyone involved with this Mary Alice Tate thing. Find out who benefited from her suicide."

Candy licked her spoon. "It was suicide, wasn't it? I mean, what if someone knocked her off?" Those cat eyes gleamed with excitement.

I held up my hand. "Whoa. Wait just a minute. Stop this conspiracy shit. I don't care about Mary Alice Tate. It's Tommy we're focused on. Right?"

"I guess. Then why have me snooping around? Doesn't make any sense." Candy pursed her lips in a mutinous expression I was very familiar with. Time to apply a liberal dose of soft soap, lavender scented.

"Look. I thought we divided up the workload. I do the mind-numbing number crunching, and you do the personality stuff. Didn't you tell me you're far better at worming secrets out of people?"

"Well." Candy brightened as a man two tables over gave her the eye. "OK, Betts. I have a couple of ideas. The only one that stumps me is that Judge Jacob Arthur. One look at that man and you knew he never used grooming products." She sighed. "All that money, and he let himself go to pot."

"I don't suppose he had any family members in your social circle?"

Candy knew everyone worth knowing in greater Boston.

"Hmm. Let me think about that. He had two college-age daughters. I think they go to Boston College or somewhere else around here. Very Catholic, the judge was. Probably made them genuflect every day."

"What about Mrs. Arthur? Any connections to her?"

A smile eclipsed every trace of pique. "Maybe. There's a women's forum in Back Bay tomorrow. Some dreadful cause like rehabilitating women convicts. Mrs. Arthur is the chair. She's a therapist, you know, very big into self-help."

It was uncanny. I found myself reading Candy's mind. "Oh, I get it. Sweet Nothings might offer free products to these poor unfortunates. Very public spirited."

Candy nodded. "The awesome Candace Ott might even be persuaded to conduct a session for them." She gathered her things. "Let me make some calls tonight. I feel lucky."

Eleven

Lucian didn't call that evening, not that I expected him to. I didn't want to hear from him. He had probably found some simpler woman to pester, one without a murdered friend and an otherworldly husband. I busied myself with research. Mental exertion is just the ticket when personal demons overwhelm me. Tonight my target was Secretary of State Richard Chernikova. The Internet fairly buzzed with information about him. He was both lionized and vilified for his positions on virtually every issue except one: Liberals and conservatives agreed that his advocacy for stem cell research and diabetes prevention was admirable.

Everywhere Chernikova went, he was surrounded by a phalanx of armed agents who were part of his protective detail. He wasn't an easy target, and Tommy knew that. Why had he included Chernikova on his list? Perhaps the enemy was an unseen intruder within the Secretary's own body.

I rubbed my eyes as exhaustion overcame me. Candy would blow a gasket if she saw that. Rubbing one's eyes is a cardinal sin punishable by sagging, aged lids. Guilty!

Della had already curled up on her bed. At least one of us would get her beauty sleep tonight. I stifled a yawn and rose to join her. Then I saw it. According to the *Boston Globe*, the Honorable Richard Chernikova was the guest speaker tomorrow night at the High Hopes Ball, a fundraiser for the Joslin Diabetes Center. Kai's family foundation gave generously to all types of charities in the Boston area, particularly the ones affiliated with Harvard. I leapt up, propelled by a sudden burst of energy. Mail still arrived addressed to Mr. Kai Buckley. My pulse quickened each time I saw those paper tributes, almost as if he were still alive. I stacked the flyers, solicitations and announcements neatly on his desk just as I'd done before that awful day. Candy considered it barbaric, but the ritual comforted me. Kai's continual presence was something that sustained and nurtured me as it always had before. We were joined, irrevocably bound in life and death.

I skimmed the solicitation pile and found it, an invitation to the High Hopes Ball. Each ticket was a pricey five hundred dollars. Several months ago, almost without thinking, I'd written a check, purchasing two seats in the names of Mr. and Mrs. Kai Buckley. Funny. I didn't mind using his name, didn't feel diminished at all. My husband was everything to me even now.

Tomorrow — tonight, actually — I would see Richard Chernikova in person. Don't ask me why. It wouldn't resolve any questions about Tommy's death, but it might motivate me. Besides, as a partner of CYBER-MED, it was my duty. Tommy was always big on duty.

I flopped into bed with my head full of plans. Sleep immediately overwhelmed me until the persistent ringing of the phone brought me back.

"Hello."

"Were you dreaming?" Even half asleep, I recognized that voice.

"Are you mad? It's three o'clock."

Lucian laughed. "I can join you. Share your dreams, perhaps."

"Go away." I disconnected and burrowed into my pillows. Inspiration struck just before Morpheus claimed me. I grabbed my phone and stabbed the redial button. Lucian answered immediately, sounding disgustingly chipper.

"Are you free for dinner tonight?" I asked.

"For you?" He gave that throaty laugh. *"Oui, Elisa, toujours."*

"I'm serious. It's a formal event, black tie, and I need an escort." I deliberately avoided the more daunting term *date*.

"How charming. What time shall I pick you up?"

"Don't bother. I'll meet you at the Copley Plaza at eight o'clock."

"I insist on picking you up, if you want an escort."

"Oh, for Christ's sake, you're not my guardian angel, you know."

"Are you so sure about that? Maybe I am."

Another throaty chuckle. Lucian must think I'm a riot.

"Fine. I'll see you at eight. Goodnight."

"A bientot. 'Til then, *ma belle."*

~

Five hours later, after two double espressos and a cold shower, I still couldn't believe it. What was I thinking? Did I think at all when it came to Lucian Sand? The man was trouble with a capital T, yet I'd asked him out. On a date. Me, Elisabeth Buckley, hermit, martyr and grieving wife. I hugged Della, taking comfort in her silky fur.

Today's schedule was insane: a morning conference at Sweet Nothings followed by four hours of maintaining the facade at CYBER-MED and a mad dash to get ready for the ball. Most of all, I dreaded Candy's reaction to my new social life. I spent the entire morning procrastinating. It was craven and puerile, but I couldn't help it. On the way out the door, I casually mentioned the High Hopes Ball to Candy, emphasizing the chance to mingle with Richard Chernikova. I reduced an elegant social event to a dreary business obligation that might connect to Tommy. After all, sponsors were invited to an elite after-party that sounded very promising.

Candy wasn't fooled for a moment. "Oh, my God! What are you going to wear? You know the media will swarm the joint because of Chernikova." She leapt to her feet and started pacing. "I'm trying to imagine your wardrobe. Let me think for a minute."

I waited her out. Even cyclones ultimately run their course. Maybe if she agonized over my appearance, she'd forget the date issue. Fat chance.

"You can't wear black. It's way too somber for an occasion with hope as its theme. I know. That peach silk sari Kai brought back from India. Just the ticket." She sighed and plastered her face with a foolish grin. "Of course, I'll have to help you. You can't get into that thing without a dresser."

I nodded meekly and gathered my things. "Be there by six-thirty. The ball starts at eight."

"Hold on." Candy did a quick pirouette. "You can't go alone. You'd look like an outcast or an assassin." She gave me the death house stare. "Wait a minute. I get it. You have a date, don't you Mrs. Buckley? Fess up."

"An escort, not a date."

Candy waved her arms. "Pish tosh. You're going with the devastating Doctor, aren't you? Oh, Lord, Lucian Sand in a tuxedo. What a sight. Men always look like a million bucks in a penguin suit anyway. Remember when we launched Sweet Nothings?"

My heart contracted into a sodden heap. How could I ever forget? Kai and Tommy had looked like gods in their finery, especially Kai. I recalled the moonlight twinkling off those silver streaks in his hair. We danced and drank champagne until dawn, then went to the harbor to watch the sunrise.

Candy touched my arm. "Hey, don't be sad. Those were happy times, but they're in the past. Kai and Tommy moved on. You need to make new memories, too, Betts. Kai would want that."

I blinked back yesterday and faced forward. "You're right, of course. See you tonight."

Through divine intervention or something very like it, I snagged a cab immediately. The driver lurched through the streets, jabbering into a cell phone in some foreign tongue while I put on my game face. In all likelihood, someone at CYBER-MED had taken my friend's life, someone who thought murder was fun. I shivered at the memory of the cassette and that raucous laugh. Tommy had sounded surprised, puzzled even. That meant the murderer was unlikely, not the stock movie character that radiates menace. Who knows? Maybe a petite, pixyish woman with a rich husband might fit the bill.

I finalized my plans before entering CYBER-MED. Today was definitely a research day. I had four hours to pore over Tommy's private files and glean whatever information I could from them. One inconsistency plagued me. If his murderer was at CYBER-MED, why were Tommy's personal files left intact? Wiping a computer clean is no big deal in a place loaded with brainy techno-geeks. I had theories, not answers. A crafty killer might leave the files there, particularly if they seemed innocent enough. A blank computer could shine a bright neon light on CYBER-MED. Time may also have been a factor. Andrews and his crew had sealed the office almost immediately. Their forensic squad sifted through most of Tommy's stuff within two days of his murder. According to Arun Rao, they had removed the crime scene tape on the day that Candy and I first arrived.

I flashed my badge and stabbed the button for the fourth floor. Through bad luck or rotten timing, Meg Cahill, clutching a stainless steel thermos, was waiting on floor three. We both nodded, assuming the masks of civility that avoid workplace bloodshed.

"Mrs. Buckley ... Elisabeth. I didn't expect to see you today." Her voice was as perky as ever. "I feared that our dull routine had driven you away." She did a quick appraisal of my outfit without dropping her smile one inch. I was wearing a classic, an olive Chanel pantsuit that contrasted nicely with my hair. Kai had bought it in Paris, along with a Hermes scarf. Even Candy approved of me when I wore it.

I upped the wattage of my smile, picturing Meg Cahill wearing the leather teddy that Tommy had so vividly described in his diary.

"CYBER-MED is fascinating. I have so much to learn that it's humbling. Was the whole thing your idea, Meg?"

Dr. Cahill lowered her eyes like a penitent. "I had lots of help. So many of my patients had pacemakers and the like that when the technology changed, I saw both a need and a business opportunity."

I held the door for her when we reached four.

Not everyone succumbs to flattery, but my instincts told me that Meg Cahill just might.

"I'm not very creative," I said. "That's my partner Candy's bailiwick. She's a genius."

Meg's lip curled a bit. "Yes, I can see that. Makeup is a challenging venture." She gave a little wave and strode toward her office, heels clicking on the limestone floors.

Fortunately, I'm not the violent type. Candy would have sensed the scorn and decked her. I comforted myself by comparing the profit margin at Sweet Nothings with CYBER-MED's. No contest.

I closed Tommy's office door, fired up his computer and opened those private files. No need to peruse his black book today. That vicarious trip through his love life would sustain me for months. The other directories looked commonplace. I scrolled down his personal calendar, looking for anomalies. He had scheduled daily exercise sessions. No surprise there. Tommy and Kai were both gym rats with the bodies to prove it. My pulse quickened as I saw a notation made one week before his murder. "CC and Giraffe, KillerStartups." What the hell? CC meant only one thing, Cotton Candy, our special name for Candace Ott. Giraffe was my much-loathed moniker. It was probably his snide way of mocking us, a jab at Sweet Nothings and all it stood for. I hadn't seen Tommy at all that week, hadn't taken his calls. That was a millstone that weighed heavily upon me. Perhaps Candy had the answer.

I was deep in thought until a brisk knock ushered in Arun Rao.

"Hi," he said. "Got a minute?"

His suit was exceedingly well cut, Oxford Clothiers if I was correct. As he took his seat, I noticed square gold cufflinks and a fetching set of dimples. Rao was a hottie, but Candy was welcome to him. Something just didn't ring true to me. He was too polished, too schooled in pleasing women. A mechanized sex toy complete with batteries.

"What brings you here?" I clothed the question in a smile.

He furrowed his brow and spoke softly. "I want to help." He straightened his cuffs and turned liquid brown eyes on me. "Tommy's murderer. I can help you find him."

"Why don't you tell the police? Sergeant Andrews seems very competent. Candy and I aren't detectives, and neither are you. It might be dangerous."

Arun swallowed twice before answering. "I have some skills that might help. Applied and Theoretical Cryptography is my academic discipline, you know."

I threw up my hands. "You'll have to be more specific, Arun. I've haven't a clue what you're talking about."

That drew a big smile. "You sound just like Tommy. He told me that, too." Arun leaned forward, palms on knees. "It's pretty simple really. I decipher messages. Kind of like the old code-breakers but with computer data. A perfect fit for CYBER-MED, that's what Dr. Meg always says. Anyhow, I help safeguard our patients' information." His sudden frown looked like a thundercloud. "That's why Lucian Sand is such a lying bastard. Our data isn't compromised. I wouldn't allow it. Neither would Rand. He's studying the same thing."

My silence spoke volumes. Rao abruptly stopped his tirade and wound down.

"What does this have to do with Tommy?"

He tugged his ear. "I'm not sure. Maybe nothing. If you find something, anything at all, bring it to me. If I can't figure it out, I'll find someone who can."

I studied him for a minute. "And Dr. Cahill approves of this?"

He hesitated. "Don't involve Meg. Just bring it to me. She wouldn't understand. CYBER-MED is her whole world."

"Why take a risk?" I asked. "After all, the murderer might be right here."

Rao's lips formed a thin line. "Tommy was my only real friend in Boston. He'd take a risk for me. I know that." With a curt nod, he loped out of the office.

Rao puzzled me. He seemed earnest enough. On the other hand, his offer of help guaranteed him access to every aspect of Tommy's murder. That generous offer might also be a very clever ploy by someone who murdered for fun. On that dreadful recording, Tommy had asked the killer why, said that the killer didn't need the money. Neither Arun nor Dr. Meg needed money. According to Candy, Arun's family was very comfortable, and her definition of comfort always involved lots of zeros. Meg and Carter Cahill were obscenely rich, if the Boston financial press was accurate. I gave myself a mental pinch for that display of Socialism. Everything depends on perspective. Some people might call the Buckley Trust obscenely rich. Kai had teased me about it, calling me his Bolshevik.

I spent the balance of the afternoon slogging through the balance sheet for CYBER-MED. It was boring, tedious work that yielded absolutely nothing. Four hours of mind-numbing activity had yielded only one tangible clue. Alas, "CC and Giraffe, KillerStartups" meant absolutely nothing to me.

Twelve

My pulse raced as I rushed home. Candy would be here any minute, armed with her makeup kit and Velcro rollers. I felt sick to my stomach. Maybe it was a touch of flu, but more likely the gut-clenching, mind-blowing realization that I would soon be with a man for the first time in a year. Not just any man, either. Lucian Sand shook me up at a cellular level. He knew things that no stranger should know, touched me as if we were longtime lovers.

I did my yoga routine, forcing myself into abdominal low breathing as Kai's words echoed in my brain. He had taken me mountain climbing, insisted on it. Just one time. I'd begged him to forget it. My nickname's Giraffe, not Nijinsky. Kai prevailed, as he always had, and one spring weekend we had motored to Jaffrey, New Hampshire, home of Mt. Monadnock. We ascended part of the White Cross trail, the easy one. Trouble started during the descent. My terror grew until I froze, paralyzed by fear. Kai reached out his arms to me and spoke softly. "Don't be afraid, Lizzie Mae. You can do anything. You're Wonder Woman. Take my hand. I'll always be here."

He lied.

Tears streamed down my face, but I didn't feel them. They cleansed my soul like a gentle rain, renewing my spirit. By the time Candy arrived I was resolute and composed. Tonight's engagement was a mere blip on life's radar screen. Lucian Sand was just another man.

Talk about your whirling dervish. Candy swept into my living room, hauling a treasure trove of self-improvement items. My face was a blank canvas, waiting to absorb whatever paint and spackle she applied. That made her suspicious.

"What, no whining about looking like a clown? OK, Betts, spill. How many Xanax did you take today?"

"None. I did yoga and meditated. Tonight is strictly business. "

Candy snorted. "Trying selling that to the hot Frenchman you're dating."

"I told you, he's not my date." Even I knew that sounded lame.

"Yeah, yeah, yeah." Candy waxed my brows with an expert flick of her wrist.

"Ouch! That hurt."

"Much better," she grinned. "At least now I know you're still alive. By the way, Arun called me today." She dabbed eye cream and moisturizer on me. "He's going solo to that shindig. Apparently, Dr. Meg demands that they dance attendance on her. Not surprising."

"Yeah. Rand's going, too. Looks like half of CYBER-MED will be there."

"Quiet now," Candy ordered. "I can't do your eyes if you're babbling." She proceeded to apply shadow, liner and mascara with dazzling precision. After a puff of powder and a splash of scent, she held up a mirror for me.

"Very nice, Mrs. Buckley. Although I think you need a new fragrance. This one is too tied up with Kai. You need something young and lively. French, of course."

"Forget it. Fleurissimo is a classic. If it was good enough for Princess Grace, it's fine for me, too."

Candy heaved a gigantic sigh and attacked my hair with her brush. "Thank goodness you have great hair, not that you appreciate it. When was the last time you went to a salon?"

"Hey. I'm not like you. Spas are your mother ship, not mine. By the way, did you contact Mrs. Arthur? I thought that prison thing was today."

"Tomorrow. I called her, and the woman was pathetically grateful. Used a lot of psycho-babble, you know the drill." Candy's smile verged on sinister. "Don't worry. I'll peel her like a grape. After all these years I'm an expert on shrinks. Here, time to drape your sari." She fingered the exquisite peach silk emblazoned with gold. "Oh, my God, this is so gorgeous. Kai must have spent a fortune on it."

"I guess. I've never worn it."

"Now, now, don't get all weepy on me. Stand still while I do this." After draping, folding and tucking, Candy stood back, surveyed her handiwork and nodded. "Another miraculous transformation by Candace Ott. Take my word. You're officially awesome."

She was right. Awesome might be a stretch, but I looked different, unlike the sober lawyer and policy wonk of yore. For once I didn't fight Candy's attempt to glamorize me. Tonight I was playing the role of undercover operative. Lucian Sand was a prop, part of the scenery. Nothing more.

Lucian was punctual. Candy met him at the door, giving him a hug, a low wolf-whistle and a hero's welcome. I couldn't fault her judgment: the man was magnificent. He glided into my home, looking like every maiden's fervent prayer. His tuxedo was traditional, a beautifully tailored Armani with notched satin collar and one-button front. Contrary to the old adage, this man made the clothes, not the other way around. When he turned toward me, I gasped. No more beard! That scruffy face hair had concealed baby smooth cheeks and a fetching chin cleft. His startling teal eyes met mine in a blaze of fire.

"You … you look amazing," I said. An unaccustomed tingling swept over me, lodging somewhere south of my waistline.

Lucian took my hand, brushing each finger with his lips. "And you, Elisa. You are a vision. As the poem says, you walk in beauty like the night."

I felt a surge of anger at the Byron reference. Kai had loved that verse. We'd spent many nights holding each other and reading poetry. Now a stranger was intruding on something sacred.

"Oh, my Lord, I feel goose bumps." Candy saved the day. "You're a man of many parts, Dr. Sand. Science and the arts are a potent combination." She put her arm through his and tugged him toward the sofa. "Our Betts is quite the beauty, isn't she? Who said redheads can't wear peach? Nonsense."

I finally gathered my scattered wits. "We can't stay, Candy. The dinner starts at nine, and I don't want to miss Chernikova's speech."

Lucian pinned me with an icy stare. "Ah. You are a fan of American imperialism?"

When I glared at him, he laughed. So did Candy. Apparently, I was the only one not in on the joke.

"You're so easy, Betts. Lucian was only teasing." Candy gave him a playful shove. "That's the same way Kai and Tommy used to ruffle your feathers. You never learn."

She was right. How had Lucian figured that out? He must think me a humorless prig.

"Ready, Mrs. Buckley?" He fixed an agate stare on me. Blue lace agate, that's what his eyes looked like now. Calming, restorative. I keep a blue agate on my desk to soothe me. It's gotten quite a workout since Kai's death.

"Sure." I gathered a cashmere wrap, my purse and some attitude. Tonight's mission concerned Tommy and the scoundrel who murdered him, nothing else. I had no right to flirt and flutter like some aimless coquette.

The elevator was packed with Boston's upper crust, taking in the night air. Lucian stood beside me, resting his hand lightly on my shoulder. It felt good, rather like Della's stolid presence. For the first time in ages, I didn't feel lonely and sad.

He'd left his Porsche parked at the curb. Our aged doorman leapt to assist us with an alacrity born of a well-placed bribe and the hope for more. Some folks inspire that kind of treatment, but I had never mastered the knack.

"We could have walked, you know, or taken a cab. The hotel's not very far from here."

He shook his head and made the risky transition into Boston traffic. "You look much too exquisite for a stroll, no? And cabs ..." His brows raised. "That simply would not do. Let me handle the transport while you tell me the plan. The truth, this time."

I'd flunked Prevarication 101. That made lying an unappealing option. Lucian would peel apart my story layer by layer until he exposed the truth. Better to get it over with.

"Tommy had a concern or a connection, something with Richard Chernikova. I don't understand it, but he left me a clue. I hoped that seeing Chernikova might help somehow. I know it sounds stupid."

Lucian looked straight ahead. "There's more. You're hiding something."

It was risky telling him things. Lucian was a stranger and might well be the killer. True, he had given me the disk, but that could be a clever ploy or a cynical sleight of hand. My social skills are limited, but I've always had keen business instincts. Why else would Kai have called me Wonder Woman? I went with my gut and trusted Lucian.

"Tommy sent me a list of four names. Three of them are already dead, and Chernikova is the fourth."

"Hmm, names. Nothing else?" He applied the brake and turned toward me. "Who were the others?"

"No one particularly famous. You probably read about one of them, Judge Jacob Arthur. He died during a big tax fraud trial. Another guy made the news, too. Ian Cotter dropped dead in some bimbo's bed. Lots of jokes about that one, you know, dying with a smile on his face."

Lucian wedged the Porsche between a stalled pickup and a motorcycle. "And the third?" His voice showed absolutely no emotion.

I sighed. "That was a suicide, a friend of Candy's actually. Mary Alice Tate."

He swung into the hotel entrance, joining the line for valet parking. "Why did this woman take her life?"

"It was a money thing. Word got out that she wasn't really related to the Tates, and that meant she wouldn't share in the estate. Someone got the results of a DNA test."

"There is a connection, I presume."

Now came the hard part. It was supposition, not fact. He could demolish any argument I made with one spurt of logic. Good thing I went to law school. Banter is my stock in trade.

"The three dead people were clients of CYBER-MED. I'm not sure about Chernikova."

Lucian waited for me as the attendant helped me alight. My movements were ungainly, more lurch than light. It's not easy to navigate a sports car when wearing a sari.

He gripped me firmly around the waist, keeping me steady.

I liked feeling his arm around me. It was comforting, familiar. I shook off sentiment the way Della shed water, vigorously. *Easy does it, Lizzie Mae.*

As we followed the crowd toward the Grand Ballroom, I saw a familiar face. Rand Lindsay, looking surprisingly svelte, was checking invitations. He grinned like a Cheshire cat when he saw us.

"Mrs. Buckley. Luc, my man." He gave my escort a bro-hug and checked our table number. "Wow, you're at the head table. I'm impressed. That's where Dr. Meg and her hubby always land."

Lucian looked unperturbed. I wasn't as sanguine.

"Maybe this isn't such a great idea. We don't have to stay, if you'd rather not."

"Nonsense," Lucian said. "I enjoy seeing old friends. Will Arun Rao be there also?"

Rand did a quick shuffle. "Nope. He'll be sitting way back in Siberia. That's part of our job tonight, filling in for absent guests and paying attention to single ladies." He took my hand and twirled me around. "I declare, Ms. Elisabeth, you are a knockout. Dr. Meg will claw your eyes out."

It was my turn to flush. I'm not good at accepting compliments. I always suspect their sincerity. Tonight was a different matter, though. Lucian's reaction buoyed my spirits and helped me believe in myself. If not an outright knockout, I might be at least a TKO.

"You're a terrible flirt, you know, but thanks anyway." I winked at Rand and followed the waiter to our seats.

Meg and Carter Cahill were enthroned in the middle seats of a large, elaborately decorated table. Beautiful silver candelabra highlighted a centerpiece of orchids and baby's breath. I recognized the man across from them as Cap Coleman, the president of the Harvard Medical Center. He had once been Kai's squash partner in a charity tourney.

Meg's jaw dropped slightly when she saw us. She recovered nicely, stretching her lips into a seamless faux smile. Her husband was oblivious. Carter Cahill, a large, florid fellow, sized us up with the challenging stare common to little league coaches. He had already drained his wine glass and was actively seeking more.

"Elisabeth, how nice of you to come." Meg checked my sari with a practiced eye. "And Dr. Sand. An unexpected pleasure."

Lucian gave her a half bow and shook hands with her husband and the other guests. I renewed my acquaintance with the Harvard honcho, who reminisced about Kai and his tragic loss. Lucian eyed me speculatively as though gauging Kai's impact on my psyche.

I don't discuss Kai's death with strangers. They never understand. Kai died, but he's never left me. Even now, as my cheeks glowed from Lucian's kiss, my husband was by my side, cheering me on. "I'm your number one fan, Lizzie Mae." That's what he'd always said.

Shortly before nine the lights dimmed. A pair of muscular agents preceded the Secretary of State as he ascended the dais and took his seat. His tablemates, all executives of the Joslin Center, gave Richard Chernikova a hearty welcome. A phalanx of waiters immediately circulated with our blameless, tasteless repast of boiled scrod, squash and red cabbage.

"Meg tells me you're the new honcho at CYBER-MED." Carter Cahill's tone was one notch short of snide. Like many self-made men, he occasionally dipped a toe over the line between audacious and obnoxious.

I activated my charm initiative. "I'm trying to learn the ropes with Meg's help. It's quite an enterprise."

Lucian barely moved. He dabbed the corners of his mouth as they twitched in a smile. His foot gently nudged my toe in appreciation of a superior snow job.

Cahill nodded vigorously. "You bet it is. My wife left one of the best practices in the nation to start CYBER-MED. We expect a payback, right, Hon?"

A faint tinge colored Meg's cheeks as she patted her husband's arm. Lucian and the Harvard honcho jousted about the relative merits of Harvard versus MIT, a debate that had raged for decades.

I was fascinated by our guest of honor. He picked at his food while fixing the crowd with a bright, unwavering gaze. His prominent nose and skeletal hands reminded me of a raptor, a bird of prey prepared to devour any enemy.

Why was his name on Tommy's list? This man had already survived two assassination attempts and was as closely guarded as the President himself. CYBER-MED was the least of his concerns.

The evening's host tapped the microphone and made a few self-deprecatory remarks. No one paid much attention. The crowd was focused on our guest of honor. The Secretary of State approached the podium, acknowledged the applause and surveyed the crowd. A hush descended on the room.

"I've spent my life fighting the enemies of our great nation," Chernikova said. "Tonight we're here, Democrat and Republican, to battle another one: diabetes." He thumped his chest. "If it weren't for this little pump, I probably wouldn't be standing at all."

Nervous laughter swept through the ballroom, but our table bucked the trend. Meg's face was a stone sculpture. Her husband took refuge in his wineglass.

"I've been called a lot of things in my Washington days," Chernikova grinned, "but one of them doesn't bother me at all — guinea pig. Yep, I'm one of the lucky ones testing an implantable insulin pump that allows me to jet all over the world. Thanks to my doctors and the fine staff at CYBER-MED, I'll be plaguing my detractors for at least another decade."

That answered one of my questions. Tommy knew that Richard Chernikova was a client of CYBER-MED, and something made him think the Secretary was in peril. Lucian gave me a quick, enquiring glance. Meg exhaled, looking as if an enormous boulder had come off her perky little shoulders.

"Nice plug for CYBER-MED," she beamed. "Another satisfied A-list client."

I didn't mention the dissatisfied ones. That would be rude. Jacob Arthur, Ian Cotter and Mary Alice Tate wouldn't speak up. Death had put paid to that. After a few more rah-rah speeches, a top-flight jazz quartet appeared. I knew from experience just how good they were. I'd heard them once before.

"Dance, Elisabeth?" Lucian asked. He put his arm around my waist, guiding me toward the dance floor. Meg left her husband's side and claimed Arun Rao as her partner. Despite the age gap, they made a handsome couple. Rao's dark hair played brilliantly off Meg's platinum locks. If only he hadn't spoiled the effect by scowling at Lucian.

The first selection was so familiar it stung my heart, that old Billy Holiday tune, "But Not For Me."

Lucian maneuvered us to a secluded spot and held me closer than dancing demanded. For once in my post-Kai life, I didn't fight it. I closed my eyes and rested my head on his shoulder until a whiff of Creed jolted me.

"What's wrong?" he asked.

"Nothing, it's just your cologne."

He stopped dancing and cocked his head. "It offends you?"

Embarrassment swept through me like a brush fire. "No, no. It isn't that."

"What then?" Lucian wouldn't let it go.

I hate stammering. It's so uncouth. "I thought it smelled like Creed, Silver Mountain Water." How gauche I am. I'd offended him and probably spoiled our evening.

Lucian's face was untroubled. "Bon. Not many people would recognize it. I spent a lot of time in Switzerland as a boy, and that scent reminds me of the Alps."

I turned my head, blinking back tears. "Forgive me, Lucian. That was Kai's favorite fragrance, too. Forget about it. Let's get back to Chernikova."

"I'd rather resume dancing for the moment. Do you mind? Arun is glaring at us. Let's keep him guessing."

Lucian was a superior dancer, transcending my lackluster performance by whirling me around as if I were an expert. When the set ended, he squeezed my hand and guided me back to our table. Immediately, I went on alert: Meg was entertaining the guest of honor.

"Good thing your husband's here tonight, little lady, or I'd be tempted to tuck you under my arm and steal you away." Chernikova's sparkling eyes radiated mischief and a whiff of entitlement. "Give your favorite client a big hug."

Meg fluttered what I knew were false eyelashes at him. Oh oh. From the vibes she was putting out, I'd bet Sir Richard was very familiar with that leather bustier.

Carter Cahill stifled a yawn. No spousal jealousy there. He shrugged as Chernikova playfully tugged his wife toward the dance floor. It seemed like a typical charity gala until the screaming started.

Thirteen

Lucian knocked me flat on my back, shielding me with his body. For a moment I couldn't breathe or make sense of anything except that shrill voice shrieking, "Murderer!"

A lithe, smartly dressed woman brandishing a broken wine glass advanced toward Meg Cahill. "CYBER-MED murdered my husband!" She got no second chances. Chernikova's bodyguards pounced on her, wrestling the would-be assassin to the ground.

As partygoers stampeded for the exits, the master of ceremonies rushed to the podium, begging for calm. "Everything's under control, folks. Relax. Just a little misunderstanding." Pleas for calm seldom work, but in this case, the well-heeled crowd showed remarkable fortitude. Instead of vanishing, most of them milled around the bar, energized by the unexpected entertainment.

His agents hustled Chernikova out the side door before I could catch my breath or introduce myself. Hotel security ringed our table while the disarmed culprit continued her tirade.

"They killed him. Ian was perfectly healthy until they murdered him."

Aha! Now it made sense. This must be the betrayed wife, Mrs. Ian Cotter. She was quite a looker, although tears hadn't improved her makeup much. Screaming was no beauty plus either.

The biggest surprise was Dr. Margaret Cahill. After the initial hubbub, she exhibited an icy calm that put snowmen to shame. I saw her beckon to Arun Rao and speak softly to him. Then she approached the sobbing widow and hugged her.

"Oh, Katherine," Meg said, "I'm so sorry. I know how much you miss Ian. We all do." She gave an imperious nod to Arun. "Dr. Rao will deal with the authorities. Mrs. Cotter is under a physician's care. She needs rest."

If I hadn't been there, I wouldn't have believed it. Within five minutes, Katherine Cotter vanished, music started, and the dance floor filled with chattering couples. The show was officially over.

~

"We've got to find her!" I was so excited I couldn't unfasten my seatbelt. "Katherine Cotter holds the key to Tommy's murder."

Lucian pulled the Porsche into my driveway and tossed the keys to the doorman.

"What makes you so sure, Elisabeth? She seemed to love her husband." His arm was around me again. He hadn't let me go since the trouble started.

"You don't get it. She said CYBER-MED is involved. The manufacturer paid off the family, but that widow isn't satisfied. She knows something."

"Consider this. She may have murdered your friend or tried to attack you. It might well be a vendetta against CYBER-MED and those who run it. On the other hand, maybe she's just lonely for her husband." He gently stroked my cheek. "You can identify with that, can't you?"

I had to slow things down. Lucian was reading my mind, seeing private things I never intended. He had insights into me that didn't make sense, otherworldly things.

"Let me escort you to your door." He walked over to my side and helped me out.

Sunstreaked tendrils escaped from his ponytail, but his tux was still pristine. I smiled at Lucian's formality. It was like a 1940s-era film, anything with Charles Boyer.

"I have to walk Della," I said as the elevator wheezed up to my floor. "Candy's probably long gone." Butterflies were spawning in my stomach. It made no sense to feel this nervous. Lucian Sand was just another man. I needed to seize control of the situation and my emotions.

"I never thanked you," I said, holding out my hand.

Instead of squeezing it, he slowly kissed my fingers one by one. "For what?"

"Saving my life, of course. That's the second time. I keep count."

"Your life is worth saving, *ma belle*. Worth so much." Those solemn blue eyes held me in their thrall. I almost felt giddy. How long had it been since a man held me? How long since Kai left me?

Hearing Della's warning bark, I fumbled with my keys and succeeded in dumping my purse on the floor. A glut of feminine frippery splayed out on the carpet: brush, mirror, blush and lipstick. Lucian scooped up the keys and put his arms around me. His kiss was soft and gentle as he explored my lips, mouth and tongue. My heartbeat accelerated to an alarming rate. I had to stop it right now.

He brushed my bangs out of my eyes and smiled. "Don't be afraid, Elisabeth. I won't hurt you. A woman like you belongs with someone who will cherish her, take care of her. Someone who can give her what she really needs."

I took a deep breath and exhaled as a wave of longing swept over me. "I don't need anything. I can take care of myself." Della's barking intensified as she stormed the door.

Like Kai, Lucian unlocked it with one quick twist of his wrist. It usually took me several tries. Della, my steadfast watchdog, didn't even try to bark. She rolled over, prostituting herself before the Frenchman for a tummy scratch. So much for female solidarity.

I rooted around in the closet, searching for her leash, while Lucian patiently waited for a different answer. Where in the world had Candy put it?

"Is this what you're looking for?"

He dangled Della's special red lead high above his head. It was custom made, Kai had insisted, of braided mountain climbing rope just like his. I should have tossed it, should have let it go, but I couldn't bear to. Kai loved that thing, said it reminded him of my red hair.

Lucian chuckled. "Della must be a pretty tough customer. I've used these myself on hiking trips." He saw the stricken look on my face and quickly closed the gap between us. "No, no. Don't be sad. Your husband's memory will be always with you. That's OK." He massaged the aching muscles in my neck. "Just open up your heart. Let someone else in."

"Della. I have to walk her." Even I thought that sounded feeble.

"She's fine. Never mind Della." He led me to the sofa, gently lowering me onto the down cushions. Our eyes met in the timeless language of desire as Lucian slowly unwrapped the folds of the sari. When he reached my skin, his fingers brushed the contours of my body like a tender breeze. I shivered as a dreamy haze of pain and pleasure consumed me. It had been so long, and I was so needy.

"*La Belle Dame Sans Merci*," he murmured. "Will you break my heart?"

I gasped as he peeled off my soft lace undergarments. This was surreal, a virtual stranger quoting Keats while he undressed me. He mapped out every sweet spot and sensitive point on my body as his lips and tongue inched down my skin. The intensity of my response overwhelmed me. I felt bloodless, boneless, otherworldly. Nothing could forestall the inevitable now. I couldn't stop it, didn't even try.

"So soft, so beautiful." Lucian flooded me with hot kisses and sweet words. He stopped for a moment and gazed out the window at the sparkling nightscape. "I know you still love him, my Elisa, but just for tonight, give yourself to me."

I closed my eyes and freed my senses. The night passed slowly in a sweet, sensual fog.

~

I felt like an awkward schoolgirl the next morning. Strange men don't stay in my home. I'm not like that. The living room told a different tale. It was littered with the debris of lovemaking with clothes, shoes and underclothes scattered everywhere. Della had found a new bed on the beautiful peach sari from last night.

Lucian bustled about the kitchen with her at his heels. He wore the unisex robe from the Four Seasons that hung on the bathroom peg and had helped himself to the toiletries, as well. I watched him firing up the espresso machine like a pro. He seemed perfectly at ease, too much so.

"Good morning, Elisabeth. You slept well?"

I flushed when I realized how disheveled I was. Clinging to shreds of dignity, I hustled into the bedroom and grabbed a peignoir. While I was there, I removed my smeared and splattered makeup and brushed my hair.

We hadn't used the bedroom. I was glad about that. I couldn't bear to bring another man into Kai's bed. Not yet, anyway.

The door chime caught me totally unprepared. What the hell?

"Ignore it," I called to Lucian. "Whoever it is will just go away."

"I don't think so," he said, sotto voce. "It's Ms. Ott."

Shit! Ignoring Candy was a losing proposition. She was impervious to the slights and snubs that would wither more sensitive souls. Plus, she had her own key.

"OK. Wait just a minute. I'll let her in. She needs to hear about last night anyway." Not everything, of course.

I stood in front of the armoire, paralyzed by indecision. Lucian couldn't wear a bathrobe or a tuxedo all morning. There were plenty of shirts and slacks, neatly folded, in Kai's dresser. They had lain there undisturbed since the day he died. Was it a betrayal to offer them to another man?

I reached in and found a flannel Brioni shirt and jeans. They'd probably fit just fine. Lucian tapped on the door and handed me a steaming cup of espresso. His hair was a tousled nimbus of curls, framing those amazing eyes. Chiseled abs peaked out from the terrycloth, causing lusty thoughts to surge through my body.

"Maybe you'd better change clothes," I suggested without meeting his eyes. "These might fit OK. The dressing room is to the left. You can store your things in this tote bag."

For a moment he hesitated. "Of course," he said. "That's very kind of you." He kissed my fingers as I handed him the clothes. "Don't worry, my Elisa. Everything will be just fine."

If only I could be that certain.

Nothing deterred Candy. She swept into the foyer with a fervor only hurricanes can muster, stopping short while she viewed the disarray.

"What's all this, Mrs. Buckley? A burglary in process?"

I chose the high road. "Oh, that? I was rearranging the furniture."

"Yeah. That always happens." Candy gave me the gimlet eye. "Things went well last night?" She stooped down to ruffle Della's silky coat. "I can't stay long. Today's that luncheon with Mrs. Jacob Arthur and the other bleeding hearts."

"Espresso?" I asked, walking over to the machine. "I know that I need one."

Before she could blurt out something rude, Lucian strolled from the dressing room, clad in Kai's old clothes. They fit him perfectly, almost like a second skin.

"Good morning, Ms. Ott," he said. "You look lovely."

Compliments always disarm her. Candy beamed a mile wide smile and preened. Appearance is important to her, and she always looks the part. Today's ensemble, a bright red suit with navy piping and big white buttons, struck a patriotic note.

We clustered around the kitchen table, sipping the magic brew as I recounted last night's events. Naturally Candy got a redacted version. Everything else was personal.

"Arun called me first thing," she admitted, "but he didn't know much because he was way in the back. This is thrilling."

"Actually, it was scary. Meg was phenomenal, though. Cold as ice. No wonder she was a top-flight surgeon." I shivered as I contemplated Dr. Margaret Cahill wielding a scalpel. "I plan to contact Mrs. Cotter today. That woman has a story to tell."

"Maybe," Candy said, staring at me. "She may just be a nut job. You know how obsessive some widows can be."

Few people ever accuse Candy of subtlety.

"Listen, Ms. Know-it-all. When you question Mrs. Arthur, and I know you will, try to gauge her feelings about CYBER-MED. You know what I mean. Tommy thought there was something fishy involving the Judge's death."

Lucian thoughtfully sipped his espresso. "CYBER-MED was cleared of negligence," he said. "I was there at the time.

Judge Arthur's pacemaker went wild and jolted him into eternity. Manufacturer's error."

"Well, something went wrong. Three deaths linked to the same company. Suspicious, don't you think?" I tried to marshal my facts and think like a prosecutor. What if Tommy sounded the alarm, tried to stop the negligence. Meg and Arun would have erupted. Carter Cahill might have joined them. He'd spoken quite openly about a return on his investment. Would they murder Tommy to protect CYBER-MED?

Candy fixed her green cat eyes on Lucian. "I don't really understand this stuff, but wouldn't it be impossible to monkey with one of those IMD things?"

"Normally." Lucian was quiet, almost brooding. "Not impossible, just extremely difficult. And why would someone go to the trouble?"

I considered that chilling conversation. Tommy had accused someone of deliberate murder, not an accident or carelessness. Was a lunatic loose at CYBER-MED, someone who got his kicks hurting others?

"I thought they just monitored things there," Candy said. "That seems harmless enough, unless someone was fooling around. Remember, my friend Mary Alice's medical data got out somehow. That was a really mean trick."

Lucian morphed seamlessly from suitor to professor. "Things can happen. I've replicated incidents in my lab, but conditions have to be just right."

"Incidents," Candy asked. "You mean you stopped someone's pacemaker? That's sick, man."

He leapt up and started pacing. "You don't understand. Everything was closely monitored. We used components from Radio Shack on a test instrument. No one was in danger."

"Who else was involved?" I asked. Suspicion resurfaced. What better way to insinuate yourself into an investigation than by seducing the clueless widow, thrilling a woman wedded to a ghost?

Lucian waved his hand impatiently. "Our team at LIPS participated."

"Lips!" Candy showed her manic side. "Sounds more like my neck of the woods."

"It's the group that studies the safety of IMDs," I said. "I presume you shared your results with Meg."

No more tenderness from Lucian. He resumed his role as the abrasive scientist.

"I told her," he muttered. "That was the last time we spoke before last night." He brushed off his jeans and carried his cup to the sink. "I have to leave. I'm teaching a seminar this afternoon."

"Oh, good," Candy said. "I'm going your way. Let's share a cab."

"I have my car out front," Lucian said. "I'll drop you."

"Even better." She linked arms with Lucian, blew me an air-kiss, and skipped out the door.

Fourteen

Solitude was comforting, allowing me to collect my thoughts and make plans without carnal distractions. My boon companions aided that process: Della and the memories of what used to be.

I found my briefcase and searched frantically for the disk. My cheeks burned as I realized that it had vanished. No wonder Lucian Sand had bustled around showcasing his domestic skills. That bastard stole them! OK, he'd gotten what he came for. Sex was an unexpected bonus, a ruse to soothe the horny widow and get his rocks off. *You're a prize fool, Lizzie Mae.*

Foolish I may be, but I'm still a lawyer. I had made three copies of that disk and locked them in my safe. Lucian Sand could have saved his virtue.

~

My first stop was Boston Police Headquarters. Mark Andrews wasn't there, but I got lucky anyway. Francie Cohen answered his page and admitted me to the squad room. I saw immediately that she'd put Candy's beauty tips to good use. No more shy wallflower. Officer Cohen had blossomed into a babe.

"I have something for you," I said. "It's for Sergeant Andrews, actually, about the investigation."

Francie ducked her head as if she were hiding something. "I'm really not on the case anymore, Mrs. Buckley. The Sarge likes to work alone."

"Oh. I'm sure he wouldn't mind if I gave you an important piece of evidence."

Her artfully lined eyes lit up. "I guess that would be OK." She motioned me to a seat in front of Andrews' desk. Every file was neatly stacked; not a paper was out of place. Who knew? Andrews was a neat freak.

"It's been almost two weeks since my friend died. Andrews said you haven't made much progress." I gave Francie a hard stare that made her flush.

"I know Sergeant Andrews is working on it." Her voice trailed off.

"Here's what I know," I said. "I won't stop until my friend's murderer is caught and punished, even if I have to do it myself." I leaned forward, speaking in a low, firm voice. "You can give him that message for me. After he listens to this, have Sergeant Andrews call me. I have some other ideas to share."

I reached CYBER-MED after lunch, just as Rand and Tony "Tornado" Torres were ambling back to work. Rand swooped down on me like an angry crow.

"Mrs. B, I was so worried about you! You and the Sandman just disappeared."

His twinkling eyes belied his words. Rand hadn't worried one bit. He nudged me toward the elevators while Tony walked behind us. "You were right there. Weren't you scared out of your mind?" Rand stopped. "I heard that Dr. Sand knocked you flat and covered you with his body. Mmm, lucky girl to have Lucian Sand as your personal protector."

Tornado chimed in. "Hey, man, that sounds like that *Bodyguard* movie. Cool."

I sensed an opportunity here.

"Dr. Cahill was the brave one. I didn't know what hit me." I lowered my eyes. "That poor woman, Mrs. Cotter. She was bereft. I know what that's like when you lose your husband." I didn't have to fake emotion. It was easy to empathize.

Rand patted my shoulder. "She really loved him, you know, even though he cheated with every woman in Boston." He glanced down at me. "Well, not every woman, but that's only because he didn't know you, Mrs. B."

I shook my head in mock sorrow. "Why does she blame CYBER-MED? I don't understand. Meg said the manufacturer settled with the family."

Tornado smirked. "That's the company line. Dr. Meg knows the whole story."

"Hush," Rand interrupted. "We can't discuss it, or we'll lose our jobs." The elevator opened on the fourth floor, admitting two women. When we exited, Rand stage whispered, "I'll stop by later."

I headed straight for the executive conference room where Meg, Arun and a third man were hunched over, engaged in what looked like a serious conversation.

"Sergeant Andrews. I just went to your office looking for you." I gave him my best smile, sunny side up. "Oh, am I interrupting?"

Meg's eyes looked scalpel sharp. She pulled out a chair and forced a smile. "You're always welcome, Elisabeth. After all, you were a witness to that mess last night."

Andrews rolled his eyes. "I know all about your visit to the station, Mrs. Buckley. Officer Cohen texted me. Texting! After all these years I finally found something that helps me out on the job."

I held my breath, hoping he wouldn't mention the disk. He didn't. Most of his questions concerned Katherine Cotter and her possible motive for murdering Tommy.

"You have evidence?" I asked. "That woman killed Mr. Yancey?"

"Nonsense," Meg Cahill said. "Katherine wouldn't hurt a flea. She never got near me. The woman needs help, not police harassment."

Arun chimed in. "Ian Cotter died a natural death, Sergeant. Check it out."

Cops are trained to control themselves. Mark Andrews compressed his lips, using every bit of training to restrain himself. Arun finished his part, nodded and looked to Dr. Meg for approval.

"There's just one thing, Dr. Rao." Andrews spoke softly, choosing his words with care. "Your staff dropped the ball. When Cotter's defibrillator went bonkers, your guys were twiddling their thumbs." He leaned back in his chair. "At least, that's what Mrs. Cotter believes."

Two blooms of color dotted Meg's cheeks. Candy would have heartily approved of the natural blush. "That's unfortunate, Sergeant. Now, if there's nothing else ..."

Andrews reminded me of a crocodile lying in wait. "Perhaps we should speak privately, Doctor. This is a delicate issue."

"Nonsense," Meg said. "My partners can hear anything you have to say."

"Do you want your attorney present?"

What the hell! Was Andrews planning to drop some bombshell?

Meg turned to me. "Mrs. Buckley is an attorney. She'll look out for my interests. Now for heaven's sake, spit it out."

"If you insist." Andrews took his time thumbing through his file folder. "Dr. Cahill, were you and Ian Cotter lovers? According to his wife, he confessed to an affair."

I was so enthralled by the process that I forgot to object. Holy smokes, Rand was right. I expected Meg to faint, yell or stalk out of the room. I never expected her to laugh.

Hearty peals of laughter rang out. Soon, Arun joined in. Andrews and I were the outsiders, stumped, unsure of what had just happened.

Meg dabbed at her eyes as she regained her composure. "I'm so sorry, Sergeant, but you have no idea how amusing that is. Ian having an affair? How in the world did he have enough time?" She leapt to her feet, the image of the perky temptress Rand had described. "The man was a whoremaster, a real hounddog. You'd have an easier time counting the women in Boston he didn't screw around with."

Andrews put on his game face, but it was too late. He had lost the initiative.

"So you admit that you had an affair with him."

She smirked. "I admit no such thing. Ian told me about his conquests. Ask Arun, he told him, too. The man couldn't shut up. He was hardly discreet. Remember, he died in the bed of some celebrity's wife. She's the one you should be questioning, not me."

"Back to CYBER-MED, Dr. Cahill. It must be difficult to lose a patient, especially a high profile one like Ian Cotter."

Arun leapt to the rescue. "You don't get it, do you? We monitor the IMDs, confer with the primary care physician, and make inputs as directed by them. Everything's documented. No one runs amuck or ignores patients in distress. Check it out. You'll see."

Meg steepled her hands and grew pensive. "You asked about losing patients. It's always hard, Sergeant. High profile or not, they become part of our family. I'm a physician, and I realize the inevitability of death, but that doesn't make it any easier. When the patient is a friend like Ian Cotter, things are even more difficult."

She grasped her coffee cup like a lifeline. "If you'll excuse me, I have another commitment." Meg strode from the room with the dignity of a monarch. Arun trailed in her wake.

"Hmm," Andrews said. "That didn't go so well." As he rose, I grabbed his arm.

"Do you have a moment? It's important. I think I can help about Mrs. Cotter."

Andrews got a wary look in his eyes. "OK, let's hear it. Nothing surprises me today."

"She didn't do it," I said. "Couldn't have."

His eyes called me a lunatic, but his lips said all the right things. "I'm sorry, Mrs. Buckley. I don't understand."

"Listen to the disk. I should have given it to you before, but I haven't felt up to it." That was true enough.

Andrews' back was ramrod straight. I had his attention now.

"It's my friend, Mr. Yancey, confronting the murderer. At least, I think it's the murderer. Anyhow, it couldn't be Katherine Cotter. These weren't revenge killings."

Andrews stayed statue still. "These, plural? Are you suggesting more than one murder occurred?"

I answered him like a lawyer, cautiously. "I'm not certain. Maybe."

Andrews leapt from his seat. "OK, that does it. You're coming with me, Mrs. Buckley. Right now."

I held my ground. "I'm staying here. After you listen to it call me, and we'll talk. I've told you everything I know. Anything else is supposition."

"Oh, yeah? Who was your source? Who gave you that tape?"

I should have ratted him out. I should have let Lucian Sand fry, but something stopped me, and I chose instead to protect him.

"A dead man sent it to me. Thomas Yancey."

Andrews stormed out of the office and slammed the door. He had barely cleared the corridor before Rand Lindsay rushed in.

"Lordy, Ms. Elisabeth, what did you do to that man?" He grinned to take the syrup off his southern act. "I hope he didn't pistol whip you."

"You have quite an imagination, sir. Sergeant Andrews just tried to rattle my cage. He's obsessed with pinning something on Lucian Sand. Who knows why?"

Rand pulled up a chair and settled in. "Oh, I can tell you that. Luc raised all kinds of hell when his brother died. Sued the manufacturer, tried to proceed criminally. He ran afoul of Andrews some way, and he never forgot it. Andrews, I mean, although Luc still holds a grudge, too." He gave me that jack-o-lantern grin again. "Sandman really likes you, Mrs. B. He never let you go last night. I saw everything."

I doubted that Lucian would have any more use for me now that he'd found that disk. Of course, he still wanted my shares in CYBER-MED, so that might warrant an investment of time. He'd done me a huge favor. Now instead of mooning over some ruthless con man, I could focus on the task at hand, finding Tommy's murderer.

"Rand, I need your help on something. Find me the insurance policies on all the top execs, especially the key person policies. Andrews said Tommy had one for five million bucks. I want to study the wording before asking Meg anything."

"Will do," Rand said. He looked toward the door and lowered his head. Guilt was smeared all over his face like jam.

"Just one thing, Mrs. B. Rao said … that is I have to check with him before giving you that kind of stuff. I'm sorry."

The oh-so-helpful Arun Rao, how interesting. Between monitoring my activities and romancing Candy, he had the new partners well in hand.

"Not a problem," I said, picking up the phone. My smile combined sweetness with steely reserve. "Arun, sorry to interrupt. Can you stop by my office? Thanks."

I winked at Rand. "Don't say a word. Everything is under control."

Five minutes later, Arun poked his head into the room. "Here I am, at your service." His gleaming black hair was combed straight back today, and his banker's grey suit projected confidence and competence. No wonder Candy was hooked on him. He was an exotic, alluring package. Too bad I didn't trust him one inch.

"I want to review CYBER-MED's insurance portfolio," I said, "starting with that key person policy you had on Tommy."

Rao stiffened slightly. "OK. Anything wrong, Mrs. Buckley?"

Rand slowly backed out of the room, leaving us to confront each other.

"Oh, no," I said. "It's standard industry practice. After I study it, I'll discuss it with Meg and you. After all, five million dollars is a big chunk. Investing it wisely is what strategic finance is all about."

Rao's face knotted in a frown. "Blood money, that's all it is. I know I shouldn't be emotional about money, but it's like a bounty on Tommy." He shuddered. "Meg is much more philosophical, of course. Comes from being a doctor, I guess. And Carter's chomping at the bit, always talking about the bottom line."

"Carter seems like quite a businessman," I said. "Did he invest much in CYBER-MED?"

Another shrug. "I guess. Mostly he contributed business expertise. He and Tommy clashed more than once, I can tell you that."

Another insight into life at CYBER-MED. Tommy never mentioned strife or conflict with investors. A horrific thought struck me. Maybe he had tried to tell me, and I was too absorbed in my own selfish concerns to react.

"Tommy lived for conflict," I said, "always called himself a gladiator. Carter Cahill couldn't shake his confidence, believe me."

Arun spent some time twisting his cufflink while I sat patiently awaiting the storm.

"Forgive me, Elisabeth. I know this is none of my business, but ..."

I got a flash straight from the psychic hotline. Operative word: awkward. "OK, Arun. Does this have anything to do with Lucian Sand?"

He stammered some kind of gutless response. "I'm concerned. Candy and I discussed it."

"Candy? You and Candy discussed my private life? Oh, that's just great."

He held out his hand in protest. "No, it wasn't like that, really it wasn't. Candy's happy for you. She said he would do you good. I just wanted you to know the truth. That's all."

My gaze pinned him like a specimen on a slide. "And what is the truth, Arun?"

"Don't trust him. Lucian Sand can't be trusted. He would do anything to get control of CYBER-MED."

The queasiness I felt was probably indigestion. Lucian Sand was a stranger, a rare error in judgment for someone as cautious as I. No big deal.

"Dr. Sand is merely an acquaintance," I said, "nothing to worry about."

Arun's relief was palpable. "OK, then. I'll leave you alone to read this stuff. Call me if you need anything else."

I donned my reading glasses and settled in for a long afternoon. It was chilling, reading the cold, dispassionate document with Tommy's name on it, one that put a dollar value on his life. When Kai died, I had sleepwalked through the paperwork, guided by a battery of attorneys for the Buckley Trust. None of it mattered to me. Money was valueless without my husband.

Tommy's key person policy was quite specific. The proceeds were payable to CYBER-MED Corporation with one exception: one million dollars went directly to Carter Cahill, identified in the document as a primary lender. No wonder he had been so emphatic about return on investment. It was time to talk money with Meg.

Fifteen

She was waiting for me, hands folded, ankles crossed, the very picture of a well-bred lady. Even her smile was letter perfect.

"Arun tells me you have questions, Elisabeth. Come on in. Please, take a seat."

Our eyes met, telegraphing an unspoken challenge. *I'm ready for you, Doctor. Time* to set *things straight.*

I'd handled plenty of business negotiations at Sweet Nothings. Few things bothered me anymore. As long as I focused on Tommy, everything would be just fine. I channeled my inner waif, hoping to allay Meg's suspicions. It didn't fool her for a minute.

"Let's talk money," I said. "How do you plan to use the proceeds from Tommy's insurance policy?"

Meg uncrossed her ankles and leaned forward. "Isn't that discussion premature? Until his murder is resolved, there is no money. Arun spoke with the insurance company today."

"Surely you've considered the issue," I said. "You're an excellent planner."

Meg shook her shiny platinum hair. "Perhaps I should call Arun. He's a partner, too."

"As you wish. I'll speak for myself and Ms. Ott. It's all theoretical anyway."

She buzzed Rao's number and poured herself more coffee. The woman mainlined caffeine. Shouldn't a doctor be abstemious?

Arun flew through the doorway as if Meg had some strange, hypnotic hold on him. He nodded to me and claimed a seat next to his mentor.

"We're discussing strategy, Arun. Tell Mrs. Buckley our proposal for using the insurance proceeds." Meg leaned toward him. She had crossed her legs, letting a lacey black slip peek out over shapely knees.

Dr. Arun Rao, prize pupil and automaton, recited his lines perfectly. "The funds were always meant to support CYBER-MED. We'll use them to buy out you and Candy ... Ms. Ott."

"Really? We'd consider that, of course, but we're also entertaining another offer."

Meg's body coiled like a striking serpent. I'd played a different card in the deck.

"Another offer? May I ask who made this offer? We'll match or exceed any reasonable bid. The survival of this company is critical."

I shook my head. "It's still very preliminary, and I'm not at liberty to disclose any specifics."

"It's Lucian Sand. I know it!" Arun leapt to his feet and started pacing. "He's conning you, don't you see? You can't trust anything that guy says."

Meg pasted a frozen smile on her face and held up her hand. "Let's remain civil. I know this has been difficult for you, Elisabeth, what with Thomas's death and ... "

"His *murder*, Meg. Don't you forget it. I never will."

"Of course. Please forgive me." Meg was in soothing healer mode. Arun leaned against the wall, a scowl marring his handsome features.

"You think it's one of us, don't you?" His eyes were feverish. "What did Tommy tell you? I was his best friend."

My self-control tore like a gently frayed garment. "No, Arun. I was his best friend. Candy, too. Maybe I wasn't there for him when he needed me, but I sure as hell am now. Count on it." I rose unsteadily, bracing myself against the chair. "If you or anyone else at CYBER-MED was responsible for taking my friend's life, watch out."

~

I took a cab straight over to Sweet Nothings, praying that Candy could make sense of things. Despite her unorthodox approach to life, she often spotted things that eluded the rest of us. Besides, I'd never asked her about that notation on Tommy's computer: CC and Giraffe, KillerStartups.

She had just concluded her weekly conference call with vendors and waved me in, her eyes aglow with triumph.

"Why so glum, Betts? Wait 'til you hear what I did!" She kicked off her stilettos and sighed. "First things first. I cozied up to Mrs. Jacob Arthur as directed." She pursed her well-moistened lips.

"And? Don't keep me in suspense, for God's sake."

Candy's cat eyes sparkled. "I peeled her like a grape. Told you I would. Anyhow, she said her husband's death was totally unexpected. He had just been given an all clear by his cardiologist. That pacemaker was his fail-safe, you know."

Her big coup looked smaller every minute. "So, no suspicion of foul play or malfeasance?"

"Well, maybe. Mrs. A. says the defendant in that tax case was a nasty piece of work. You know the type, government conspiracy, trumped up evidence, the works. He'd made veiled threats against the judge and the prosecutor. Nothing concrete, though."

I hated to dampen Candy's spirits. "Maybe it's a dead end. Tommy might have been wrong, you know." I felt a pang of conscience at my disloyalty. Tommy was not fanciful. He was a hardheaded realist. He and Kai accused both me and Candy of being romantics, mystery buffs who read too many books. That list was important to Tommy, and the tape supported it. My task was to fit the pieces of this lethal puzzle together.

I waved the printout at Candy. "Hey, look at this. CC and Giraffe, KillerStartups. I found it in Tommy's personal files yesterday, but it has me stumped. It connects to us somehow. I just don't know how. Probably something about Sweet Nothings."

I'd racked my brain for any blade of inspiration. Safety deposit box? I'd checked those. They had all the standard boring stuff we all put in the bank, a copy of Tommy's will, deeds, bonds and some more pictures. Nothing that linked up to CYBER-MED.

Candy stirred her tea as she studied the printout. Anyone else would have frowned, and wrinkles be damned. Naturally, elegant Candace Ott, beauty seer to the stars, would never do that. She allowed herself several massive sighs and a cleansing breath. I watched transfixed as her face lit up with the glow of a morning sunrise.

"You really don't get it, do you?" She hugged her pillow, swaying merrily from side to side. "Unbelievable! For once I'm the smart one."

My nerves had reached the precipice. One more smirk, and Candy would be a beautifully groomed corpse.

"Yeah, you're a genius. Stop stalling and spit it out before I pole-axe you."

"Geez, what a grouch." Candy rolled her eyes, playing the scene for every ounce of drama. "Look Betts, it's simple. When Tommy was here, he experimented with all kinds of social media. You must remember that. He loved to twitter, and he posted on Facebook more than he used the telephone. Said it enhanced business, but personally I think Tommy used it to troll for dates. Most of his so-called friends were female. Check it out, if you don't believe me. His Facebook account is still active."

I closed my eyes and leaned back. Once Candy went off track, nothing could pull her back. No way would I endure another disjointed piece of Tommy's life. I missed him too much to confront that grim reality so late in the day.

"What does all that have to do with this CC and Giraffe business?" My voice was gruff. "Why conceal something that was in the public domain anyhow?"

Candy ignored my bad temper. "I don't know. Maybe he left a clue or something." She snapped her fingers. "I've got an idea. Let's ask Arun's opinion. After all, he knew Tommy almost as well as we did."

I snatched her iPhone before she could dial. "Absolutely not. Arun Rao is way too cozy with Meg Cahill for my taste. Those two practically inhale each other's air."

That stopped Candy cold. I shouldn't have hinted about Rao and Meg's relationship without solid proof. It was downright mean, and I regretted it instantly. Fortunately, Candy was focused on the task at hand.

"We could always call the delectable Dr. Sand," she purred. "I'll bet he'd have plenty of exotic suggestions."

"Forget it. I have nothing to say to Lucian Sand. Besides, like Arun, he's a suspect. They all had a motive to silence Tommy."

Pouting is always unattractive, particularly when the pouter in question is a thirty-year-old business executive. Candy's brief vale of sunshine was eclipsed by a sudden storm.

"You're no help at all, Betts. Didn't they teach you anything at Harvard?" She leapt up and tackled her computer. "Let's just see what Google has to say about that." Candy typed something in and waited. Then she uttered a strangled cry. "Oh, my God! Look, Betts, I was right." Her finger shook as she pointed at the screen. KillerStartups was a social networking site devoted to all manner of new business ventures. It had hundreds of applications, any one of which Tommy might have used to send us a message. On the other hand, perhaps it was just a joke. Only in detective fiction is everything tinged with meaning.

As we assessed it, our assistant poked her head in the office. "Phone call for you, Mrs. Buckley. Dr. Lucian Sand."

I immediately panicked. "Tell him I'm busy. Take a message." I wrung my hands until they hurt.

Her patient smile never faltered. "It's the second time he's called today."

She was right, of course. I'm not some maladjusted teen coping with lost love. I'm a lawyer and business executive, for heaven's sake. I cleared my throat and picked up the phone.

"Mrs. Buckley." My voice was decidedly neutral, suitable for an acquaintance not a lover. Chilly, but not frigid.

"I missed you, Elisa." The breathy growl stirred my senses. Damn all Frenchmen.

"Lucian, how are you?" *Enjoying that tape, you bastard?*

"When can I see you? It's been ten hours already."

I could feel the flush spreading up my neck and the benign, faintly patronizing looks that Candy shot my way. I turned my back and grasped the phone.

"Things are hectic around here, Lucian."

"I can't stop thinking about you, your soft, soft skin and beautiful hair. Don't deprive a starving man of sustenance." He chuckled, knowing how absurd that sounded. "After all, Della must get her walk, no?"

What a low blow, using my dog as leverage. I had to seize control and end the charade with this con man once and for all. Sensing my loneliness, he had wielded it like a club. He'd battered my defenses and released a year's worth of yearning.

In his arms I had felt alive for the first time since Kai's death. There would be no second helpings, no more orgasmic bliss.

"Let me cook for you this time," I said. "Nothing fancy. Just broiled fish."

"Are you sure? You sound so tired, ma petite."

I ignored his solicitude, the big phony. "Is eight o'clock too late?"

"Of course not. I will bring dessert."

"See you then." I disconnected without another word.

By six p.m. I'd fled the office and cabbed it to the nearest gourmet market. Tuna, I'd serve him tuna and hope it came filled with mercury. Lucian couldn't charm me anymore. My heart was armor plated, bulletproof. Once he confessed to stealing the tape, I'd pack him a doggie bag and boot his elegant ass out the door.

I primped a bit, nothing that would meet Candy's standards but enough to satisfy most men. My attire was simple but stylish, black jeans and cashmere sweater with a beautiful Bulgari necklace that Kai had given me on our second anniversary. I applied lipstick with the certainty that it would not be disturbed. No passionate kisses or sensuous slow dancing allowed.

He rang my doorbell promptly at eight looking like every woman's wet dream. It must have been pheromones or something, because even Della seemed enamored by him. Lucian's sun-streaked hair spilled over his shoulders, nearly obscuring that diamond stud twinkling in his ear. I did a quick appraisal of his clothing. We looked like twins in our black jeans and sweaters.

"How elegant you are, ma belle." He gently brushed the loose strands out of my eyes in a gesture that felt more like a caress. I shivered as he handed me the evening's dessert.

"Crème brûlée," Lucian whispered, "smooth and silky like your beautiful skin."

"Did you make this yourself?" I felt flustered and out of sorts. Time to rein in my libido.

He laughed. "Alas, no, but I swear I paid for it." He presented me with a beautiful spray of lilies and orchids. "A small tribute."

I'm no good at game playing. Chalk it up to my Irish ancestry or too much Catholic education. Kai always said my face was an open book, an easy read for any opponent. Lucian had the upper hand as long as we avoided the truth and fenced. I finally blurted out the truth.

"Why are you here? You already got what you wanted."

His muscles tensed like a caged beast's. No more soft glowing looks. Lucian turned to stone.

"Is that what you think of me, Elisa? Am I a man who seeks conquests?" He tilted my chin up to meet his eyes. "Did we make love against your will?"

Shame coursed through my veins. I was flustered, confused, and beet red. "No, of course not. I mean, I take full responsibility for what happened."

His eyes were arctic cold. "Explain yourself."

"It doesn't matter. Just leave, Lucian. Please."

He shook his head. "Not before you tell me what's wrong." He stroked my hair again. "I care about you more than you know. You cannot dismiss me."

I whirled around and faced him. "You have the disk. Isn't that what you wanted? Protecting your interests, right? Thrilling the horny widow was just part of the job."

Lucian sighed. He put his arms around me and rocked back and forth. "How can anyone so beautiful even think that? Look into my eyes."

Against my will I gazed at him, mesmerized by his passion. His strong arms reassured me, giving me the solace I so badly needed. For a moment I saw Kai's glistening eyes staring back at me. I blinked, fearing for my sanity.

"I took nothing from this house except beautiful memories. Believe me." Lucian pressed me to him in a fierce hug.

I was tongue-tied, unable to respond. Before I collected my wits, the doorbell rang.

For once in a very long while, Candace Ott saved the day.

Sixteen

"I had to come. You'll forgive me, won't you Lucian?" Candy hugged Della and sauntered into the living room. Appearance is key in Candy-land. One look at her told me something was very wrong. Her curls spiraled out against flushed cheeks like Medusa's spawn, and her fleece jacket sported a conspicuous coffee stain on the lapel. My stomach clenched. *Please God, no more death.*

"Can't it wait, Candace?" I tried giving her the eye. "Dr. Sand was just leaving."

"Already? I want him to hear this too."

Her cat eyes widened, pupils dilated. Candy eschews recreational drugs, so that wasn't the problem. Something had her spooked.

"Sit down, mon cher. Calm yourself." Lucian put his arms on her shoulders to steady her. "Now tell us. What happened?"

Candy collapsed on the sofa, taking several cleansing breaths as she fought to regain control. "I found it, the key to Tommy's clue. It was right there in front of us."

Lucian Sand had so firmly taken root that I'd need a shotgun to make him leave now. He settled into Kai's favorite wingchair and crossed his legs, his gestures firm and deliberate.

"I was frantic," Candy said. "Arun was gone, or I'd have told him. That disk bothered him enough …"

"Disk?" I held up my hand like a crossing guard. "What disk?"

My friend and partner morphed instantly from crazed adult to guilty, stubborn adolescent. She lowered her head in a sullen pout that spoke volumes. I read her like the CliffsNotes on *War and Peace*.

"You took that? I don't believe it! How could you, Candy?" I shot a glance at Lucian. His smile was beatific.

"Don't blame me," Candy said. "Someone had to do something. You couldn't make a decision, so I did. Besides, Arun wanted to help."

"Oh, for God's sake. That means Meg knows everything, too. How in the world can I face them if they're on to me?"

Lucian Sand leaned forward, pinning Candy with his glare. "Did you tell them how you got it? I'm worried about my contact."

"Give me some credit," Candy said. "I never reveal my sources. Arun didn't care about that anyhow. He said it was a joke, a set-up." She shrugged. "Maybe he's right."

Too late, I remembered my hostess duties. I scuttled to the kitchen and grabbed a bottle of Pouilly-Fumé. It was French, white and supposedly complemented grilled fish. That was the full extent of my knowledge and interest. Lucian glided over to the bar and examined the bottle closely. When I handed him the corkscrew, he wielded it like a sommelier.

"Voila! Sauvignon Blanc, an excellent choice." He poured a glass, swirling the pale golden liquid around. "Sensuous and delicate," he said with a smile. "So lovely in wine and beautiful women."

I hid my confusion by taking a healthy slug of vino. What a fool I'd been, making baseless accusations. Lucian must either loathe or pity me, maybe both.

"Hey, aren't you a little bit curious? Remember why I'm here, Tommy's clue." Candy helped herself to wine and headed toward Kai's study. My office.

"Wait! Don't go in there."

She whirled around and faced me. "It's an office, Betts. A study, not a shrine. Besides, that's where the computer is."

"Computer?" Lucian's frown was a storm cloud. "What's this about a clue?"

I filled him in as we filed into the room. "Use my computer," I said.

No one used Kai's iMac but me. I'd updated the programs but left everything else intact. Even the history section went untouched. The emails from one year ago remained unanswered, just as he'd left them. I knew them all by heart. It made me feel connected to him, as if someday he would magically appear to reclaim them and me.

Candy fired up Google and typed in the now familiar phrase, KillerStartups. As her fingers flew over the keys, she grew positively giddy.

"That's so like Tommy, always the joker, no matter what. I remembered how much he liked to video things, so that's what I studied." She clicked on that section, typing in the password Topper. "Sit down, Betts. This is ... difficult."

I grasped the corner of my desk, steadying myself as his image appeared on the screen.

He looked alive, ready to spring right into my office. Thomas Yancey, very much the Harvard MBA, wore a navy Brooks Brothers suit, white shirt and rep tie. Nothing, not even the grim subject matter, extinguished the gleam in his eyes or that errant wing of straight brown hair that flopped over his forehead. I drew back to avoid touching his face on the screen.

"I hoped you wouldn't see this, ladies. That can't be good for me." Tommy chuckled. "Oh, well, *c'est la vie* or something equally profound. You're both the controlling partners in CYBER-MED by now, so you need to know this. My advice — no, my command — is to turn this thing over to the cops and get the hell out of the way. If only Kai were there ..." He swallowed and regained his composure. "Something's wrong at that place. Very wrong. I sensed it right away. Oh, the metrics are sound enough. All startups take a while to make a profit, but CYBER-MED is different. People are dying. Our clients. I noticed a disturbing pattern, and I've been poking around trying to flesh it out." He nodded. "I even got Kai involved. You see, we lost some very high profile clients, people who shouldn't have died."

Tommy gave that megawatt grin. "I know what you're thinking, Lizzie Mae. You lawyers are all alike. And no, I don't have proof. Not incontrovertible proof, anyhow. I admit I'm not a doctor. Hell, I'm not even much of a computer geek, but I excel at puzzles. You know that."

Tears trickled down my cheeks. Candy had a similar reaction. I recalled how often we'd played Scrabble, Trivial Pursuit and other board games. In college we didn't have much money to do anything else. Tommy was a relentless competitor. Granted, I usually beat him, but he never gave up. He found every angle, even a few that required chicanery. He would have been a gifted lawyer.

"Anyhow, here's the deal. There's no other way to say this."

He didn't use notes. Tommy never did. He prided himself on making flawless presentations that sold the customer without a lot of confusing statistics. We had kidded him about that, and his response never varied. Why confuse them with facts?

"Someone at CYBER-MED is running a sophisticated, very low key, murder-for-hire scheme. I know it sounds crazy, but I'm convinced of it. Think about it. It's the perfect murder. Check out those names I gave you."

He blinked back a drop of sweat. "I'm not a computer geek, so I can't say for sure how they do it. Monkeying around with the parameters on certain patients, I suspect. I don't know who the murderer is, not for sure. There may be more than one, an insider and an outside contact. Tonight, I'm going to confront the person I suspect. Sounds stupid, I know, but I can't justify accusing someone with only supposition. If it works out, I'll go right to the cops, and you lovely ladies will have to wait another fifty years to get my money." Tommy's eyes glistened. "I love both of you. You know that without getting mushy. You're my family, always have been. Well, wish me luck." He gave one jaunty wave, and the screen went dark.

No one said a word. We sat in stunned silence, assessing our wounds like train wreck survivors. Our space felt crowded, too small to contain the three of us and the two men whose vibrant spirits populated it. Kai and Tommy, together again. It seemed so right.

Lucian took my hand and gently squeezed it. Candy chose her normal coping mechanism. She closed her eyes, curled up in a ball, and rocked back and forth, chanting some unintelligible mantra. The tragedy of losing our friend was compounded by the taint of other murders and their stunning implications. Damn Tommy and his arrogance! He had confronted a murderer alone and sealed his own doom. How many times had he walked away from disasters, leaving me to soothe outraged professors or shaken customers. I was sick and tired of cleaning up his messes.

"No wonder he sent us that list," I said. "Typical Tommy. His version of a scavenger hunt, a lethal one."

"But why not name the murderer?" Lucian asked. "He could always amend the tape if he got it wrong."

Candy emerged from her cocoon with something approaching a grin. "Proves you didn't really know him. Tommy was scrupulously fair. He would never say something that damaging without proof, even if it endangered him. He was just that kind of guy."

"At least we now know what that disk meant." I replayed it in my mind. "Seems like he underestimated the murderer. Tommy always thought he could charm the birds out of the trees." I filled our glasses with more wine. "Funny thing was, he usually could." I caught myself snuggling up to Lucian and hastily drew back.

You pick some weird times for romance, Lizzie Mae. Does danger excite you?

I turned and faced him, disregarding that sexy smile he wore. For all I knew Lucian Sand might still be the murderer. He had means, opportunity and tons of motive. Cop shows always stress that. Was he Mr. Outside?

"You have to tell us, Lucian. Who sent you the disk? At the very least it can help us exclude someone at CYBER-MED."

"Yeah," Candy chimed in. "Stop screwing with us. Betts or I might be next on the hit parade."

He let go of my hand and slowly sipped his wine, seemingly untroubled by a dead man's words. Lucian was either very cool or very guilty. I watched anxiously as Candy gripped her glass like a baseball and lobbed it at his head.

"Hey! Are you crazy? Stop that shit." I was prepared to slap her, if necessary.

"What's the matter, Betts? Afraid I'll hurt your boyfriend?"

I shivered as the lamplight glistened on the crystal shards. Candy's aim was as bad as her taunts. She had missed him by a country mile and splattered wine all over my wall.

"I'm concerned about that Baccarat," I told her with a tight smile. "We got it as a wedding present. Empire ... they've retired that pattern, you know."

That made Lucian smile. "I'm honored that a fine French crystal was used to assault me." He nodded pleasantly to Candy. "You win. I will tell you what you seek."

His language grew more formal, and his accent more pronounced, as he spoke. Hurrah! We were finally reaching the imperturbable Dr. Sand.

"I did it myself," he said. "It was child's play. I planted recorders in the offices of the principals at CYBER-MED and waited for something to happen. They had no suspicions. The security at that place is laughable, as you yourself have observed."

"What? You've violated at least two state statutes that I can think of offhand and probably a federal one, too. Are they still there?" I didn't like Lucian monitoring my private conversations, even though they were innocuous. Boring.

"Alas, no. I had everything removed when I learned of Tommy's murder." He answered the question before I could ask it. "You know I am *persona non grata* at CYBER-MED, but a friend, someone totally removed from the process, retrieved the equipment for me."

"How convenient," Candy snapped. "Well, tell us. What else did you learn, Mr. Snooper?"

"Nothing germane. Office relationships hold no charm for me, even the salacious ones." Lucian's face betrayed no emotion.

Whatever his shortcomings, at least Lucian was a gentleman. I'm sure his tapes had caught the moans and groans coming from Drs. Rao and Cahill. Candy didn't need to hear about that.

"Yo, Betts. You still with us?" Candy started her toe tapping routine. "We have to decide. Take this stuff to Andrews or keep it quiet. We know what Tommy wanted, and Kai would have hit the roof if you played detective."

I bit my lip so hard it bled. The answer was laughably clear. Turn CYBER-MED, the tape and everything else over to the cops. My conscience wouldn't allow anything else.

"This time I agree with Tommy. We can't take the chance that someone might die while we screw around. That doesn't mean I'll stop digging, though. Someone killed Tommy, and I won't forget it."

Seventeen

Lucian stared quizzically at me but said nothing. I'm not a vengeful person. Not really. I accepted Kai's death, even though I'd felt like dying myself. Murder was different. Tommy's death unleashed a primitive rage so intense it threatened to consume me. Lizzie Mae, Warrior Princess, was a new role, one that I embraced. Somehow I would avenge my friend and find his killer. The weapons in my arsenal weren't tempered steel and gunpowder. I would use the skills that had distinguished me in school and business to bring down this coward: brains, tenacity and imagination. Mercy and compassion weren't on the agenda. Leave that to the Lord.

"Let me try Andrews' number." I checked the time on Grandmother Buckley's ormolu mantle clock. You could always set your watch by that beautiful hunk of bronze. Like Kai, the clock was artfully constructed and devastatingly accurate. I doubted that either Andrews or the perky Francie Cohen was still on the job. No blowing police overtime to unmask Thomas Yancey's killer, no sir.

"Wait a minute," Candy said. She thrust Andrews' card under my nose. "He gave us his cell and home number. Try those first."

She was right, of course. Andrews answered his cell without hesitation although his vigor faded when he heard my voice. I brought out the big guns, forcing him to arrange a meeting with Candy and me the next day. He complied reluctantly and with poor grace.

"There's nothing new I can tell you, Mrs. Buckley."

"OK, but there's something important we can tell you, Sergeant."

He didn't bother to mask a yawn. "If it's about that disk ..."

"This is new evidence, a video made by Mr. Yancey. Some might call it a dying declaration. That has probative value in most courts."

"Let me be frank with you."

Uh oh. When anyone starts a conversation like that, bad news is sure to follow. I gave Andrews my best business school line.

"I applaud candor, Sergeant, especially when it concerns my friend's murder."

"We're inclined to think it was some joyriding kid who stole that old lady's car, hit Mr. Yancey and panicked. Those cases are hardly ever solved."

"Interesting theory," I said. "I'm afraid I can't accept that. Ms. Ott and I will see you tomorrow morning at nine."

"Wait a minute," Candy whined when I hung up. "I have plans tomorrow."

"Tough." I gave her the evil eye. "Personal plans aren't important. This is Tommy we're talking about."

Lucian kept silent until Candy prodded him.

"What do you think, Dr. Sand? Set Mrs. Buckley straight, please."

We faced off from opposite ends of Kai's leather couch. "Andrews is looking for an easy out," Lucian said. "Otherwise, he risks stepping on some very big toes. You can hardly blame him."

"Wait a minute. I can blame him, and I do. It's his job to investigate no matter where it leads him or to whom." I forced myself to remain calm, using logic rather than emotion. I'd worked in the land of men long enough to know the power of a cool, articulate female.

Lucian's face looked grave. "I'm afraid for you. This killer is ruthless, willing to take chances. You're so vulnerable at CYBER-MED."

I knew he was right, but I'd never admit it. Remember the saying, "The unexamined life is not worth living"? Socrates hit a bull's-eye with that one. Tommy's murder had catapulted me into the real world again, forcing me to re-evaluate everything in my life. Lucian was right. I was vulnerable at CYBER-MED, but I was also at risk as I had been, living my soulless existence, waiting for death to reunite me with Kai.

"I'll be careful," I said. "If Andrews follows the leads we give him, I won't have to worry. We've made some good contacts that might help him. I still want to chat up Ian Cotter's wife somehow. She's the most vocal one."

Lucian raked his fingers through his thick, wavy hair. "I can help you with that. Mrs. Cotter trains at the same gym that I do."

"Why isn't that woman in jail?" Candy asked. "She's a nut."

"Meg got the charges dropped," I said. "She's one cool customer, let me tell you. Meg, that is. When Andrews accused her of having an affair with Ian, she laughed in his face."

"How tight are you with this Mrs. Cotter?" Candy asked Lucian.

He shrugged. "We speak." His soft azure eyes twinkled.

I'll just bet they did. Lucian Sand in workout attire was a tasty prospect that any warm-blooded woman would respond to, even a bereaved widow.

"Don't tell me you trained with Ian Cotter, too."

Lucian's connection to yet another CYBER-MED casualty made me uneasy. Talk about six degrees of separation. There were far too many coincidences in this case.

I tried to laugh it off. "Pretty soon you'll be telling us that you knew Judge Arthur, too."

His silence spoke more eloquently than words.

"You palled around with the Judge?" Candy squealed. "My head is spinning. I'd better go get my beauty sleep if we have to see Andrews tomorrow." She yawned.

"Wait a minute. You didn't even have dinner yet," I said. "I can grill the fish in ten minutes."

She gathered her things and shook her head. "No, thanks, I'm exhausted. Plus, maybe I'll lose a few pounds by starving. Della can come home with me tonight. That way I won't feel scared. Come on, Sweetness, your auntie needs you." She snapped on Della's lead and walked swiftly out the door.

"I should leave, too," Lucian said touching my cheek. "You've had enough excitement for one day."

An unexpected wave of loneliness swamped me. Kai, Tommy … I felt so isolated. I yearned for comfort, the kind I'd found in Lucian's arms.

"Don't go," I said. "Stay with me tonight." I led him slowly into the guest room, dousing the outside lights.

"I can just hold you if you want to sleep," Lucian said. His fingers filtered through my hair like a mountain breeze.

"Not tonight," I whispered. "Please. Make me forget all this pain."

The bedside lamp cast soft pink shadows on his face. Such a handsome face, with strong Gallic features framed by luxuriant curls. He touched me gently as if it were the first time.

"My beautiful Elisabeth," he murmured. "Do you still distrust me?"

"Forgive me," I said. "I'm so confused. You came from out of the blue, saving me like some guardian angel. I still don't understand your connection to all this. Before we met I never missed ... that is, I never thought about another man. Kai has always been with me."

"And now?" he asked, stroking my cheek. "How is it now?" Lucian brushed his lips down my neck, making me shiver. His fingertips were magic as they grazed my breasts. I felt limp, oblivious to everything but this man's touch. He raised my sweater over my head, folding it neatly on the side table. His tongue found every part of me that ached, teasing me until I yielded to him. The faint scent of Creed captivated me as it always had.

Our kiss seemed neverending as we melded into a sensuous union that felt so right.

I closed my eyes, willing my battered senses to take control of my body. As he entered me, filling me with the familiar pleasure, I said a silent prayer of thanks. *I love you Kai, love you so much. Please forgive me.*

~

I awakened the next morning in Lucian's arms, listening to his gentle snores. Kai had snored too, even though he wouldn't admit it. Lucian didn't stir as I slipped out of his grasp and found my robe. *Maybe we should have used my bedroom.* But no, that was out of the question. Kai inhabited every square inch of that room from his bathroom to the perfectly appointed closet housing his clothes.

Someday, I'll be ready. Not right now.

I got dressed in record time, just in case there was another interruption. Lucian had seen enough of my skin to last him all week. I chose a sober black suit and brushed my hair into a twist. Sergeant Andrews wouldn't notice no matter what I wore. That man was all business. In deference to Candy, I swiped my mouth with lip gloss and dabbed on green eye shadow and mascara. Redheads look dead without some kind of color. Police stations had surely seen worse, but I didn't want to be measured against a corpse.

When Lucian reached the breakfast table, I was suitably attired in widow's weeds. He took my hand and trained those gorgeous eyes on me.

"Ah, you look so grown up, Elisabeth. No school girl now." His smile told me it was all an act.

"I am grown up."

He chuckled. "Yes, I noticed that this morning. I have still not recovered from patting honey gel on your beautiful skin."

"Don't make fun of me. I'm not a fool." I turned away to suppress the hint of tears.

"No, no, no. Look at me." Lucian turned me toward him. "You are a beautiful, brilliant woman. See yourself as others see you, just this once."

I swallowed hard and summoned a smile. "I promise I'll try. But Lucian, this is serious. We need your help with CYBER-MED."

"I wondered if you would ask," he said. "You are so strong, so brave. Sometimes we all must ask for help, ma belle."

"You're the computer expert. Tell me how these murders, if they were murders, took place. In the case of Richard Chernikova, we may save a life."

He sighed. "Bon. I will review the autopsy reports for Judge Arthur and Ian Cotter."

"Wait a minute. How will you get them? We don't have time for a Freedom of Information request, you know."

Another sigh. "Computers hold every bit of information about all of us." He stroked my hand. "Except what is in our hearts. I can access anything I need to get. Give me a day or two. I'll verify my findings by doing some experiments at the LIPS office."

I decided not to ask more questions. Hacking is a violation of federal and state statutes. It's absolutely abhorrent and just what we needed.

"That policeman, Andrews, he will suspect me, you know. Even you still aren't certain." Lucian seemed amused, not alarmed.

"No doubt your name will come up."

He rose, dangling his keychain like a talisman. It was made of steel and leather embossed with the Cayenne logo. Strong and elegant, just like him.

"I am motivated, Mrs. Buckley. If I can find the method, perhaps you will find the culprit. Then you will be free from distractions." He kissed my cheek, giving me that soulful look again. "Just be careful. I cannot lose you now."

Eighteen

Mark Andrews stomped down the battered hallway of Boston police headquarters stuffing his bony arms into his pockets. He didn't believe a word we said. Maybe he just didn't care. It hadn't begun well. Candy and I arrived promptly at nine o'clock like upright, respectable citizens resolved to do their duty. Andrews was nowhere to be found.

At nine-fifteen, Francie Cohen retrieved us from the waiting room, trying hard to wipe the guilt off her well-rouged face.

"I'm so sorry, ladies. The Sergeant is running late. Come with me, and you can wait in his office." She hung her head as she delivered the lie.

Candy beamed a megawatt smile at her and linked arms. "Francie, you look stunning! You've been using our hair masque, too, I can tell."

"Uh, Officer Cohen, any idea when Andrews will make an appearance?" I liked Francie, but she was in the enemy camp. She probably knew exactly where the boss was. "We spoke with him less than twelve hours ago, you know. This is really important."

"I'm sorry, Mrs. Buckley. Do you want to reschedule?"

I'd had enough evasion and condescension from the Boston PD. If Andrews wouldn't help us, someone higher up would. Everyone has a boss. Kai had taught me that.

"Take us to your boss, please. Lives are at stake here."

The young officer came close to panic. She blanched under the artfully arranged cosmetics. I'm no bully, but this case called for leverage.

"Let me text him one more time, Mrs. Buckley. Please."

Candy nodded benevolently. "Go ahead, Francie."

Within five minutes, Mark Andrews, the Hub's very own Ichabod Crane, finally materialized. He made no apologies. In fact, he barely acknowledged us. His frosty gaze would have chilled most people, unless one was named Candace Ott. She immediately went into charm mode, sweeping aside the cop's rudeness like an errant bug.

"Wait 'til you see this, Sergeant. I brought my computer in case yours isn't updated. I know how hard it is for public servants to get equipment. Of course, Betts is the techie, not me." Sometimes Candy overplays her ditzy mode, but Andrews seemed satisfied.

I watched in silence as she romanced that machine like a pro. Even Andrews raised a brow in disbelief or admiration. I leaned back in the faux leather chair, steeling myself for another painful encounter with Tommy. Even though we had seen it all last night, the pain felt just as fresh.

Tears welled up in both of us as the lively visage of our friend appeared. Andrews didn't react other than to summon Francie Cohen to the meeting.

"Take down this information," he told her as he coolly appraised Candy and me.

"Ladies, this is very interesting. Thank you for bringing this to my attention. Officer Cohen will escort you out and answer any other questions you may have."

"That's it?" Candy asked. "After all this, you're giving us the bum's rush? I don't believe it."

I grasped her wrist, hoping she would power down. Assaulting a cop is always bad form, particularly in the police station.

"Surely you have questions for us," I said. "Mr. Yancey's dying words …"

"This conspiracy stuff is nothing but speculation," Andrews said. "Mr. Yancey was the victim of a hit and run driver, probably some drunk kid. Period."

"Aren't you going to investigate CYBER-MED, Sergeant?" I still couldn't believe it. "Those allegations are very serious."

For a moment I thought I had him. Then Andrews glanced at his desk piled with file folders that consumed the surface like a spreading rash.

"You see that, Mrs. Buckley? Those aren't hypotheticals. They're homicides, real Boston murders assigned to me. Murders with victims every bit as important as your friend." His hand shook a bit as he pointed. "I'm not wasting time chasing after potential deaths when I've got actual ones to deal with."

That's when he stomped out the door, leaving Francie Cohen to deal with us.

"I'm so sorry, ladies. He's had a hard week." She dipped a toe over that solid blue line. "Maybe I could help you. You know, on my own time."

"Thanks," I said. "That means a lot. We'll keep you in the loop."

Candy hugged her after we packed up the computer and prepared to leave. We remained silent all the way down to the lobby, each of us lost to her thoughts. Andrews' attitude hadn't devastated me at all. In fact, I found it liberating. His laissez-faire approach opened the door to almost anything we might do. My conscience was officially clear.

~

"What's our plan?" Candy asked. "I know you won't give up."

We'd ducked into the nearest Starbucks for a badly needed latte. It was a strange place for a war council, but it served the purpose.

"Ground rules first," I said. "Top secret, need to know. Stamp that on your shiny little forehead."

"Shiny?" Candy dug into her bag and got her mirror.

"Stop being silly. That means no Arun Rao. At least he can't know our plans."

Candy got that mulish look. "I suppose Lucian Sand is part of our cabal. Nice for you."

"We need Lucian for his technical skills. Don't worry, I don't trust him one hundred percent either."

"Hmm. I'll bet he practiced those technical skills on you last night, didn't he?"

I could feel the blush spreading up my neck. "Come on. Let's apportion the duties. I'll report back to CYBER-MED. You're tasked with pursuing Mrs. Ian Cotter and squeezing Judge Arthur's wife some more. I just wish I had some allies in CYBER-MED. It's hard creeping around without an idea of where I'm going."

"What about Mary Alice Tate?" Candy asked. "Maybe that was a setup, too. After all, Tommy sent you her name on that list."

"Who benefitted from her death?" I asked. "We should probably start there."

Candy thought about it for a moment. "Terrell Tate scooped the lot once poor Mary Alice got the heave-ho. Man, I'm telling you, everyone was shocked at that one. Mary Alice grew up in that house. Old man Tate called her his daughter, same as Terrell." She paused. "You know, Terrell has at least one glaring flaw. She's horribly conceited. Maybe I'll talk to her about appearing in some publicity stills for Sweet Nothings, you know, the real women who use our products."

"Good idea," I said. "What about the Cotters?"

"That's a toughie," Candy said. "I thought your boy Lucian had it covered. Or was it uncovered?"

I ignore tasteless remarks, particularly when they ring with truth. Lucian was a free agent, a sexy, single man. I'd never asked him about his love life. It was strictly off limits, none of my business. He had never asked me about Kai either, not really.

"Yo, Lizzie Mae." Candy waved her hand in front of my eyes. "I just thought of something. What if I connect with Tatiana Lake?" She noticed my blank stare. "You know, she's the unlucky woman whose bed Ian Cotter croaked in, the fashion designer. I'll propose some tie-ins between her clothes and our products."

"Oh. Good idea. Maybe she knows if Mrs. Cotter was the jealous type."

Candy sighed. "That's not all. I'll nose around and find out if Todd Brantley was the jealous type. He has enough money to hire a hit."

I couldn't fault her logic. "Just be careful, Candy. Someone has a lot to protect."

"No problemo," Candy purred. "Everyone loves makeup."

~

CYBER-MED felt alien today. Nothing specific. It was probably only my nerves. Unless Andrews commandeered their speakerphone, he couldn't have told them about Tommy's video. Hell, who knew if he would ever risk offending Dr. Meg Cahill and her deep pockets spouse with the tawdry facts of murder. Meg had cautioned me before about the effect of rumors in the high-tech sector. It was nothing too surprising. Any business, even cosmetics, can take a hit from unsavory gossip, but murder would sink CYBER-MED in a New York minute. Clients generally shy away from the threat of homicide, especially their own. As major players in this enterprise, Candy and I had fiduciary responsibilities. That's business school mumble jumble that sounds good and masks reality. I didn't really need an excuse. After all, Meg and Arun had to be told about Tommy's video. Suppose someone else found the damn thing and took it viral?

Candy needed some persuading. She loathes unpleasant scenes unless they really interest her. Try unloading a lead lipstick on her, and she'd fight like a tigress. CYBER-MED and its patient disposal service didn't engage her one bit.

"It's for Tommy," I growled. "Stop thinking of yourself. We have to present a united front. Besides, I thought you needed the money."

Her cat eyes brightened immediately. "You're right, Betts. After all, they're our partners."

I phoned Meg while we were en route. Her faithful gatekeeper swore that Dr. Cahill hadn't arrived and had a packed scheduled today.

"Change it," I snapped. "Ms. Ott and I must see Drs. Cahill and Rao immediately. Tell her it's about Mr. Yancey's murder."

When we entered CYBER-MED, we were met by the looming presence of Rand Lindsay. He was somber, far removed from his jovial self. I suspected that Meg had warned him about us.

"Miss Elisabeth," Rand nodded pleasantly. His eyes sparkled when he saw Candy, but he quickly extinguished the glow. "Love that color on you," he said. "Polka dots sure spice up gabardine."

That made Candy beam. "You're a smooth operator, Dr. Lindsay."

"Ooh, not yet. Can't call me Doctor 'til June, assuming my dissertation passes muster." Rand grimaced as he said the words.

"Are you our escort or our bodyguard?" I asked him in the elevator.

He didn't smile when he answered. "Your friend, I hope. Come on, ladies. She's waiting for you."

"What about Arun?" Candy asked.

"Him, too. I don't know what's going on, but I'm warning you. Dr. M. is on a very tight tether today." He looked furtively around the hallway, lowering his voice. "She brought in the big guns. Carter Cahill is up there, too."

That made things even more interesting.

"Good," I said. "I'll be curious to hear his reaction."

Rand knocked softly on the conference room door and ushered us in. "Good luck, ladies."

The three of them sat side by side at the conference table. Meg, clad in crisp pinstripes nodded briskly and took command. Carter gave us the once over and sank slowly into his chair like an alligator sizing up his prey. After flashing Candy a smile, Arun faded into the background, his normally ebullient spirit subdued by the occasion.

"Ladies," Meg said, "what's so urgent? My assistant said you insisted on this meeting."

I said nothing for a full half-minute. The dismissal by the great Doctor got on my last nerve. Candy followed my lead and stayed silent. After watching Carter twitch, I made my move.

"Last night a voice from the grave contacted us." I spoke softly and wielded a humongous stick. "Thomas Yancey gave us the motive for his murder."

Their expressions were priceless. Meg's perpetual smile almost masked her disdain while Carter's features contorted in a malicious grin. Arun's liquid brown eyes widened in horror.

"Let them have it, Candy," I said. "It's time for show and tell."

She adjusted her computer and called up KillerStartups. When she clicked on the video section, Tommy's face appeared on the screen.

I had committed his words to memory. That allowed me to focus on the reactions of my three colleagues as they heard my friend's accusations. Meg maintained a perfect poker face throughout the presentation. You would almost think that she was listening to a dry medical treatise. Her husband tried a different tack: Carter's face contorted with each word Tommy uttered. I fully expected steam to belch from his outsized ears. Arun was harder to read. He masked his feelings by folding his arms and lowering his eyes. After seven minutes of torture, the video concluded. Stunned silence consumed the room.

"This isn't real," Meg said, leaning back in her seat. "Thomas always joked. You two know that better than I do. He probably contrived this thing to throw a scare into you. Us, too." Her pixie grin was a failed attempt at gallows humor. "For heaven's sake, you'd think we were Murder Incorporated here." She nudged Arun Rao to include him in the fun. "I'm a physician. Do I look like some kind of hit woman?"

Candy shed her fluffy persona like a snake molting its skin. The reptile that emerged was fearsome indeed.

"What does a hit woman look like, I wonder? After all, Jack the Ripper was supposedly a doctor, right?" She flashed her beguiling smile and continued. "Tommy wasn't playing a prank. He would never do that to us. He loved us."

Meg rubbed her throat as if it were dry while Carter leapt to his wife's defense.

"See here, you two. Stop this irresponsible speculation right now, or I'll sue you for slander."

I hate bullies. That's why I had to butt in when Carter's smug self-righteousness hit the third rail on my subway system.

"Actually, Carter, the term is libel. These days courts equate video charges with libel even though they're spoken." I packaged my barb in a sunny smile that no one bought.

Cahill sputtered until his wife's gentle squeeze short-circuited his ire. Meg tugged her skirt and got down to business.

"OK, ladies. What's your proposal? Do we allow this unsubstantiated item to destroy the firm or forge on? Thomas believed in CYBER-MED, you know."

I could tell that Candy had reached the boiling point. Her face had the volcanic look of Mt. St. Helens pre-eruption. Lava would spew any moment now.

"Now let me get this straight," she said. Calm. She was far too calm. "You're willing to risk lives of helpless patients to preserve your company." Candy rose slowly, like an undulating cobra, and stood squarely in front of Dr. Meg. "Doesn't that violate the Hippocratic Oath or something?"

A rosy wash of color stained Meg's cheeks. I recognized the shade instantly: Sweet Nothings Come Hither #3. Candy should bottle it and sell it.

"You're wrong," Meg said. "We would never compromise lives."

Arun joined the fray. He clenched his fists, turning his flashing eyes on me.

"That bastard Sand's behind all this, I know it. He's your lover; you're in cahoots with him."

I kicked Candy under the table to stem any violent reaction. Emotion was useful to us. People lose focus when they're upset.

"It's extortion," Carter growled, pounding the table, "highway robbery, trying to drive up the price of your shares. Well, it won't work, girls. My attorneys will make mincemeat out of you."

Kai had the self-confidence born of great wealth and the ability to kick almost anyone's ass. He would have laughed in Cahill's face. I'm not that cocky, but I am a lawyer. I used the weapons I knew best.

"Calm down," I said. "You're wasting your time, folks."

"What are you talking about?" Arun barked. "Tell us."

I held out my hands, palms up. "It's simple. This morning we turned that information over to Sergeant Andrews. I'm an officer of the court. I had no other choice."

Candy nodded sagely as if the plan had been hers alone. "I think it's time for some contingency planning." Her smile radiated pride in the business school palaver.

For a moment Meg's iron control wilted. Her head sank between her hands as she ran slender fingers through her shining bob. Carter put his arm around her in a clumsy embrace.

"OK," she said squaring her shoulders. "Let me think. There's no proof to all this. We know that. After all, we monitor several hundred patients. Some have died. More will. That's the nature of dealing with the critically ill. They die. If we had some specifics …"

When Candy passed her Tommy's death list, Meg's complexion lost its rosy glow. For a moment I thought she might faint. Her husband's next words provided little comfort.

"We have to consider the possibility that the media will find out. I suggest you prepare a press release just in case, Meggy. It's the smart thing to do."

"And don't forget cyberspace," Rao cautioned. "This thing could go viral any time."

I smiled, thinking of one million people downloading Tommy's final words. How perfect. He'd always been a ham.

"These people weren't murdered," Meg said. "One is still alive. For crying out loud, Richard Chernikova was just here. You saw him, Elisabeth."

"Are you so sure?" I asked. "About the other three, I mean. There were reasons people would want them dead, and Secretary Chernikova has tons of enemies."

"No, no, no." Meg dug her nails into the palms of her hands. "If we're so slick, where's the money? You studied our balance sheet. We're running on hot air and my husband's largesse until we get established." Her eyes pleaded for understanding.

"I'd hardly expect a ledger entry for hits," I said.

Meg's wintery smile told me she got the joke. "Start a complete review of our procedures. Rao, you're in charge. I want everything tightened up, especially if it's connected with Richard." She turned to me. "Would you speak with Rand? He can whip out a press release without breaking a sweat."

"Are you sure?" Arun asked. "Why let another person in on this?"

"He's my assistant and my friend. We have to trust someone." Meg rose and walked stiffly out the door with her husband trailing behind her.

Arun Rao gathered his iPad and glasses. "Candy, forgive me. I don't know what came over me. It's just that my life's work is CYBER-MED. It's my identity. If it implodes, I may go with it." He took her hand and rubbed it softly against his cheek. "Call you soon."

Nineteen

The Cayenne was draped in front of my building like a peacock strutting its stuff. Lucian could claim my doorman as a tax deduction if he kept that up. I acted nonchalant or tried to. It wasn't easy when he hopped out of the car, all flowing hair, black sunglasses and manly muscles. Lucian was quite a dish, if you liked an exotic blend.

"I thought you'd never come home," he said. "May I come up with you?"

I should have said no or at least acted indifferent. All I could think of was the strength of his arms around me and the feel of his lips as they brushed against my skin. If Lucian was a murderer, my goose was cooked. He could kill me with those sensuous looks or strain my heart with the pleasure of his touch.

Cool it, Lizzie Mae. You're utterly pathetic.

I'm not the fanciful type. That's Candy's domain. The last time I'd felt this silly ... I gulped, willing my heart rate under control. My senses hadn't been this wild since the miraculous day that I'd met Kai. I know how to act. *Stop fantasizing, and focus on the business at hand.* Lucian and I had a murder to solve, possibly several murders. That took precedence over romantic flings and girlish giggles. I couldn't count on Andrews and company. They wanted a neat and tidy solution that would wrap everything up without entangling Boston Brahmins like Carter Cahill and his wife. From Andrews' perspective it made sense. Why stir a caldron that might bubble over into a major political scandal? The deaths of Ian Cotter, Mary Alice Tate and Jacob Arthur were yesterday's news.

Lucian stared at me with that ridiculous half-smile. "Are you ill, Elisabeth? We've been standing here for quite a while." He placed his hand at the small of my back, urging me forward.

Damn. Could the man read my mind? I shivered when he touched me.

"We dropped Tommy's bombshell today," I said. "First on Andrews, then the CYBER-MED crew. Andrews was indifferent, and my partners were livid. Arun blamed you."

"Of course." Lucian nodded. "I did some research this morning that you need to see. It won't answer all our questions, but it suggests a method. With your permission, I'd like my assistant to help me demonstrate."

"Assistant? I thought we'd keep this between the two of us."

Lucian pinned me with an icy stare. "Do you not trust me yet?"

I returned his glare with interest. "I don't have much choice, do I?"

We passed my beaming concierge and commandeered the elevator. I positioned myself in one corner where I could study Lucian's face. If he had a guilty conscience, you would never know it by his placid expression. I reminded myself that sociopaths felt none of the emotions that ruled normal beings. Maybe Lucian was worse, a charming psychopath who could subdue his enemies with a ripple of those spectacular muscles. Psych 101 had been a long time ago. I forgot what the distinction was between the terms, and frankly I didn't care.

While I fished in my purse for my house keys, Lucian stood guard. It unnerved me, causing me to fumble with the door.

"May I?" he asked. Lucian placed the gold elephant key lock in his palm and stroked it. "Ah," he said. "Hermes is one of my favorites. It suits you. Looks a bit battered though."

He swung open the door with one twist of the Medco lock, leaving me to ponder once again how familiar this man seemed. The key lock had belonged to Kai. He had loved elephants. He'd dangled it in front of me as he was leaving that final day.

"They're admirable creatures, Lizzie Mae, symbols of luck and fidelity." Kai had winked at me and patted my stomach. "Fertility too."

This particular elephant hadn't brought him much luck. The key lock was one of the personal effects they'd found with my husband's body. Few people would realize that it was from Hermes. Points to Lucian for that.

Della greeted us with her frenzied, scolding bark, letting us know that she'd been neglected. Faithless minx, she ignored me and hurled herself into Lucian's open arms.

"She's always preferred men," I said, "a big daddy's girl."

He locked eyes with me. "I love animals. They can sense it, I think. In many ways, they're far more intelligent than humans."

That warmth on my cheeks meant only one thing, the redhead's curse. Someday I might master my emotions. No more blushing, flushing or swooning. Until then I'd have to ignore it and soldier on.

"I'll get us something to drink. Then we can discuss your experiment." I busied myself with hostess chores while Lucian examined the marble fireplace surround.

"This is beautiful," he said. "It is French, no?"

I nodded. "Imported from an old chateau in Avignon. Getting it up here was quite a feat, I can tell you."

"Your husband was a man of great discernment in furnishings and in women." Lucian grinned. "I can tell that."

"Yes, well." I handed him a tray with three Baccarat wineglasses and a bottle of Château Latour. "Will you do the honors, please? Then as soon as your buddy arrives, we can get down to business."

"Gladly." Lucian uncorked the wine and poured both of us a glass. After a perfunctory toast we settled in.

He reached into his attaché case and produced a strange object. "Here it is," Lucian said. "I got this and a few other components at Radio Shack this morning. If you can wait a minute, it will be worth your while."

The house phone shrilled, announcing the arrival of a visitor. "Send him up," I said.

Five minutes later I opened the door to Rand Lindsay.

"Thanks, Miss Elisabeth," he said as he accepted his wine. "This place is phenomenal. I couldn't even afford a closet." He chuckled. "Not that I could ever fit in most closets. Good thing I'm out. That's a gay joke, in case you hadn't noticed."

"Very droll. Someday, Rand, you'll own the whole building. By the way, aren't you taking a big chance coming here?" I recalled Arun's reaction to Lucian.

He shrugged. "There's so much chaos at CYBER-MED, they'll never miss me. I did that press release for Dr. Meg and skedaddled. Everyone was keyed up, even the Tornado."

Lucian grinned at the nickname. "Rand has a code name for everyone. It's part of his charm." He brought out what I assumed was some implantable device and a simple-looking radio. "Ready, Rand? Mrs. Buckley wants a show."

"On it, Sandman." He produced a complicated diagram that left me stumped. "A few basics, Miss Elisabeth. I watched that video after you left. Dr. Meg and I reviewed every word Tommy said." He patted my hand. "Anything's possible, I know that, but I think this is a software issue."

"Software? Make it simple, Rand. My interest in science is very limited and my patience even more so." I drummed my fingers on the table. It was rude, quite unlike the behavior of the refined Mrs. Kai Buckley. It felt good.

I saw that sly smile on Lucian's face. He sipped his wine and helped out his protégé. "My warnings last year concerned safety issues. Nothing malicious, just the possibility of malfunctions in the software. The hardware, pacemakers and the like, is closely regulated, but there's a vacuum. No one polices the software until it's too late." He raked his impossibly thick hair again.

Does he know how sexy that gesture is? Kai did that same thing until I called him on it.

"This is no malfunction, not if Tommy was right. We're talking hits, targeted murders for hire." I still couldn't believe it. The whole thing was preposterous, Candy and I blundering into a ring of murderers.

"Tell me how they would do it, Lucian. I want to understand."

He closed his eyes for a second and regrouped. "Rand was correct about the software issues. Much research has been devoted to the devices themselves, safety and such." He held up an ordinary looking radio. "See this? We did a bench test today using this software radio."

His frown told me the news was not good. Tommy's instincts had been right on the mark.

"First, we intercepted data, signals from the device itself. In this case we replicated the cardiac defibrillator that Ian Cotter used. Same make and model."

"How could you possibly know that you were accessing the right device? After all, thousands of patients in Boston alone must have them."

Rand jumped in with unseemly zeal. "That's the cool thing, Mrs. B. Sandman and I got the name, age, medical ID, all that personal stuff, right off the implant. It was easy."

I'm no scientist, but my training had taught me to analyze problems. "OK, so in a case like Mary Alice Tate, someone could find out blood type, maybe even DNA stuff. That's bad enough, but it didn't kill her. How about Cotter and the Judge?"

Lucian sighed. He spoke clinically, very much the cool, dispassionate scientist. "There's more. We went into attack mode and were able to turn off the therapy settings. In other words, we fried the device." He entered a special world inhabited by scientists and other techno-freaks like Rand, Arun and the Tornado. The door slammed shut on non-believers like me. Candy wasn't even in the bleacher seats for this show. I risked a frown. There was more, I could feel it. Something worse than mere privacy issues.

Rand beamed, oblivious to reality. "It's high-quality, original research. Boy, I wish I could use this on my professors. I'd sail right through my oral exams."

How the hell had Tommy, the least technical person I knew, stumbled upon this? There had to be a financial link somewhere. If only I could find it.

"Back to Ian Cotter's case," Lucian said. "We went further, much further than I'd ever imagined." A look passed between him and Rand. It was hard to describe: caution, fatalism, maybe even fear. "We delivered a shock that induced ventricular fibrillation — heart attack."

My throat felt drier than dust. I sipped my wine as if it were salvation itself. "Was it ... would it have killed him?"

His voice was flat, matter of fact. "It was lethal. Ian Cotter would have died instantly."

"And the Judge? Jacob Arthur." Somehow saying his name made him seem real. I felt a sickening slide in my gut.

"Him too," Lucian said. "Judge Arthur's pacemaker would have attacked the organ it was programmed to save."

I was speechless, unable to form a coherent thought.

Stop moping. Harness that spectacular mind of yours. It's a business case. Think like a lawyer, Lizzie Mae.

I heard Kai's words as clearly as if he were sitting there in that tatty leather chair sipping Château Latour. They strengthened my resolve the way his arms had always fortified my soul.

"OK, bear with me now. Some of my questions may sound elementary." I checked their faces. Lucian's was an unreadable mask, Rand's aglow with scientific endorphins.

"This type of attack would require special expertise, right?" They both nodded. "Surely other scientists could do this, too." The nerd herd in Boston alone could fill a stadium. Maybe one of them went for the cash and became a killer.

"That is true," Lucian said. "We are gifted, but so many in the scientific community are also." He reached for the wine and poured another glass for him and Rand. His movements seemed stiff, mechanical. Was he hiding the truth from me?

I recalled something Tony "Tornado" Torres had mentioned about proximity. "Isn't there a distance issue? How close would you have to get to do this? The Judge was presiding over the trial when he died. An audience of fifty people saw that."

Both men relaxed as the conversation switched to pedagogy. That role was as comfortable for them as a pair of well-worn boots. Rand looked to Lucian before answering.

"That's where it gets really interesting," he said. "At one time not too long ago, you had to stand close, within three centimeters, to interact with an IMD. Not anymore." He rubbed his hands together. "These new devices are way cool. You know Latin, Mrs. B., so you'll get this. It's called malware. We tried it from several points. One time we were almost a third of a mile away."

Lucian's frown subdued Rand's high spirits. If circumstances were different, that frown would have sent me on an estrogen high. I felt giddy, skating on ice so thin it could crack without warning, plunging me into the icy waters of reality.

My eyes locked on Lucian's. The scientific sheen had temporarily blinded me to reality. Tommy didn't pal around with a gang of techno-nerds. He'd been too busy servicing every Boston female with a pulse to do that. My old pal knew the murderer, felt comfortable having a civilized discussion about his or her crimes. I couldn't exclude my own gender. Anyone can drive a car or program death. Like it or not, it was inescapable: the murderer worked at CYBER-MED.

Twenty

As they headed out the door, Candy called. Her voice cracked; that always happens when she's verging on hysteria. I signaled to the guys and put her on speaker.

"What's wrong?" I asked, dreading the answer.

"Arun's here. I'll let him tell you."

Arun cleared his throat. "Mrs. Buckley. Are we disturbing you?"

"Not at all. Dr. Sand is here. Full disclosure policy and all." Rand exhaled, mouthing a silent thank you when his name wasn't mentioned.

Arun's voice deepened. "OK. It doesn't matter anyway. Nothing does."

The man was a drama queen. King. Whatever. Either way, he spent far too much time moaning for my taste. Something had gone wrong, that was obvious. If only he would man up and spit it out.

"Tell me about it, Arun," I said. "After the last year nothing shocks me anymore."

I'd had my fill of phone calls. Two of them had been death calls, actually. First Tommy phoned me about Kai. I recalled every word he said as if it were yesterday. I had clutched the phone to my chest and fainted on the spot. Later I'd awakened in a hospital bed, bereft of my husband and son.

Tommy's death was even more vivid. Painful vignettes flitted through my mind. The theme was always the same: Tommy, Kai, Candy and me. They all melded into one amorphous mass that spelled grief. After that, nothing Arun said would shock me. I was Teflon tough, inured to hurt.

"It happened," Arun said. "We're ruined."

"What are you talking about? I suppressed the urge to slam the phone.

Lucian listened without saying a word. Rand put a hand over his mouth to keep from blurting out a reaction.

"Tommy's video went viral. It's all over YouTube and God only knows where else." His heavy breathing filled the room. I expected him to hyperventilate any second. "The calls started this afternoon from clients, prospective clients and every physician we deal with. They had the same question: what the hell is going on at CYBER-MED?"

"Not a total surprise," I said. "These days, privacy is an illusion. I'm afraid the cops will swarm all over CYBER-MED. Have many patients switched providers yet?"

"A few," Arun answered, "but its early days. Worst case, we'll lose the majority and have to go Chapter 11. Maybe even Chapter 7."

"Any white knights in the offing?" I asked. "After all, the public's attention span is short, and no one can prove anything. Yet."

"Maybe. Meg already got a third-party offer for a majority of our shares. Rock bottom price, though. Ten million bucks. Wouldn't even cover our outstanding debt."

I considered that development carefully. What better way to bring CYBER-MED to its knees than by leaking Tommy's video? I logged on to my computer and typed in YouTube. Thomas Yancey's last words were prominently displayed, listed under Featured Video. It had already racked up over two million hits.

"Switch on the news," Lucian said. Rand lumbered over to the flat screen and clicked on the New England News channel. There it was, bigger than life. The station recounted the CYBER-MED controversy, complete with statements by the grieving widows and a taut, coolly professional interview with Dr. Margaret Cahill. The song "Cold as Ice" swept through my mind as I watched her. In a weird way I admired Meg's inexorable strength. She would be near the top of my heroes list in any crisis. Of course, loyalty was out of the question. Meg would jettison you in a hurry if it suited her.

For a moment I forgot that Arun and Candy were still on speakerphone. "Are you guys there?" I asked.

"Barely," Candy whined. "What should we do, Betts?"

"Get your bony little ass in gear and meet me at CYBER-MED. We have to strategize."

I asked Lucian Sand to join us at CYBER-MED. Mentioning Cahill's name made Rand flee as fast as his bulk allowed. "Meet you at the office," he panted. "Dr. Meg will be looking for me." His fear was almost palpable.

It took every ounce of my poise to keep from screaming.

"Is something wrong?" Lucian asked, giving me a gentle squeeze.

"Nope. Everything is hunky dory. My best friend was murdered, and now Candy and I are ensnared by a murderous cabal of cyber-thugs. Nothing's wrong."

His response was sharper than a slap. "Believe it or not," he said calmly, "there's now a machine algorithm that detects sarcasm. The Israelis developed it. SASI they call it." His turquoise eyes twinkled. "Computers can do anything, Elisabeth. Almost." Lucian lifted my chin toward him, kissing my forehead

"I told you before, ma belle. I will never leave your side unless you ask. Count on that." He thrust a sheet of plain printer paper at me. "Here. I found this taped to your front door when I went back for your gloves. I put it in one of your plastic bags to preserve evidence."

The message was succinct. In neatly printed letters someone warned: BACK OFF BITCH OR YOU'LL DIE.

Porsche's have superior heaters, but that didn't help me. My body shook as if I were stranded in the Arctic. Someone, a murderer perhaps, had breached my supposedly secure building and threatened me. Anyone with sense would have called the cops right away. Not me, the newly galvanized Lizzie Mae. I was consumed by a rage so volcanic I almost swooned.

"That does it," I growled. "I'll never back off now. Screw Andrews and all the other cops. I'll handle this myself."

"Too late," Lucian said. "I dialed the Sergeant on my way down. He said he'd meet us at CYBER-MED."

This time there were no sly jokes or innuendos. Lucian's handsome features were etched in stone.

"Maybe you should give it up," he said, "leave everything to the authorities. That's what Tommy asked you to do." He slid into his seat and fired up the engine.

A momentary suspicion flashed through me. Could Lucian himself have penned that note? What a perfect way to scare me off without hurting me or Della. It was printed so it was hard to tell who wrote it. I summoned the lawyer's look: a smooth, impenetrable mask.

"You don't get it. Nothing scares me anymore. Hasn't for a long time."

Lucian paused, warily scanning my face. "Would Kai accept that? Risking your life? I thought he cherished you."

I hugged Della's silky fur, pulling her close for a nose kiss. "Don't act like you knew him. Kai was willing enough to risk his own life and our son's." As always whenever I thought of that, renegade tears welled up in my eyes. I swiped at them with my sleeve.

Lucian reached across the gearbox and gathered me in his arms. "You're very brave. I know that, but you don't have to do this alone. Let me help you."

I pulled away, fighting every instinct inside me. "You can help. Just don't get in my way. This is something I must do for Tommy and for me."

He gave a brisk nod, shifted the powerful beast and edged into traffic. "D'accord. Next stop, CYBER-MED."

The two-mile drive was unendurable. Lucian kept his eyes on the road, even while we waited for traffic lights. I barely noticed. Today's drama engulfed me so much that I felt disembodied. Before long I would face a building full of potential murderers. Virtually everyone at CYBER-MED had the skills and information to mastermind this monstrous crime. I suspected there were at least two conspirators, one to target potential customers and one to effect the crime. I don't subscribe to *Soldier of Fortune Magazine*. I have no idea what the fee schedule is for murder. Pretty steep, I bet, especially with the possibility of life without parole staring you in the face. Murder one carries a hefty penalty, even in this bluest of states.

"I forgot to tell you," Lucian said. "I spoke with Katherine today at my club."

"Katherine? I'm drawing a blank."

He gifted me with his winsome smile. "Mrs. Cotter. You know, Ian Cotter's wife."

"Ah. Did she brandish a weapon or have anything valuable to say?"

His grin widened. "No weapon, but she had plenty to say. According to her, Ian was inoffensive, harmless. Played around but always crawled home to her begging forgiveness. She swears the womanizing was part of his public persona. You know, a way to entice the clients."

"Yeah. I love a man who knows how to beg." I smiled sweetly. "Ian must have been some actor, enticing Tatiana Lake right into her bed."

Lucian made a quick turn despite the squealing tires and clenched fists of other drivers. "Kat said that Ian frequently got threats from boyfriends and husbands." He shrugged. "It was *par le cours* for him. No big deal. Most of the time they'd have a beer together and part friends. That's how they handle these things in France. Many men have a mistress or someone on the side. Women do, too."

"Interesting. Any suspects? Guys who don't like beer, for instance?"

"Not really," Lucian said. "Although one guy, older, wouldn't play ball. Ian worried a bit about him. No name, but like most of them he was wealthy."

"Was she telling the truth?" I asked. "That's pretty sensitive information to blurt out to a stranger."

His smile was priceless. "Did I say that we were strangers?"

"No, of course not," I stammered.

I'm a woeful interrogator. Nosy questions and sly hints give me hives. What if he thought I was jealous or possessive? Nothing could be further from the truth.

"Kat is a sensitive woman," Lucian said. "Losing control the other night embarrassed her. She has no love for Margaret Cahill, although she didn't say why."

"I can think of a dozen reasons, especially if the good doctor was toying with Ian."

Lucian swung into a space on the street adjoining CYBER-MED just as Candy alighted from a cab wearing a media savvy red power suit with subdued black piping. Without much effort she'd nailed it, a serious but stylish venture into corporate America.

I gave Della the down-stay command and wiggled out of my seatbelt. "Just one more thing," I told Lucian. "This is America, not France, and I don't buy Mrs. Cotter's blasé act one bit. If she loved her husband, she cared about his carousing. Believe me."

We locked eyes. "A woman like you would not tolerate that, my Elisa, but not everyone is so strong." Lucian walked over and opened the passenger side door. "Come. We must discuss this some other time. Ms. Ott awaits us."

Despite the publicity, the media were conspicuously absent. I scanned the streets around CYBER-MED, looking for telltale vans, helicopters or lurking scribes. In the scheme of things, I suppose our story was less compelling than war, terrorism or economic ruin unless you had an IMD inside your body.

There was no welcome party to greet us in the lobby, just a lone guard whose dour expression dared us to make a false move. He handed Lucian a visitor's pass and waved the three of us toward the elevator.

"Meg must be expecting you," I told Lucian. "That woman is on the ball even when a crisis looms."

Candy snorted. "Let's just hope she hasn't booby-trapped the elevator. Arun said she doesn't like you, Betts."

"Really? Boo hoo. I can live without her approval. Need I mention that she's our junior partner?"

That's another lesson that Kai had taught me: stop agonizing over other people's opinion of you. It's one obsession that can drive you nuts.

We reached the executive floor without mishap. When the elevator doors opened, Tony Torres awaited us. He was friendly enough, but something about his looming presence disturbed me. He was always there, lurking on the fringes of CYBER-MED like a migraine.

"Sandman! Great to see you, guy." He gave Lucian a man-hug and lowered his voice. "Watch your step in there. They're on the warpath. Sent me down to the lobby to wait for the cops. Just what I want to do. Maybe a change at the top wouldn't be such a bad thing."

Candy glanced at his muscular hindquarters as he retreated. "Wow, that Tornado stays in shape. No loafing around the donut box for him. Stairmaster all the way." She strode down the corridor, stilettos clicking , knocked briskly at the conference room door and glided in with Lucian and me trailing in her wake.

It was all quiet on the meeting front. Meg sat with her ankles crossed like a superior student awaiting praise. Her husband's eyes never left her. Carter snarled a greeting and inched closer to his wife, angling his body as if to shield her. Arun, his fingers flying over the keyboard, worked his iPhone. He glanced up, eyes aglow, when Candy entered the room.

"How are you?" I asked. "We came as soon as we heard. Maybe with some contingency planning ..."

"Don't worry, Elisabeth. Everything's under control."

Meg's voice was calm, friendly even. Was her euphoria natural or chemically induced? I'd expected something different, a war council, not a slumber party.

"Aren't you worried?" Candy asked. "CYBER-MED just imploded. By tomorrow every client will pull up stakes."

Meg's smugness irritated me. This was no trivial matter to dismiss or will away. The survival of the company, our company, was at stake.

Lucian chose a corner seat. He was a lynx, languidly stretching his long, elegant limbs as he surveyed his adversaries with practiced ease.

"I hope you're satisfied," Carter growled my way. "You had to do it, didn't you?"

"I beg your pardon."

"The video. You had to tip them off." He held a snowy linen handkerchief to his nose. "Well, it won't work. We've already turned down your offer, Mrs. Buckley."

"You can't talk to her like that." Candy wheeled around, ready to pounce. "Betts had nothing to do with this."

"Maybe we should just wait for Sergeant Andrews," I said. "No sense in repeating ourselves."

"Of course not, but the exodus you spoke of won't be happening." Meg patted her perfect bob. "I just finished speaking with our most prominent client. For your information, Secretary Chernikova will remain with CYBER-MED. Once that word gets out, the rest will fall in line."

Everything made sense. Meg, the master tactician, had called in the big guns to save her. Why dither when you have both right and might on your side? Richard Chernikova had paid his debt, but at what price? It might cost him his life.

"What about the murders? Tommy died to prevent more from happening."

"Unproven, irresponsible nonsense." Carter did his table-pounding act again. His antics must take quite a toll on the family furniture. I reacted by ignoring him.

"Let's think strategically," I said. "You need to listen to what Dr. Sand has to say, all of you. I commissioned him to check out the methodology of this scheme, assuming it exists, of course."

Lucian discussed the same material I'd heard before. Candy gasped at the implications, Meg and Arun grunted politely, and Carter drummed his fingers.

"That's all very illuminating, Dr. Sand, but your theories fail to link CYBER-MED to anything illegal." Meg gave a tight little smile that was more like a dismissal. "I realize you ladies have controlling interest, but Arun and I know the medical community. Let us handle this for all our sakes."

I value self-control even under difficult conditions. Deep breathing, yoga style, came in handy during tough times like this. Rather than savage Meg, I took a cleansing breath.

"My concern is for the victims past and present. Doesn't that bother you?"

"Not at all," she said. "There are no victims, Mrs. Buckley, only suppositions."

Candy didn't practice yoga. She leapt right into the fray. "Now just one minute. Our friend Tommy was murdered."

Arun leaned over and patted her hand. I didn't trust him or even like him much, but I had to admit his concern seemed genuine. He stopped texting and cleared his throat.

"As a scientist I have to say this is disturbing. However, everything Dr. Sand mentioned can also have a less sinister explanation. Not everyone is a conspiracy theorist."

"And yet," Lucian interjected smoothly, "only today someone threatened Mrs. Buckley's life." He held up the plastic envelope containing the note. "Is this not disturbing?"

Before anyone could react, the door opened. Rand entered the room with Sergeant Andrews and Francie Cohen in tow.

"Excuse me, everyone," Rand said. "He insisted on seeing you." He lowered his eyes and slowly backed out of the room.

"Now see here," Carter growled. "We want our attorney present for any interrogations."

I had to admire Andrews' poise. He was undeterred by the rich man's tantrum. After motioning Francie to a seat in the back, he calmly faced our group.

Twenty-One

"Pardon the interruption, folks. This isn't an interrogation. More of an inquiry, actually. Since your firm made the news, I have to follow up." Andrews grinned. "Now, Dr. Sand here reports a threat to Mrs. Buckley. Things are heating up."

"It's nonsense," Carter Cahill sniffed. "Poppycock."

Andrews shrugged. "It may very well be, sir, but that doesn't change the fact that a man was murdered, your colleague, Thomas Yancey." He scrutinized each of our faces. "What can you tell me about this recording the victim made?"

Meg spread out her hands, palms up. "He had a very lively imagination, Sergeant. We all loved him, but Tommy had his quirks, as we all do."

"I understand that, Doctor, but the legal guys tell me that tape is more than a whim. It's what they call a dying declaration. That has some weight to it." He nodded at me.

"You're right," I said. "The Federal Rules of Evidence allow it, even though it's hearsay. Most states do, too."

Carter gave me a sour look. "I've got my own lawyers, Mrs. Buckley, a whole team of them. Corporate guys, not makeup artists. They tell me we don't have to answer any questions."

Francie Cohen frowned and ducked her head. Her ringlets were especially shiny today. Score another hit for Candy. The atmosphere in the room intensified, even though the temperature remained crisp. Arun wiped his shiny forehead with a pocket square.

"Let me ask you, Mrs. Buckley. What do you think is going on here?" Andrews had a few smooth moves of his own. He threw that hot potato right into my lap.

I knew what Kai would have done—stood toe to toe with Meg, her cretinous hubby and anyone else who opposed him. I didn't have Kai's strength, but I'm no coward.

"Dr. Sand can explain things better," I said, "but I believe that someone at CYBER-MED is a murderer, arranging targeted hits. My friend Tommy figured it out somehow and confronted that person. He died because of it."

"Outrageous!" Arun exploded. "Where's the proof? Show it to me, Mrs. Buckley. You studied our financial statement."

Andrews smirked but stayed silent. He appeared to be enjoying the show.

I watched Meg carefully. She had folded her hands again in that faux schoolgirl pose and pasted a mask of compassion on her face. Fortunately, her eyes betrayed her. She was loaded and ready to fire.

"Sergeant," she said calmly, "we must consider Mrs. Buckley's situation. Having suffered two tragic losses in a year," she turned toward me, "her reaction is only natural. As a medical professional ..."

"Stop." I rose slowly, deliberately, and approached the whiteboard. "Dr. Cahill's wrong. It was three tragic losses, actually. She forgot my miscarriage." My hands were steady as I held the marker. Lucian caught my eye and gave me thumbs up. "None of that matters now except to me. Let's focus on the big picture. Dr. Rao is correct. The corporate books don't have a ledger entry for murder. No one would go that far. I suspect there are at least two people involved, one insider and one outsider. That would make sense. Tommy knew the insider. He told us that on the video. It's the only way to explain his death."

"Wait just a minute," Arun said. "You're making an assumption here. Maybe Tommy's death was collateral damage. You know, the unintended byproduct of another crime. We know someone stole that old lady's car. Some kid, probably. I say he panicked and lost control of it. Check other crimes in the area that night, Sergeant. That's where you'll find him. Stop this nonsense about a high tech conspiracy."

I turned toward the board and wrote down four names: Ian Cotter, Mary Alice Tate, Judge Jacob Arthur, and Thomas Yancey. I then added Richard Chernikova's name with a question mark.

"Thomas Yancey loved puzzles. He was masterful at solving them. Somehow he linked these names to an unthinkable truth. Our task is to pool our skills and do the same thing."

"Count me out." Carter curled his lip at me. "Damned nonsense, that's what it is. Is that what they taught you at Harvard, Mrs. Buckley? One pathetic woman's fantasy." He held his arm out to his wife. "Come on, Meggy. Let's go call our lawyer."

It stung, but I bounced right back. I was Wonder Woman, using my magic bracelets to deflect enemy arrows.

"I'll help you," Arun said, playing Prince Charming. "Tommy was my friend. We can probably get Rand to join in too, if he's not too scared of Meg."

Candy beamed at him and moved closer. Arun was in for a good night.

Before we started the exercise, Andrews stood and gathered his things. "You guys can do this without me," he said. "Officer Cohen can help you." He stabbed his bony finger at Francie. "I'll expect a full report tomorrow."

"You look disappointed," Lucian said. "Did you expect more? A confession, perhaps?"

I refused to dignify his sarcasm. Actually, I had hoped for some telltale sign of guilt from someone. That was unrealistic. Silly. Fictional sleuths were lucky, but the rest of us had to stumble through reality scratching for clues. Maybe Carter was right. Perhaps I am pathetic.

Lucian took some getting used to. He's pushy in the self-assured manner of gorgeous men everywhere, automatically making decisions for both of us without a second thought. It was familiar territory for me. Kai had possessed that same attitude in spades.

"What did you make of Meg's reaction?" I asked. "She was so calm. Weird."

His lips twisted in a half-smile. "You have to know le bon Doctor. She never shows her cards until the last play of the night, but she's always thinking."

"You seem to know her very well."

A smug smile was his only response. It was preferable to Tommy's seamy details about Dr. Meg in her leather bustier and whip.

Arun recovered quickly. He recited one of those textbook answers that consumed airtime without adding content.

"Naturally, we're committed to accountability. Meg was right on top of things. She always is. I personally interviewed the operators on all three shifts. They're highly reputable industry professionals of the highest caliber."

"And?" Candy went on red alert. "Did you find anything hinky? Massive debt, unexplained wealth? You know the drill."

Tornado locked eyes with Rand but stayed mute.

"Arun, I'm talking to you." Candy can be merciless when the occasion demands. Tonight was one of those times.

Arun hemmed and hawed, unnerved by her withering gaze. "We started a thorough review, but the truth is, once the manufacturer paid off, we sort of let things slide. After all, the FDA only cares about the reliability of the device. We stopped investigating our people. Bad for morale and all that."

"So," I said. "Tommy might have alerted the murder."

"Only if he or she worked at CYBER-MED," Rand said. His cheeks flushed as a coughing spell hit him. No one wanted to go there, but I had no choice.

"Who was working here then? I assume you'd need high level clearance to access those two patients."

"Three, actually." Candy's ferocity startled even Francie Cohen. She leaned back as if to avoid the anger radiating from my friend. "Don't forget Mary Alice Tate," Candy said. "Someone here leaked confidential medical information about her. I think it was a dry run. You know, get a payoff and see if anyone figures it out."

Lucian's French accent intensified as he responded. "I was here and had the necessary clearances. I assume everyone else here plus Dr. Cahill did as well."

"Not Carter," Arun said. "He's strictly hands off, the silent partner type. Wouldn't know a bit from a byte."

Carter had been anything but silent tonight. A more doting husband was hard to imagine. How far would he go to protect his precious Meggy?

"Of course, anyone could team up and split the proceeds." Candy assumed the mantle of avenging angel. I'd seen that persona emerge when other companies tried to screw with Sweet Nothings. Her transformation from makeup maven to femme formidable was truly frightening.

Della issued a low growl as she sensed tension in the conference room. She inched closer to me, training her gaze on the Tornado.

"Hey, what's wrong with that mutt?" he asked. "Keep her away from me." His eyes darted back and forth between me and my dog. Odd that a fifty-pound furball like Della could intimidate such a big man.

"Do you not like dogs?" Lucian asked. "That surprises me, Tony."

Tornado wiped his brow with a tissue. "They're vicious beasts. Dirty, too. Listen, are we about finished here? I've got a family, you know."

"Of course," I said. "I just want to confirm one more thing. Do we all agree that it's possible to tamper with IMDs?"

"Technically possible, realistically improbable. Highly improbable, I must stress that." Arun gave new meaning to the word pedantic. "You have absolutely no proof that this ... this plot is anything other than a fantasy, Tommy's fantasy and yours."

I wanted to slap that sneer right off his face, but I didn't. That's where training took over. I silently repeated Kai's mantra: lose control, lose the issue. Losing was not an option, not when Tommy's killer might be facing me.

"Thomas Yancey was a man of many parts," I said, "but one thing I know. He would never mix fantasy with business. Trust me on this, Arun. If one of you killed my friend, I won't rest until you're caught and punished. Count on it."

"Me, too," Candy chimed in, pumping her fist.

A wall of silence confronted me. The space seemed airless, more tomb than conference room. Even Officer Francie Cohen gulped a big lungful of air. Lucian was the exception. He didn't try to hide his smile or the conspicuous wink he gave me.

"Ready?" he asked.

Candy gathered her purse and joined us. We made a fearsome quartet as we filed out, three grim adults and one herding dog. Streetlights illuminated the sidewalk, casting their ghostly shadows on the pavements. It was ten o'clock, the time of night Tommy last walked this slice of earth. I felt his spirit, linked forever with Kai's, cheering me on. Let others scoff. I felt it.

Lucian's frown expressed another opinion. "I'm concerned about you, Elisa. You may have placed your life in danger. Taunting a murderer is unwise."

"You forget," I said, matching his frown, "nothing scares me, not anymore."

Lucian squeezed my shoulder. "Except, perhaps, the thought of loving again, having a normal life. Alors, I must be your protector then, your guardian angel." He smiled without soft-pedaling his meaning.

"Lucky girl," Candy said. "Guess I'll have to rely on this." She reached into her purse and retrieved a canister of pepper spray. "Just let him get near me!"

Brave talk. Somehow it sounded perilously close to hubris. The thought of petite Candace Ott tangling with a murderer made me shudder. Tommy had had a black belt in karate, for all the good it did him. The thought of losing another friend was unendurable.

"Come," Lucian said. "We will take Ms. Ott to her car." He escorted us, arm in arm, toward the street.

Twenty-Two

Lucian came back to check my home for intruders. That was the official reason. I confess that the thought of having his arms around me was both thrilling and disquieting. My transformation from wan widow to blushing ingénue had rocked my tranquil life, resurrecting emotions I'd buried with my husband. Kai had made me feel beloved. His tenderness aroused my passion, and his playfulness awakened a wry humor I'd never dared show any other man. When he died, the droll, sensual Lizzie Mae left with him. Until now.

I lit the bronze torchère and switched on the Bose, flooding the room with the soft, sexy sounds of Diana Krall.

"Do you want me to stay?" Lucian asked, gently stroking my hair. "You may need protection."

"Are you up for that?"

"Perhaps I should demonstrate." His lips swept down my neck like a feather, making me shiver with delight. "Do you not feel safer now?"

"Maybe. Show me more."

Fortunately, the dim lights hid my blushes. Lucian spun me around, gently kissing my forehead, nose and lips. I stood on tiptoe, welcoming his touch, pressing his head toward me.

"You are so special. Stop fighting me. This was meant to be." The intensity of his blazing azure eyes riveted me.

"I ... it's too soon for me, Lucian. I can't."

He flashed that grin again. "Tonight I saw a lioness, unafraid of death. Can you not face a man who loves you?"

He gathered me in his arms and carried me to the sofa. "Come, ma petite. Open your heart."

I was drowning, swept away by euphoria. Intellect and reason ruled the life of Elisabeth Buckley, MBA, JD. Tonight this sober, sensible woman had been banished by a wild, passionate creature without boundaries. Had my ears deceived me? Had Lucian Sand told me that he loved me? I cleared my mind, focusing only on the pleasure his body brought me.

The sofa enveloped me in a velvet cocoon as Lucian caressed my every part. I bit my lip to avoid crying out. It was maddening, pulse-pounding torture, and I wanted more. He winced as I raked his back with my nails. How incongruous to see those pale pink nails raise welts on his skin. That shade was way too neutral, a relic of the starchy Elisabeth of yesteryear. They should be blood red talons with a touch of black. Chanel's Vamp nail varnish would be perfect.

"Your skin is silk, pure silk." Lucian slowly stroked my collarbone until I moaned. "Are you ready? Tell me and I will stop."

I gritted my teeth, unwilling to yield to him. My body was wedged against the sofa's arm, and it wasn't comfortable. There was only one answer, one I'd tried to avoid.

"Follow me." I took his hand, leading him and Della up the stairs. The bed was waiting, clothed in layers of down and fine Italian sheeting. Queen sized. Kai hadn't wanted anything larger. "I need to touch you in the night, Lizzie Mae," he'd said. "I need to know you're there."

I turned down the comforter and switched off the lamp. Lucian slid in beside me and held me tight.

~

I spent the next morning working feverishly and mooning about Lucian. Did he really love me? Did I care? Despite my growing attachment to him, I couldn't banish one nagging thought: Lucian met every test for the outside man in the murder scheme. His motive, if he did it, was revenge, the destruction of CYBER-MED, pure and simple. I was collateral damage, an unavoidable wrinkle in an otherwise flawless plan.

I moped through a dreary lunch of fat-free yogurt and broth, hoping that I was wrong. When Candy's call came through, I almost spilled my guts. Almost.

"I'm a genius," she trilled. "Tell me that, or I'll clam up."

"OK, you're a genius. Now earn your keep. What's up?"

She immediately sensed my mood. "Oops. Someone's awfully grumpy. What's the matter, Betts? Didn't the Love Doc put out last night?"

"Don't be absurd. Now what's going on?"

"Terrell Tate."

"Who?"

Candy's sigh was bigger than Brooklyn. "Mary Alice Tate's nearest and not so dearest. My assignment, remember?"

"Sorry. Temporary amnesia. Tell me everything."

It's difficult to pin Candy down when she's on a roll. She spends plenty of time on the setup, backstory and secondary characters. By the time she reaches the main event, you're either exhausted or asleep.

"It wasn't easy," she said. "Only a skilled trickster could even try." She waited, as if expecting applause. "I took the direct approach—after a few cocktails, of course."

I gasped. "You confronted a potential murderer? Candy!"

"Keep your shirt on, Betts. I'm smarter than that. I spent thirty minutes bitching about my partner, what a millstone you were, all that money you siphoned off."

"You used me as the tethered goat? How could you, Candy?"

She ignored everything. "Goat, smote. Bottom line, I got results. By martini three, Terrell confided in me. Seems she had a similar problem, someone who tried to muscle in on the family fortune."

"Mary Alice Tate?"

"Right you are. Anyway, Terrell found a contact at CYBER-MED, someone who outed Mary Alice and blabbed about her DNA match. Mary Alice was a flake, of course. World class. She offed herself when the money spigot turned off, leaving Terrell rich and relatively blameless."

"Oh, my God, we were actually right. Did she say who her contact was?"

"Nope, only that it cost her half a million bucks. Cheap at the price, Terrell said."

A sinking sensation overwhelmed me. That kind of money could easily buy a Porsche, fine clothes and a big bank balance. A degree from MIT meant that the skills were a foregone conclusion.

"Still there, Betts? I done good, right?"

"Yeah, sure. One more thing," I said. "How did Terrell get connected to CYBER-MED?"

"She was a bit vague about that. Some chance meeting at a charity event." Candy paused. "Oh, I remember. It was that Joslin thing you went to, the diabetes charity."

Now I really needed to think. Half of CYBER-MED attended that event, but a big bucks donor like Terrell Tate was unlikely to mix with the staff. That left Arun Rao, Meg Cahill and Dr. Lucian Sand as my best bets. Tommy may well have sensed something that night. He had probably been right there, front and center, observing his future murderer.

I had no one to confide in. Candy knew everything, but like me, she was personally involved. I needed someone with a clear head and some sense of objectivity. Only one person met the test.

My next call was to Rand Lindsay. I acted nonchalant, saying that I wanted to verify some of the firm's charitable donations. Can't screw with the IRS, you know.

"How can I help you, Miss Elisabeth?" His soft southern accent reassured me. At least one member of my new business team was friendly. Rand quickly promised to unearth the information and send it to my iPhone.

"And Rand," I said, "keep this between the two of us. No one, not even Dr. Cahill or Rao, needs to know."

"What if the Sandman asks?" He couldn't suppress a giggle.

"No one."

~

I didn't take his call. I was way too busy on a day like this to chat with Lucian. Besides, last night's tryst had roiled the waters, threatening the balance of power in our relationship. Who needed love? I was doing just fine.

Something about Tommy's death list bothered me. I retrieved it from my safe and scrutinized all four names. Excluding CYBER-MED, what common factor linked all four? It must be fairly obvious, the old hide in plain sight thing that my man Poe wrote about. Tommy with his puzzle obsession would be on that like a seal on a fish. Why, oh why didn't my friend give me more clues?

I jumped when my iPhone buzzed. Rand Lindsay's message jolted me out of my stupor, putting me on high alert.

He'd attached a list of ten names, CYBER-MED's attendees at last year's big shindig. As a bonus, he'd included names of anyone else who sat at the head table. My stomach lurched as I scanned the familiar names. He was there big as life: Lucian Sand. There were other suspects, of course. Meg, Carter and Arun had all trooped in to honor the charity. Seeing Tommy's name gave me a temporary twinge. I felt that same way every time I heard Kai's name. Emptiness. Unrelenting sorrow.

One small surprise. Tony "Tornado" Torres had attended last year. Funny. He'd said only the single guys got tapped for duty. That thrust him right back into the murder mix with everyone else. I texted Rand with a request to do a full bio and background check on Tony Torres including bank records. Top secret.

The honorary guests were also an interesting crew. "Oh, my Lord." I muttered a really bad word under my breath as I scanned their names. I'd almost missed it. The additions to the head table included Terrell and Mary Alice Tate, Judge and Mrs. Jacob Arthur, Mr. and Mrs. Ian Cotter, and the Honorable Richard Chernikova.

That was it, the missing link. Each of the victims, plus one intended target, had broken beignets together that night. The murderer was almost certainly among them. Tommy must have noticed it, pieced it together and signed his death warrant. Six months later he was gone.

Somewhere, somehow, Terrell Tate made a contact that night. Her pseudo-sister Mary Alice took her own life eight weeks later. I got a sudden brainstorm and tapped into Google. One by one I checked the *Globe's* obituaries for the three victims. Just as I thought, they had died in order: Tate, Arthur and Cotter. I shivered, taking solace in a big swallow of espresso. My theory was just supposition, but it made sense. Mary Alice Tate was a test case. The murderer tried a relatively low risk strategy that netted him or her a cool half-million. No doubt the Evil Empire ran on referrals. That was standard business practice everywhere, even at Sweet Nothings.

Candy had one more guest on her agenda. This afternoon, she was scheduled to meet Tatiana Lake about a fashion shoot. My ears rang as I imagined the distortions Candy was spreading. Oh, well, it was in a good cause. If Tatiana Lake and Terrell Tate ever compared notes, they'd have a consistent story.

When the phone rang, I answered it automatically.

"You will not take my calls," Lucian said. "Did I frighten you last night, ma belle?"

I'm a dreadful liar. Visions of mortal sin, eternal damnation and Sister Adelma zoomed through my mind.

"Not at all," I said. "I've just been busy today."

"I sensed it when I said I loved you. You weren't ready. It was too soon. No matter. I am a patient man. I can wait forever if need be. Do not shut me out."

"Don't you ever work?" I asked him, changing the subject. His supreme self-confidence made me cranky.

"Ah. You would not want a lazy husband. Not a worker like you."

"Husband! I never ..."

I imagined his cocky grin as I sputtered. Lucian was downright annoying. His hubris was off the chart.

"How can I help you, ma petite? I am at your service."

"You met every one of those victims at the Joslin last year. That's when all this started. Tommy caught on somehow."

"You suspect me, no?" He paused. "Ask me anything. I have no secrets from you."

I didn't want to do it, but I had no choice. Tommy's murder cried out for vengeance or at least justice.

"You've got plenty of money, more than any professor should have. The murderer probably cleared at least four million dollars tax free on his hits."

Lucian's voice was gruff. "You would prefer a poor man, Elisabeth? One who needs your fortune. I see. How much easier to reject such a man when he loves you."

I hate stammering. It's very unbecoming in a business executive. "No, not at all. You're wrong."

"Nevertheless, I will tell you. You must trust me, ma belle. You are at your computer? Look up this website: Sandblasters, An Innovation Factory."

"What is it?" My fingers flew over the keyboard. "Some kind of brain trust?"

This time, his mirth was genuine. "You might say that. I hold twelve patents on various computer algorithms. They have been quite successful."

My face felt warm again, but I forced myself to speak. "I'm sorry, Lucian. Forgive me."

He made a strangled sound. He was laughing. Lucian Sand was mocking me.

"What's so funny, Dr. Sand?"

"You. You are so brave, my Elisa, confronting a man you thought was a murderer and all to avenge your friend. Such loyalty is priceless. We all need friends such as you."

We spent a moment considering his words.

"I must go," Lucian said. "A graduate seminar."

"Me, too, or Candy might fire me."

"Until the next time. Take care, mon ange."

Twenty-Three

"OK," I said after Candy chowed down. "Tell me everything." She had bribed me into having a late night snack at one of Boston's toniest restaurants.

Candy gulped her martini and reprised her showdown with Tatiana Lake.

"Not as satisfying, I'm afraid. I tried everything I could think of, but I couldn't crack her. Tattie stuck with her story that Todd Brantley knew about her affair with Ian and didn't really care. She cried on my shoulder a bit and told me they have a sham marriage. Todd keeps a mistress in every city." Candy gave us an eye roll. "Goodness, that boy must have energy."

"Why stay married? They both have money."

I knew the answer even before I heard it.

"She loves him," Candy said. "Who knows why, but she does. So I guess we struck out on that one."

"Not necessarily. Ian Colter pissed off a string of husbands. Not everyone's as forgiving as Todd Brantley. We have to expand our search. Wasn't Ian's wife at the head table?"

"Yeah," Candy said. "That's kind of odd putting an exercise guru at the table with the Secretary of State. After all, this is Boston, not Hollywood."

I flashed back to something Lucian had said about a wealthy older man who worried Ian. That ballroom was probably full of likely suspects.

"Too bad Terrell Tate won't give a statement," I said. "Andrews would have to listen to us then. I know he thinks I'm some sort of wacky conspiracy theorist."

"Who says she won't?" Candy wore her Cheshire cat look. She reached into her purse and extracted her iPhone. "I just happened to record this when we had our girl-to-girl chat. That should put the fear of God into her."

"Hold on," I said. "You just broke the law. Massachusetts has a two-party consent statute, meaning that what you have is an illegal recording. Terrell Tate could sue you, my dear girl."

Candy shrugged. "BFD. Put the cuffs on me now. We're not going to use it. I just want to convince Andrews." She pressed the button, sharing a perfect rendition of Terrell Tate's conversation.

"It's frustrating," I said. "There should be some common thread here, a motive we can unearth, but other than CYBER-MED I can't think of one."

"I'll have another crack at Mrs. Jacob Arthur," Candy said, "although I have to say that unlike you, Betts, she doesn't seem to miss her late husband one bit."

"Find out more about that trial, if she knows. Meanwhile, I'll dig around the public records and check out the guy who was on trial. Didn't they say he was connected or something?"

Candy took a healthy swig of her martini. "I guess I'm glad I'm not married. All this bed-hopping, and nobody cares. Ian's wife, Tatiana's husband, even Meg Cahill. What's wrong with these people?"

I flashed back to my conversation with Lucian. Most spouses, male and female, would be jealous or at least mildly put out if their marital partner screwed around. I would have died if Kai had cheated on me. Maybe infidelity was the link.

Even the lugubrious Judge Jacob Arthur might have strayed occasionally.

"Wait a minute, Candy. Change of tactics. Use your wiles to find out if the Judge ever polluted the marital bed. I have confidence in you. You'll think of something."

Her eyes got way too bright. "I just thought of a bombshell, but you won't like it."

After two minutes of silence, she caved. "OK, here it is. I'll tell Mrs. Arthur about my dear friend Elisabeth who was so devastated to find that her late husband dicked the world."

"Candy! You wouldn't!"

Her smug smile told me that she would. Naturally, she would also swear the widow to secrecy.

"Come on, Betts. You know how it is. You have to give to get. Besides, Kai and Tommy would love it."

She was right. Kai would relish the part of roué, despoiler, dickwad, especially if it helped nail Tommy's murderer. Maybe if I went with her, it would minimize the damage.

My iPhone buzzed just as I got ready to pay the check. Rand Lindsay on the case. I couldn't read the text in the dim bar light. Besides, no detective worth her salt ever burns a confidential source. Rand's big scoop would have to wait.

~

Candy wasted no time. She hailed a cab, pulled me into it, and spit out a staccato Beacon Hill address I'd never heard of before.

"What's going on?" I asked. "I have a headache, and I'm tired. It's almost ten o'clock."

Whining is unattractive but inevitable when dealing with Candace Ott. She leveled me with one withering glare.

"Tough. Your headache has more to do with those martinis than anything else. Besides, you said you wanted to end this thing."

The driver lurched to a stop in front of an imposing brick townhouse that screamed big, big money. It looked vaguely familiar, a particle of memory from the distant past.

"Wait a minute, I've been here before. A long time ago with Kai. Some charity thing."

"Bingo. Your synapses are still firing after all." Candy paid the driver and sprang out of the cab. "Come on, slowpoke. Mrs. Jacob Arthur awaits."

She sprinted halfway up the steep brick stairs before I caught her. Considering the height of her heels, that was a pretty nifty trick.

"You're not going to do the tethered goat thing again, are you? Please tell me I'm wrong."

She shot an unrepentant look my way. "I could tell you that, but I'd be lying. Look, Betts, suck it up. As you're always saying, this is about Tommy, not us."

I knew when I was beaten. Having your own words thrown back at you is a dirty trick but very effective. I bowed in weary resignation.

"OK, but don't be too hard on Kai. Neither one of us ever looked at anyone else."

Candy squeezed my arm and pressed the buzzer. It was answered by a rara avis, something akin to the dodo — an honest-to God-British butler.

"Good evening, Bunter," Candy said, brushing past him. "We're expected. Come along, Elisabeth." Candy gave me a superior smirk. "Our hostess awaits."

Bunter kept his cool, swept in front of us, and led the way to the drawing room.

The furnishings were Georgian and the carpets Persian. Like most Boston Brahmins, the Arthurs had arrayed a number of ancestral portraits on the walls. A kind observer would have praised the strength of character evident in their faces. I fixated on the alarming jaws, prominent noses and beady eyes of these forebears. Kai had joked that it was no wonder Jacob became a jurist. He had the right equipment to stare down any criminal.

Lynette Arthur was a handsome woman with raven hair and obsidian eyes. She sat on a delicate satin settee with a posture Queen Victoria herself would cheer. I tried to focus on her face, but her enormous breasts mesmerized me.

Dear Lord! The woman can barely stand. Glancing down at my meager chest, I felt chastened.

"Lynette," Candy simpered. "Forgive us for intruding. I just had to discuss the program with you." She tugged me forward. "You've met my partner, Elisabeth Buckley, I believe. You know, Kai's wife. She wants to help us."

Mrs. Arthur's expression softened instantly. "Oh, my dear. I'm sorry about your husband. He was so charming."

I caught a whiff of alcohol on her breath. The widow had started without us.

I didn't have to act. Just hearing Kai's name left me misty-eyed. I turned away, staring at some hook-nosed Arthur ancestor for balance.

"Tea. Shall we have tea?" Lynette asked. She rang a discreet buzzer that summoned Bunter. "Perhaps brandy would do better. Jacob loved his brandy. Armagnac was his favorite." She nodded to Bunter, who did the honors. After he whisked noiselessly away, Lynette sank back on the cushions and sighed.

"God, I got so sick of hearing about brandy. Jacob ranted on for hours about the grapes, blah, blah, blah. The man took field trips to France just to check out the vineyards."

The Judge had died two months before Kai's accident. Lynette's recovery was quite remarkable, considering that her husband had popped off so spectacularly. On the other hand, my own devastation might seem excessive to most people.

"Your marriage was different, wasn't it, dear? You really loved him." Lynette's face crinkled with compassion.

"More than she should have," Candy spat. "Kai Buckley was just like most men, couldn't be satisfied with one woman and broke her heart."

I gulped down my brandy. "No, Candy."

"It's okay, honey. Jacob was the same way." Lynette poured us another round. "That bastard didn't go to France alone, and it wasn't only vineyards he explored." Her face hardened as she relived her marriage. "Every woman was fair game, no matter who she was. Even married ones."

"See, Betts? I told you not to grieve." Candy winked at me as she turned away. "You weren't the only one."

"I would have divorced him. Should have." Lynette paused and spread out her arms. "But why let some bimbo have all this? I earned it, believe you me, and I had my girls to consider."

"Kai wasn't alone when he died," Candy said, with a small, tight smile. "So tragic."

I leapt up, ready to spring at Candy. "That's enough. Please. I can't take anymore."

Lynette was oblivious. "Honey, I get it. Believe me, I do. Jacob invented every excuse in the book, especially after his heart problem. Called his extracurricular activities medical consultations. Huh! He didn't have a heart. Anyone who ever met him knew that."

Candy dug in her tote and produced an embossed folder. "I'd better get her home. Here, Lynette. Check this out and get back to me. You can count on Sweet Nothings to help with your program."

"How generous of you." Lynette was glassy eyed by now. "And Mrs. Buckley, I promise things will get better. Trust me."

Bunter appeared out of the ethos and escorted us to a cab, all the while maintaining his stiff upper lip.

"That went well," Candy said, "if I do say so myself. Add the Judge to the cheaters' club."

I maintained a stubborn, stony silence until I thought I'd burst. "How could you? Kai was your friend."

"Big deal. Kai would have done anything to avenge Tommy, you know that. Plus, there are worse things to call a man than a stud. What if I'd said Kai couldn't get it up?"

"Candy!"

"Calm down. You're home. We'll discuss this at work tomorrow."

I stepped out of the cab and watched her disappear.

Twenty-Four

After walking Della, I crawled into bed and crashed. Three cheers for booze, the ultimate soporific. Kai joined me in my dreams that night, wearing a grin and nothing else. He held out his arms, enveloping me in a cloud of Creed, Silver Mountain Water. As I snuggled up to him, he whispered, "Good job, Lizzie Mae. That's my girl."

I love you, Kai. I always will.

The next morning I felt exceptionally fit, body and mind. In view of last night's alcohol consumption, that qualified as a near miracle. Two cups of espresso later, I recalled Rand's unread text message. I floated downstairs on a wave of optimism. Every day brought me closer to finding Tommy's murderer. I knew with astounding clarity that by avenging my friend, I would save myself, too. Kai and Tommy, best buddies in this life, were together in the afterworld, cheering me on.

Rand's message puzzled me. The first part was routine: Tornado's name, age and marital status. Good grief, he had four little boys under five. Another man whose equipment was in fine working order.

Then it stopped. Instead of summarizing financial data, Rand inserted three words in big bold script: CALL ME URGENT. He'd left a cell and home number. Nothing else.

What the hell?

Some unnamed dread claimed me. With trembling fingers I dialed Rand's cell. Straight to voicemail. No answer at his home number either. I paged down my directory, searching for the CYBER-MED section. It was early for most people, barely seven o'clock, but not computer types. Silence and another dump to voicemail from Rand's private line. My skyrocketing pulse and rapid heartbeat signaled a major panic attack.

I didn't want to do it. Succumbing to terror is so clichéd. Nevertheless, my fingers dialed Lucian Sand's number before my brain caught up. He answered immediately in that sultry baritone that made me quiver.

"Oui, Elisa."

"I didn't mean to disturb you, Lucian."

"A call from you is a gift. How are you?"

I felt foolish. After all, Rand wasn't a child. He had probably found a companion for the night and turned off his phone.

"Don't worry. Call me anytime, Elisabeth. You know that."

"It's Rand," I blurted out. "He doesn't answer his calls, and I'm worried about him."

It sounded feeble even to me, just a pretext to hear Dr. Sand's scintillating voice.

"Did something happen?"

Now I'd done it. I gave Lucian an expurgated account of last night's activities, ending with Rand's text message.

"You are at home? Stay there. I will be right over."

He disconnected while I was still protesting. That sent me scrambling to make myself presentable, police the house and attend to Della before he arrived.

I was applying lip-gloss (Sweet Nothings #6) when the concierge buzzed Lucian in. One look at his face confirmed my worst suspicions. He put his arms around me and drew me close.

"You were right. Rand had a misadventure last night."

Tragic news was becoming the norm for me. I'd gotten rather good at hearing it.

"Is he ... dead?"

"No, no. The doctors say he will be fine. He is at the Mass. General Hospital if you'd like to see for yourself."

I grabbed my briefcase, purse and sunglasses. "What are we waiting for."?

~

Looking inordinately cheerful, Rand was propped up in his hospital bed like a low-rent pasha. He brightened when he saw us and waved us in.

"Miss Elisabeth. Sandman. Come on in." He beamed at a young candy striper reading his blood pressure. "They're taking such good care of me here that I don't want to go home."

A dizzying array of medical devices chronicled his every move. They creeped me out, but Rand and Lucian shrugged it off.

"OK," I said when the volunteer left, "tell us what happened."

He locked eyes with Lucian and lowered his voice. "Can you shut the door? Please."

Lucian found me a chair and stood behind it like a sentry.

"I'm embarrassed," Rand said. "It's probably no big deal. I was researching that topic for you when Dr. Meg called me in. I left my screen on. When I came back, and I can't prove this, but I thought someone had scrolled through my computer."

"Who was there?" Lucian folded his arms like a hanging judge. His handsome face was Carrara marble, Michelangelo's David in street clothes.

"I can't really say. Arun breezed by before I was called in, and Tornado was back and forth. Dr. Meg is always there, of course, and Carter dropped by with some take-out for her." Rand threw his hands up. "Things were crazy last night."

I leaned forward and touched Rand's foot. "Your text sounded urgent. What did you find?"

He sighed. "You told me to look for anomalies, financial stuff that didn't make sense. Well, I did some digging— hacking—into the Tornado's bank records. People are crazy to bank on line, you know. Anyone can access it."

"Stop avoiding the issue. What did you find?"

"Money. Tons of it. Tony Torres has over fifty thousand in his checking account alone. That doesn't count the CDs and savings accounts. Those add up to several million bucks. I didn't want to put it in the text, so I asked you to call me."

Lucian's eyes narrowed. "Financial security is not criminal. It doesn't make him a murderer."

"How about his wife?" I asked. "Maybe it's her money."

"Maybe," Rand said, "but I thought Nilda was some sort of teacher. Not a big money profession."

"What does any of this have to do with your accident? Have you called the police?"

Rand's eyes grew saucer sized. "I didn't, but Dr. Meg did. Please, Mrs. B. All I know is that I left my big glass of Coke on my desk. You know I always drink a lot of that. Regular, not that diet stuff. Anyway, I was thirsty when I got back from Dr. Meg, so I chug-a-lugged it, and bam! Within about five minutes, I was sicker than I've ever been in my life."

I forced myself to power down. *Logic, Lizzie Mae. Reason will win the day.*

"What do the doctors say? Have they done your blood work yet?"

"They did it right away, and it's really weird, almost embarrassing."

Lucian's frown would have terrified most people. It sobered Rand immediately, driving him back on point. He settled back on his pillows and continued his narrative.

"It was Visine or something like it. Almost a whole bottle of the stuff got into my Coke. Can you believe it?"

"Damn." Frustration swamped my senses. What next? Most people have something like that, especially if they stare at a computer screen all day. Anybody at CYBER-MED could have had that stuff. Come to think of it, both Candy and I carried it in our purses.

Rand's grin didn't make any sense. Poison is hardly a laughing matter.

"Forgive me, Mrs. B. It's just that they found the vial already. And guess what? It came from my desk. I use eye drops a couple of times a day, especially when I'm working on my dissertation."

"You mean ...?"

"Yep. Only my prints are on the bottle. Kind of funny, don't you think? So much for clues."

After Rand reassured us that he was compos mentis and ready to go home, we left him to the tender mercies of the candy striper. His brush with death had one significant upside: confirmation that the CYBER-MED conspiracy was alive and well.

Lucian hesitated as he helped me into the Cayenne, fixing those blazing azure eyes on me. "Don't go back there," he said, stroking my cheek. "Please, Elisabeth. I worry about you at CYBER-MED. You are vulnerable in there, so alone."

He was right, of course, but despite the danger, I felt exhilarated, cautious but not fearful. Fate had given me another chance to reclaim my life. Nothing would deter me, not even a clever, ruthless killer.

"You forget," I teased. "I have a protector. Rand and I can watch each other's backs."

"That does not comfort me," Lucian growled. "Rand can barely protect himself." He tenderly tucked in my skirt, bag and briefcase before closing the car door.

Funny. Kai had always done the same thing from the very first date we'd ever had. I'd said opening doors for a woman was archaic, a sexist relic of the past. He'd laughed and said that he knew better. *Let me cherish you, Lizzie Mae. You're precious to me.*

"Can you drop me at Sweet Nothings?" I asked Lucian. I need some quiet time."

I had to ponder the faithless spouse issue. Could it really be that easy? Was someone intent on eliminating every faithless spouse on the client list? To cement my theory I would have to find out more about Richard Chernikova, the kinds of things absent from official bios and position papers. I'd skip the *Wall Street Journal* and binge on *Wonkette, Gawker-Stalker,* and *Huff-Post.*

After a cursory nod to Candy, I walled myself in my office and fired up Google. *Wonkette,* a snarky DC blog, had plenty to say about Chernikova, none of it flattering. They compared him to both Ivan the Terrible and Colonel Klink in the same posting without batting a keystroke. That didn't surprise me, but I needed a more personal profile. By scrolling down the page, I found it:

Why was Richard Chernikova, aka "stiff Dick", seen exiting a posh Georgetown Hotel from the guest elevator? Was the perpetual GW Hospital patient getting a special medical check-up, or is his heart otherwise engaged?

Several other blurbs repeated the same theme. Despite the prominence and charm of his wife Lola, Richard was apparently a hound. That explained his antics with Meg the night of the Joslin Ball.

Gossip is inadmissible in court, but I subscribe to the where-there's-smoke-there's-fire adage. Chernikova had scored enough points to join the bad boys club with honors. I strolled over to Candy's office and shared the news, expecting a round of applause or at least a high five.

"Big deal," she shrugged, "another guy with a zipper problem. I keep telling you, Betts. They're all that way, at least the ones who have any opportunity."

"Not all."

I'm not naïve, but I knew with every fiber of my being that Kai loved only me. Nothing she or anyone else said would ever shake that certainty.

"Oh, Betts, get a grip. Kai was different. I know that." She twirled her pencil. "But you have to admit, Tommy fooled us. We knew he was a player but not on such a grand scale. I mean, diddling your cougar boss is risky business in any outfit."

"True, but that's not what killed him. Tommy was too smart. He figured out this murder-for-hire scheme and confronted someone." I flopped down in the guest chair facing Candy's ornate French desk. "This may sound crazy, but I suspect Tony Torres. I'm not saying he did it by himself, just that he meets the criteria for the inside man."

"Hmm, the Tornado? He's pretty tough, that's for sure, and he was front and center when Rand was poisoned." She bit her lower lip. "I don't know. Would a guy with four little boys at home take that kind of risk, even for a boatload of cash?"

A very good question. Unfortunately, one need only read the daily newspaper to answer that. I wondered what Lucian would think. Maybe I should call him.

"Betts! Hello in there." Candy rolled her eyes. "I bet I know where your mind is, Mrs. Buckley, with luscious Lucian Sand."

"You're wrong," I said. "I was thinking of something else, something you won't like."

"Pish tosh. Tell me anything."

I took her at her word. "OK. Arun was on the spot every time something happened. He has a lot to lose if CYBER-MED goes belly up. I wonder what his money situation is."

I expected an explosion, not a flood of tears. Candace Ott doesn't cry over things like that. She's indomitable, a real fighter.

"Don't do this," she sobbed. "You had Kai to love. Now you've got Lucian. I missed the boat on the whole thing."

I put my arms around my friend and hugged her. "Come on now. Is this the awesome Candace Ott speaking, the woman who brings men to their knees and makes strong guys beg?"

She sniffled noisily and blew her nose. "I'm like everyone else. I want a husband and family someday." A sudden grin eclipsed her tears. "Someday in the future. The thing is, Betts, I think Arun might be the one. We're really good together. There's got to be some other explanation."

"Are you willing to question him? I'll get his financials checked out."

Her nod was half-hearted, but it was a start. With Rand out of commission, I'd have to ask Lucian to hack into Arun's records. Somehow that thought pleased me.

Twenty-Five

He called just before six, curling my toes with the sultry sound of his voice.

"Elisa. You are well?"

"Yes, of course."

"I will pick you up in one hour."

"Wait just a minute. I'm drowning in work, Lucian. No way can I leave."

His throaty chuckle annoyed me. "You must eat, ma belle. Don't worry."

He hung up before I could say anything else. No time to protest or examine my feelings about him. The man was annoying. Pushy beyond belief. Incredibly hot.

When Lucian finally stood before me, those excuses vanished. He wore a tweedy blue blazer, charcoal slacks and a fine weave sweater that matched his eyes. No ponytail tonight. His sand-streaked hair was a tousled mass of curls that barely concealed his ear stud. The nerdy professor with elbow patches was an urban fable. He came bearing gifts, a woven picnic basket redolent with delicious smells.

"Dinner," Lucian said with a bow. He gently tucked a napkin on my lap and shrugged. "The chef is a friend from Provence. We cook together sometimes, compare recipes." He unveiled a portobello appetizer and thin crust pizza that made my mouth water.

"Heavenly! I love portobellos. How did you know?"

He cut the mushroom into tiny tidbits, feeding them to me as if I were a nestling and he the papa bird. Two crystal goblets of Perrier and a bottle of Provencal Rose completed our feast.

"Umm, that's delicious." I licked every bit of sauce off my lips and sucked the juice off the fork. Lucian hovered over me, a faint smile enveloping his face. Where were my manners? My mother would have been appalled.

"Pardon me," I said. "I'm not usually this greedy."

"Is this not a better plan?" he whispered, stroking my cheek. "A woman who appreciates fine cuisine is very sensual. You must never deprive yourself, Elisabeth. Life has so many riches to share with us."

I was drowning, submerged by waves of desire as Lucian transformed dining into foreplay. His sultry gaze mesmerized me, addling my senses. We sipped wine, exchanging fevered glances and tender touches that melted my resolve. The crème brûlèe went untouched as we enjoyed a different type of sweetness.

Afterwards, I lay in his arms filled with a bliss that had long eluded me. Sexual abandon was a relic of the past, a treasure only Kai had unearthed. Lucian was both strange and familiar, an elixir that intoxicated me even as I craved his body like a drug. I couldn't explain it and didn't want to try. For now I would live in the moment.

I rose halfway up on my elbows, breaking the spell. "I need your help, Lucian. If it makes you uncomfortable, just tell me. That's OK. I'll find another way."

His bemused smile stopped me in mid-flight. "Just ask, ma petite. I can refuse you nothing."

As I outlined my plans for Arun, Lucian remained stoic even when the word "hacking" arose.

"This is a serious thing you ask of me. I understand your motive, but have you anything tangible against Arun?'

I shook my head. "Other than opportunity, means, and a possible motive, I have nothing at all."

"OK, we will do this thing. I take this seriously," Lucian said. "Never would I violate someone's privacy for selfish reasons." He touched my hand. "Just for you."

~

It was a fascinating read that shattered Candy's dreams of happily ever after. Lucian's fax was a damning indictment of a charming trust fund baby with a past. Apparently, Arun's poor judgment in money matters had emptied his own coffers and alienated his family. They had officially turned off the fiscal spigot, leaving their pride and joy on his own. CYBER-MED was his lifeboat, and it was hemorrhaging cash.

No wonder he'd raged against Lucian. Any whiff of scandal would sink the business and Arun along with it. I saw only one ray of hope for Candy. If he were involved in the murders, Arun had absolutely nothing to show for it—no big cash deposits, real property or other tangible assets. What he did have was an abundance of debt and maxed-out credit cards, most of them in arrears. Two companies had judgments against him.

He was certainly vulnerable enough to be the inside man, but Arun has no visible assets. He would more likely bilk Candy of her money than plan a murder. That possibility sickened me.

I did a reality check. Had Lucian seduced me in my own office, fed me, and committed God only knows how many felonies for me by hacking into secure databases? Was he an entrepreneurial genius or a cunning Svengali? I didn't know, and frankly I didn't much care. Lucian was in my blood. I could either swim against the tide or drown in ecstasy.

My mind was on CYBER-MED. I intended to face down Tony Torres and Arun Rao or die trying. Wait a minute, forget the die trying part. Since I'd met Lucian my will to live had reasserted itself. I could almost feel Kai's arms hugging me. "That's my girl, Lizzie Mae. Go for it."

I dressed with care in head-to-toe black, my ninja avenger outfit. Before leaving, I forced myself to call Candy. She had every right to know what I'd found, even if it devastated her. I dialed her private line, hoping she wasn't there.

"Candace Ott." Her voice had its normal buoyancy.

"Hey. How are you feeling?" I edged gingerly into the conversation like the coward that I am.

"I don't know, Betts. You tell me." My best friend awaited the verdict stoically.

It wasn't easy but I'd shared dire news before. Let's face it. Since Kai and Tommy died, I was a pro, handmaiden to the grim reaper himself.

She didn't react. I expected anger, tears or sarcasm, not stony silence.

"Candy, you're scaring me. Say something. Please."

Her voice was atonal, subdued. "You've said it all, Betts. He's a scoundrel, possibly a fortune hunter or even a murderer." She stifled a sob. "Told you. Arun is the perfect man for me. I sure know how to pick 'em, don't I?"

"I'm coming right over. Stay put."

"Don't bother. I won't be here. I'm having lunch with Tattie Lake. She called this morning all hot and bothered. Something about Ian."

"Ian Cotter?"

"The very one. Who knows? Maybe Tattie knows something bad about Arun, too. That would give you a matched set."

"Candy …"

"See you, Betts." She hung up with an emphatic click.

~

Luckily, the first face I saw at CYBER-MED was a friendly one. Rand Lindsay was at his post, busily updating Dr. Meg's schedule.

"Hey, Miss Elisabeth," he said. "How y'all doing this morning?"

I basked in that blast of Alabama sunshine. "What are you doing back at work?" I asked him. "Shouldn't you be resting or something?"

"Nah. Doc said it was okay. Besides, Dr. Meg's here if anything goes haywire."

I looked around, noting the deserted corridor. "Look, Rand, be careful for heaven's sake. I mean it."

"Ah, come on. It was probably a prank." He grinned. "Tornado already told me I'm too tough to die."

"Come into my office. I need to speak with you about that."

He ambled into my office as if he hadn't a care in the world. "What's up, ma'am?"

"Don't ma'am me. This is serious." I lowered my voice. "Did you know Arun Rao was insolvent?"

Rand's cherubic face fell. "No. Arun has family money. He told me. Arun wouldn't lie. Not to me."

"Forget Arun for a minute. What about Tony Torres? How would a nurse practitioner with four little kids and a wife ever amass that kind of money? You tell me."

Rand squirmed in his seat. "They're my friends. I don't want to spy on them anymore. It's wrong."

"So is murder." I folded my arms and gave him the death house stare. "Man up, Rand. Can I still count on you?"

"I guess so. Yes."

"Good. I think we should lay a trap for the murderer. Francie Cohen will help us in case there's any rough stuff. I don't expect much from Andrews, but you never know. People surprise you sometimes."

Rand stared down at the floor as if his eyelids were glued to the spot. "Does Dr. Sand approve of this?"

"Never mind, leave Lucian out of it. Tommy was my friend, mine and Candy's. If you won't help, that's okay. We'll find another way." My mouth was set in a long, grim line. Ninja avengers don't fold when they get a bad hand.

His sigh shook several folds of skin. "OK, you got me, Mrs. B. How can I help?"

"Keep your ears open, especially around Arun and Tony. Secretary Chernikova's next to die, if I'm right. I did some web-crawling of my own, and apparently he's some kind of lothario."

"Chernikova?" Rand's eyes widened. "I thought he was too mean to screw around."

"Apparently not. He's tailor made for our guy or gal. Didn't you say he was sniffing around Dr. Cahill?"

"Me?" Rand started choking. "Please! I don't know anything about that. It's just gossip." He lowered his voice to a whisper. "If Dr. Meg found out I even suggested that, she'd fire me or worse."

"What could be worse than that? Are you suggesting she would kill you?"

I panicked as Rand's face turned an unhealthy shade of puce. He held up both hands in surrender. "Please, Miss Elisabeth, Dr. Meg could blacklist me. Do you understand? She could guarantee that I would never be employed by any university or think tank. My God! She'd make sure I never even got my PhD."

If it weren't a physical impossibility, Rand would have prostrated himself at my feet. Good thing, because I couldn't pick him up if he collapsed or flopped into a fleshy heap.

"Calm down, Rand. I promise not to say anything about you."

"Even to the Sandman?" His normal color returned, and his breathing slowed.

"I can't promise that. Lucian is helping me ... us. But I'll be very discreet. Now go back to work and try to act normal."

After he lumbered out the door, I did some deep thinking. Meg Cahill was a powerful woman with a healthy ego and a robust libido. It was possible that she had warmed the sheets with all the victims, at least the male ones. Mrs. Jacob Arthur had certainly hinted at it, and even Sergeant Andrews, the sloth of Boston homicide, had accused her of screwing Ian Cotter. I knew for sure that Tommy was one of her conquests. At the Joslin Ball, Richard Chernikova, the rake of the Potomac, had acted Biblically fond of his former physician. Was that the answer? There was a Shakespearean simplicity about the woman spurned angle. That didn't explain Mary Alice Tate, unless she was the test case. Crass Carter Cahill had all the money. If I was right, Meg was simultaneously lining her pockets and avenging her honor without involving her doting hubby.

I needed caffeine to clear the cobwebs from my brain. By the time I cleared the elevator and sprinted out the door, Starbucks was packed. The latte seared my fingers as I searched for a seat. The only available one was back in the corner at a pie-shaped table for two occupied by Tony Torres. He waved, flashing a lupine grin that was part grimace.

"Are you saving this?" I asked.

"Nope. Have a seat." Tony arranged his newspaper in neat folds and eyed me.

Something about him made me shudder. Perhaps it was his perpetual scowl. More likely it was my guilt at having invaded his private life.

"So," he said, "how goes the investigation? Any breaks?" His stare was impudent, hardly that of a respectful employee. Come to think of it, everything about the Tornado screamed impertinence.

I shrugged. "So, so. All I really care about is finding Tommy's murderer. We're focusing on the financial angle now. You know, seeing if anyone has unexplained wealth."

Tony Torres yawned. If he felt stress, it wasn't evident. "What do the cops think?" he asked. "They're supposed to be the experts, aren't they?"

"It's early yet. Sergeant Andrews traced the stolen car involved in Tommy's death."

"Oh, yeah. Grandmas in Wellesley always go out on the town in their Mercedeses." He chuckled, a cold and soulless sound. "Maybe Tommy insulted her little doggie. Those old broads take that stuff seriously." He gulped his latte and pushed back the chair. "Well, back to the grindstone."

He strode away, awash with swagger, leaving me speechless. How could Tony Torres describe the car that killed Tommy? That information never appeared in print.

I flipped open my iPhone and dialed Francie Cohen. Unfortunately, Mark Andrews answered the call.

"Officer Cohen, please." I toyed with using a British accent but kept my voice as anonymous as possible.

"Hello, Mrs. Buckley." Andrews couldn't control the smirk in his voice. "Francie's off today. Anything I can help you with? Pistol-whipped a perp? Gotten a confession? Whatever."

"That's your job, Sergeant. Made any progress? Or have you already given up on my friend's murder?" I leashed my temper and muzzled my mouth.

Andrews paused a moment. "Sorry. I know you want results. So do I. Francie told me about your theories, and believe it or not, I've considered them." It was a rare confession, a measure of how desperate he was.

I plunged into the abyss, asking the question that plagued me. "Just one thing, Sergeant. Did you release that information about the Mercedes? You know, the car that killed my friend."

He didn't respond for a long time. Maybe Mark Andrews knew yoga, too. Cop-like, he answered with a question.

"Why do you ask? As a matter of fact, I purposely didn't release that information."

"Someone mentioned it today. Tony Torres, a CYBER-MED employee. He fits the pattern, Sergeant. I think he might be the one." I craned my neck, making certain no one was listening. "He's got lots of unexplained income, too."

Strange squawks emanated from my iPhone. It was either bad reception or Sergeant Andrews in death throes.

"You've been very industrious, Mrs. Buckley. However, I do have news, something I should have already told you. We ran the fingerprints inside the Mercedes through AFIS and got a hit. This morning we arrested a kid from Natick. Nineteen years old, a habitual offender."

I stuttered, "But…that can't be."

"It can be. It is. He stole the old lady's car."

"This guy murdered my friend? He admitted it?" I was making a scene, thrilling the coffee crowd with an unintended show.

Andrews knew how to handle hysterical women. Angry lawyers, not so much. He made a series of clucking noises intended to soothe the savage breast. Mine.

"Calm down, Mrs. Buckley. He hasn't admitted to anything yet. Says he only borrowed the car. Claims the old doll lent it to him for the night." Andrews hooted. "Sooner or later, we'll get it out of him. He swears that he left it parked, keys in the ignition, on a side street near CYBER-MED. Never saw Mr. Yancey. Blah, blah, blah."

"So that's it? Case closed?"

Andrews went mute again. Maybe it was my phone. He couldn't leave it like that. I'm a patient woman. I could last as long as my battery did.

"Please, Mrs. Buckley. Try to understand." He was almost pleading now. I had already written off Sergeant Mark Andrews.

"Thanks for your time, Sergeant."

I knew now what I had to do and how to do it.

Twenty-Six

Candy's voice sounded normal, buoyant and brimming with vitality. No traces of post-Arun blues or recriminations. Thank God!

"I've got some hot news, Betts. Hot, hot, hot."

"That's good. If it's only tepid, I'm not interested." I was sitting in my CYBER-MED office—Tommy's actually—with the door closed and Lucian's warning echoing in my ears.

I wouldn't make much of a spy. Creeping around, infiltrating the enemy camp was nerve wracking. I'd rather be at Sweet Nothings, testing hair mousse.

"Betts, are you listening to me? This is important."

I shook off my misgivings like Della shedding rainwater. There are differences, of course. Della is fearless, a furry female version of Kai. I'm a plodder, more adept at planning than executing a caper. I could envision ten sensible reasons for caution and only one for action: avenging Tommy. Unfortunately, that's all it took.

"OK, Candy. What happened?"

"Not on the phone. I'm halfway to CYBER-MED. Wait for me in Tommy's office."

"See you soon." I hung up and gave myself a mental shake. It was time to marshal my wits and use my faculties. A jolt of courage wouldn't hurt either. I traced the one link common to every CYBER-MED death: Meg Cahill. She wouldn't soil her perfect manicure by committing the crimes, but she would enjoy manipulating the dupe who did. My lead candidate for dupe was Tony Torres. He was smart enough, possessed the necessary skills to alter the IMD settings, and had lots of surplus cash. Arun was the understudy. He fit the pattern even better than the Tornado but had nothing to show for it. Tommy had been friendly with both of them. Camaraderie may have killed him.

There was a third possibility too painful to consider. Lucian Sand. I'd been a fool to succumb to Lucian without firing a shot. What was that old slogan, trust but verify? Where was my due diligence? I would be disbarred for doing sloppy work like that for a client.

Life had been safe before I met him, safe and predictable. My career, Della and memories of Kai sustained me. Then Lucian exploded into my life, exposing my inner core. Emotions I'd submerged under widow's weeds had blossomed, leaving me vulnerable. Exhilarated. Alive.

I was too self-absorbed to hear the knock on my door. Candy flung it open and pranced in, looking very proud of herself. Her eyes sparkled with the fire that a big scoop always engendered.

"I knocked, you know."

"Sorry, I was dreaming. Come in and sit down. Tell me your news."

She pouted for a bit, waiting for me to beg. When that didn't happen, my esteemed partner and best friend cracked like Humpty Dumpty.

"OK, here it is. Tatiana Lake was half soused by the time I got there. Liquor does horrible things to one's complexion. Tattie looks bloated now, and her skin used to be pristine."

I tapped my foot until she got the message.

"Calm down, Betts. Let me tell this my way. Don't worry, it's worth it. Anyhow, Tattie was boo-hooing about Ian Cotter and how much she adored him. I played the sympathy card, you know, her tragic loss blah, blah, blah, and it worked." Candy sighed, fluffing her perfectly coiffed hair. "She said

Ian spilled his guts to her about his other clients, especially one who just wouldn't let go. Guess who that was, Betts?"

"Dr. Meg Cahill."

"How did you know?" Candy's tone told me I'd robbed her of her big surprise. "Oh, well, no matter. Meg started phoning him at home, showing up without an appointment, the whole works. Ian finally got rid of her by threatening to call her husband." Candy's head bobbed up and down as if she danced to an inaudible tune. "Pretty interesting stuff, eh? Of course, we both made lots of cougar jokes. Imagine an old bag like Meg Cahill chasing Ian Cotter. Big ick factor."

I couldn't share the joke. If Meg Cahill was masterminding a murder scheme, it was too awful even to chuckle about. Tommy died because of it. Had our friend been victimized by a sex-crazed doc with an outsized libido?

Lucian had promised to question Katherine Cotter. Maybe I should confirm Candy's findings with him. It made sense. Wouldn't take a minute.

I stopped myself before my fingers did the walking.

Meanwhile, Candy continued her monologue, extolling the facemask she had pressed on Tatiana Lake and the restorative powers of Juvaderm.

"Doesn't Lucian know Ian's wife?" Candy furrowed her brow for a nanosecond. "They use the same gym or something like that. Call him and ask, Betts."

I hung my head and mumbled something really rude. "Nope, I won't do it."

Candy's sigh was over the top. "Oh, for heaven's sake. Give me that phone." She grabbed the receiver and dialed his number from memory.

"Dr. Sand. It's Candace Ott." Her posture, tone and facial expression morphed from femme fatale to fluff ball. "Yes, Betts is fine. She's sitting right here." She gave him a highly edited version of her chat with Tatiana Lake and asked about Katherine Cotter.

"Very good. I knew you'd take care of it. Here she is." Candy handed me the phone.

The tingling inside me wouldn't stop. A tsunami-size thrill coursed through my body, leaving me weak. It was stupid, ridiculous and unbecoming a widow. I loved it.

"I've been thinking of you," he said, "worrying. You are safe, ma belle?"

"Yes, Lucian. I'm fine. Everything's OK." A warm glow suffused my every pore. I recalled that feeling. It had filled my heart when Kai smiled. I masked my tears with a cough.

"What's wrong? You are not ill?"

"No. Nothing like that. I've been strategizing, that's all. It's hard work."

"Ah, yes. Will you and Ms. Ott join me tonight for dinner? We will discuss everything."

"Tonight?" I looked over at Candy and saw her nod. "OK. Where and when."

"My home. I will pick up you ladies and Della at eight. D'accord?"

I mumbled some form of assent and disconnected.

~

Lucian lived in West Cambridge. As he swung into his driveway, Candy and I gaped at the elegant Greek revival home set on a neat corner lot in The Larches. Not what I expected from the abrasive scientist whose obsession with CYBER-MED had brought us together. Della eyed the fenced yard with a slight incline of her elegant head. She stepped daintily into the foyer like a monarch surveying her kingdom.

"Della feels at home here," Lucian said, giving me a mischievous grin. "Maybe she should stay."

"Who wouldn't?" Candy gazed upward, admiring the intricate crown moldings and ten-foot ceilings. "Your home is absolutely beautiful."

He ushered us into a walnut paneled room that served as his study. "Please sit, ladies. First we will toast our efforts." Lucian poured each of us a flute of Cristal and sat next to me on the burgundy leather couch. "To Thomas Yancey and those who went before him. Justice."

I glanced down, focusing on the creamy pattern of the Aubusson carpet. Those other names floated through my mind in an endless parade: Jacob Arthur, Mary Alice Tate, Ian Cotter, and of course, Lucian's brother. We clinked glasses as Lucian started his narrative.

"I spoke with Katherine Cotter this afternoon at my club. She grieves still for her husband, that one." He shook his head. "In the weeks before his murder, Ian Cotter was a very troubled man."

"Huh," Candy snorted. "That didn't stop him from screwing around, did it?"

Lucian moved closer to me, close enough to heat my blood. "Katherine knew about his affairs. They were of no interest to her. She also knew he loved only her."

He fixed me with that agate stare, calming and sea blue this evening. "Katherine is a passionate woman, very courageous. She blames Dr. Cahill for Ian's death and is very candid about that. Unfortunately, she has no proof, no specifics."

Meg Cahill was the perfect murderer: steely eyed, self-indulgent and egomaniacal. I'd seen her in action when Katherine Cotter brandished that crystal shard. No cucumber was cooler than Dr. Meg. Her confederate would be carefully chosen, much as a scientist chose lab specimens. Tony Torres fit that mold perfectly.

They said nothing as I made the case. Motive: revenge and money, lots of both. Opportunity: limitless. Meg had all the medical information and was the perfect conduit for an outsider with deep pockets. Tony the technician knew just how to interfere with the IMDs. Means: Lucian himself had shown us that. For a skilled professional like the Tornado, it was child's play. They had missed Richard Chernikova, thanks to Katherine Cotter's outburst, but they'd try again. I was certain of that. More importantly, Tommy had bet his life on it and lost.

When I finished, Lucian sat silently. Most men with knitted brows look menacing, but he looked positively Byronic. Heathcliff himself paled in comparison.

"I cannot accept it," Lucian said. "I know Tony, know his family. He would not do this."

"Explain that extra cash, if he's so innocent." Candy squared her shoulders, prepared for combat. "And how come he knew about the Mercedes and the dog pictures?"

Lucian webbed his strong fingers around the champagne flute. "I cannot explain either one. I admit it is a concern. Dr. Cahill, that I understand. Meg is strong willed, very hedonistic. She wants what she wants. But Tony, no, I cannot believe that he would do this terrible thing."

Pragmatism is Candy's greatest gift. She sipped her champagne slowly as if each drop were liquid gold. When she'd drained the glass, she made her play.

"Admit it, Betts. This is all theory. You're the lawyer, but I bet they'd laugh you out of court. Mark Andrews would bust a gut." She shot me a triumphant look and refilled her flute.

I hate it when she's right. It happens infrequently, but it's still painful. The time for talking was over, eclipsed by a gnawing fear that one more life hung in the balance. If

Richard Chernikova died because of our inertia, I would never recover.

I tried another approach. "OK, how about this? I read in the *Globe* that there's some big conference coming up at MIT. A really hot topic, the proliferation of nuclear arms in Iran and North Korea. Chernikova's sure to be there."

"So what?" Candy sniped. "Plan on parachuting into MIT, Mrs. Buckley?"

I felt myself flush. *Damn! I'm so transparent.*

Lucian stroked my cheek. "That I would like to see. Delicious!" He rose and beckoned us toward the kitchen. "Come, ladies, while I prepare our meal. Keep the cook company."

We entered a fantasy kitchen straight out of *Architectural Digest* with a Sub-Zero Viking range, the works. There was even a fireplace in the middle of the room.

"Wow! Candy almost drooled. "I love it, and I can't even cook."

I filled an earthenware bowl with water for Della. "Let's brainstorm about this Chernikova thing while Lucian cooks. Come on, Candy. Be a sport."

She grumbled, but it was only token resistance. We claimed two stools and sat facing the well-tended rose garden. Lucian kept his back to us while chopping, dicing and slicing an astonishing array of vegetables.

"Security will be tight at that conference," Lucian said, "impregnable."

"Agreed. We need finesse, not brute force." I thought of Tommy and his passion for CYBER-MED. "How about this? We sponsor a cocktail party and tour of CYBER-MED with Chernikova as our honored guest."

Dead silence. Candy's cat eyes widened like emerald marbles. Lucian scraped vegetables into a heavy cast iron skillet and adjusted the flame on the range.

"Impossible. Can't be done," Candy said. "Meg Cahill would never agree to it."

I spun around, enraged at my partner. "Excuse me, Cotton Candy, but you've overlooked something. You and I are the majority partners in CYBER-MED. If we propose this gala, she has to agree. Plus, she knows something's up. Say what you will about her, Meg's not stupid. She'd pretend to love the idea."

Lucian's eyes sparkled. He removed his chef's apron and scoured his hands.

"It might work," he said. "Timing will be critical, of course. Chernikova is safe at CYBER-MED. It's too risky for anyone to attack him there. They are cautious, these murderers. Intelligent. But the time right before or after the soiree ... he is most vulnerable then."

Candy's foot twitched, a sure sign of angst. "Oh, I don't know, Betts. Maybe we should just back off and let Francie take over. What if Tony Torres goes after us? He looks really tough. Mean, too."

"Don't worry. I will protect you." Lucian's smile could melt an iceberg. "But you raise a good point. We will need reinforcements. At least two."

"Francie might help us," I agreed, "and we can trust Rand."

"Huh," Candy hooted. "Some help he'd be. He can't move fast enough to do us any good. Plus, he'd probably spill his guts to the Cougar if she got him alone. What about Arun? He's plenty strong." Her dreamy smile said she spoke from experience.

Arun was still a suspect in my book. He had a money motive that wouldn't quit and the skill to manipulate medical data. Coward that I am, I couldn't hurt Candy by stating the obvious. Lucian saved me.

"No, ma petite," he said gently. "From now on, everyone at CYBER-MED must be suspect, even Arun and Rand." He flashed a bemused grin at both of us. "Do either of you have protection?"

What is it about Frenchmen? Is sex always on their minds?

Candy and I exchanged puzzled looks. Condoms seemed an unlikely topic before dinner. Lucian watched us until it dawned on him.

"Oh! I mean guns, knives, that kind of protection. I would never ask a lady anything so personal."

"Damn," Candy said, "just when this conversation was starting to sizzle. Oh, well." She grabbed an apron off the door peg and started rinsing the dishes. "To answer your question, Dr. Sand, I have only my charm and some pepper spray to protect me. No rough stuff, I'm afraid. Betts is a different matter. Kai taught her how to shoot."

"Really?" Lucian raised his brows. "Good to know."

"I have a Glock at home," I admitted, "my husband's. It's legal, properly registered and all, but it's not even loaded."

Lucian's silence frightened me more than words. I didn't need a gun. No one would try to kill me.

That's what Tommy thought, too. A strong, virile man. Someone murdered him without much trouble.

Lucian put his arms around me. "I'm not trying to frighten you. I worry about you. Ms. Ott, too. These people have taken many lives. Two more would not faze them." His eyes were stormy now, almost grey. "Perhaps you should stay here. Both of you. Della, too. Just for a while."

It was tempting. Easy to do. That's why I said no. I would take care of myself and deal with any problems. Besides, I had Della, the winged avenger, on my side. Who could ask for more?

"I can't stay," I told him. "I want to, but I can't. Not now."

He nodded. "When this is over, then we will talk, Elisa." He bent down and brushed his lips across my cheek. "We have much to say."

"Yoo hoo," Candy said. "Remember me, the other partner in this scheme? Before you lovebirds start cooing, let's get something straight. Do we all agree that we're going to trap that perky cougar and her henchman?"

Lucian and I both nodded. Even Della had her ears on alert. We spent the next hour planning our strategy.

Twenty-Seven

I phoned Meg Cahill bright and early the next day. The good doctor was obviously not a morning person. Her voice had more growl than grovel in it. After hearing my proposal she responded with forced cheer.

"How delightful of you, Elisabeth. Unfortunately, the Secretary's time is so limited."

"Great news. I spoke with Cap Coleman last night. My late husband was his squash partner, you know. Anyway, we reconnected at the Joslin party, and I called him. He was thrilled. Thought it was a great opportunity for Harvard Medical. I agreed to donate the proceeds to their stroke prevention program. Anyhow, he arranged the whole thing. Terrific, isn't it?"

Her response was barely audible. "That's such short notice, and we're so busy here. I'm not sure we can handle the arrangements."

"Don't you worry. My partner is one of the premier event planners in Boston. Candy will handle everything."

"Ah, yes. Ms. Ott."

"She's been feeling guilty, you know. After all, she is a partner in CYBER-MED, and she's been so hands off."

Meg kept her cool. "I'll just leave everything to you."

~

Candy was a whirlwind, a freak of nature. She commandeered troops, buttonholed workmen and sweet-talked bureaucrats, bending them all to her will.

The CYBER-MED Social soon became the hot ticket for Boston's elite. Candy even arranged for a gaggle of supermodels to appear, courtesy of Tatiana Lake. Everyone was ecstatic except Meg Cahill. Her unsmiling lips had the cold tightness of the Maginot Line. Only Carter Cahill dared to engage his wife in anything other than routine matters. He substituted bluster for business acumen, trailing after Candy and asking inane questions that she ignored.

The four of us had reconnoitered at Lucian's home for several evenings, planning every detail. Our cabal included Francie Cohen, who had somehow convinced Sergeant Andrews that her participation was good community relations. We excluded everyone from CYBER-MED, even Rand. There was no trust, no room for error until our mission ended.

Candy reviewed the social arrangements; Lucian talked security; I handled logistics. The goal was to lure Meg and her partner into acting while safeguarding our famous patient. Lucian's plan was simple but elegant. On the day of the party he would reprogram the Secretary's insulin pump to a different frequency known only to him. Lucian would personally monitor Chernikova's vital signs until the danger was over. He could do so from CYBER-MED or an adjoining facility. Francie's role was to shadow Tony Torres and limit his contact with Meg as much as possible. Candy and I were the public face of the event. She promised to entice Chernikova into staying by her side all night. I had no doubt that she was up to that task. We'd probably have to scrape him off her like bubble gum.

Della and I spent most nights at Lucian's house. All kinds of alarm bells sounded in my mind, but I ignored them. My experience with men was so limited that I had no natural defenses. Slowly, ineluctably, I was falling in love with Lucian. I couldn't stop myself. His tender touches and gentle words made it easy. No more insomnia. Now I longed for sleep so that I could curl up next to him, feeling his arms around me.

If he broke my heart, I would never recover. I was playing in a high stakes game that had no rules. I'm a lousy card-player anyhow. Kai used to peek openly at my hand and wipe me out every time.

Kai … he still visited my dreams, but each time it felt easier, as though he wanted this for me. Another chance at life, a chance to finish the journey we'd started together.

"You are pensive, ma belle," Lucian said, playing with tendrils of my hair. "What concerns you?"

"I just want this thing to end," I said. "Then Tommy can rest in peace."

"You are prepared for any outcome?" he asked. "Things may not go according to plan, you know."

I nodded. "But at least I will have tried. It's the only way I can live with myself."

He brushed his lips gently across mine. "Do you believe that some things are meant to be? Kismet, they call it. Destiny."

My throat tightened. "I don't know. Bad things aren't always inevitable."

His eyes were azure magnets pulling me into their depths. "Often they are followed by good things. I would not have met you without your friend's tragedy. So some good came out of that wickedness."

I buried my face in the soft folds of his sweater, content to hear his perfect heartbeat. "You saved my life, Lucian. No matter what else happens, I'll always be grateful for that."

He forced me to look up at him. "Listen to me. I told you early on, Elisa. I love you. As long as you want me, I will never leave your side."

~

It was almost time. In ten minutes the first guests would arrive at CYBER-MED, and our show would start. I shivered, even though my red dress was made of softest cashmere. I'm no glamour girl at the best of times. With today's high stakes, fussing over my appearance seemed criminally negligent. Candy had another point of view. She invoked every threat, promise and compliment in her power to inveigle me into primping. She won, of course. Her final taunt about Lucian and the chic image of French women stung me into submission. By the time she finished with me, my hair, makeup and accessories all had the Sweet Nothings seal of approval.

If the plan worked, which was a big unknown, Tommy's death would finally be avenged. It wouldn't bring him back, couldn't staunch the pain of losing him. But somewhere, he and Kai were watching, cheering us on. I knew that with every fiber of my being. Retribution is a time-honored tradition, but this wasn't revenge. Not really. I sought only justice. Thomas Yancey would have scorched the earth if I'd been murdered. I could do no less for him.

Candy was nowhere and everywhere. She flew from room to room, hectoring caterers, nudging workers, and shamelessly fawning over supermodels. Her shimmering aqua silk had a plunging neckline that would pop Chernikova's eyeballs out. No worries about where he'd be lurking, no sir.

My other partner was the poster child for poise. Meg trotted around the office, composed and perky, in a subdued satin suit that hugged her body. If she were anxious, it wasn't evident. To the contrary, her stride and fixed smile proclaimed that all was well at CYBER-MED. Even her husband's antics didn't faze her.

We had police protection, too. Officer Cohen corralled Arun, giving him the big-eyed look, absorbing his words like a reef-building sponge. I knew for a fact that around one shapely knee was a holstered Baby Glock, the ultimate power accessory.

Lucian held me tight before I left. "Do not fear, Elisa. All will be well." His palm glided down the length of my dress, skimming the neckline. "So soft and lovely," he whispered. "Take care today. You are precious to me, you and Candy." He bit his lip. "If only I were there to protect you."

"Hey. What can happen in a room full of doctors, dignitaries and security types? I promise to stay near Francie and her Glock. Besides, you've got the most important job, protecting the Secretary of State."

His caress made me yelp. "We've missed something. I know it. Something obvious. Dr. Cahill is too composed, too assured. If only I could find the key."

I stood on tiptoe, pressing my lips to his. "Don't worry, Lucian. I can handle myself. Candy, too, if I have to."

"I must worry, mon ange. I love you."

Despite innate caution and lawyerly instincts, those words made my heart quiver. My brave talk of independence was just that, talk. I'd been half-alive since Kai's death, but things were different now. I had made the transition. Kai was my beloved past, Lucian Sand, my future. I floated into CYBER-MED on a cloud of joy.

"Where is he?" Candy barked. "Where's Tony Torres?"

That brought me down to earth. "How do I know? I just got here, for heaven's sake. Maybe Tornado had to use the bathroom or something. It happens, you know."

"Maybe he's gone after Lucian. Ever think of that, genius?"

Even I wasn't sure where Lucian was. I knew he was close enough to monitor Richard Chernikova and keep him safe. That's all I cared about. I pointed Candy toward Rand Lindsay. "There. Ask Rand about it. He'll know."

Rand encased both of us in a friendly hug. "Wow, you ladies look gorgeous! Let me stand near you. I could use some glamour."

He'd worn his good blue suit with a starched white shirt. No tie. Ties violate some geek commandment.

"Where's your buddy?" Candy asked. "Why isn't he here?"

"Huh? Oh, you mean Tony. Family emergency. He'll be in later." Rand smiled as he surveyed Candy's handiwork. "This is amazing. Look at those models, my Lord. Wouldn't Tommy love this? He'd be all over those ladies." He looked guiltily at us, putting his hand over his mouth. "Sorry. It's just that he was so … alive. He even liked those stupid little dogs those girls carry."

"Tommy loved dogs," Candy said. "Cats, too. All animals."

"No one but old ladies loves those yippy little things," Rand said. "Ugh! Little rats, and their owners dress them up and put those obnoxious photos all over the place. Now your Della is my idea of a real dog. No need to dress her up like a baby."

I patted his arm. "She thanks you, sir. Now I see the security detail. Positions, everyone. It's show time."

Richard Chernikova and a spate of local celebrities swept into CYBER-MED. After Cap Coleman and I welcomed them, most of our guests vaulted over to the open bar and buffet table. Chernikova never moved. His eyes were fixed on the beauteous Candace Ott and her most prominent assets. Poor

Meg. She barely contained her fury at being displaced by a makeup artist. Everything was fine, just as we planned it, until Rand tapped me on the shoulder.

"Miss Elisabeth, may I see you?" His cheeks were mottled, and that spark of Alabama accent was now an inferno.

"Are you ill?" I asked.

He guided me toward his cubicle. "It's not that. I just heard from Tornado." Rand gulped a lungful of air. "I don't understand it. He says he's got the Sandman, that he plans to kill him."

"What? Lucian, oh my God! Let's find Francie. We need the police."

Rand clutched my arm. "No. Tony says he'll kill Lucian if you get the cops. He wants you, you and Ms. Ott. Says he has to explain something." He was babbling now, almost hysterical. "Please, ma'am. Don't push him. You don't know what Tony's like when he's angry."

I thought of Kai's Glock, nestled in my shoulder bag. It was loaded now. Lethal. I beckoned Candy with an emphatic wave. After several attempts she eluded Chernikova and joined us.

"What's wrong with you?" she groused. "He was really buying my act."

"It wasn't your act he was buying," I said, nodding toward Rand. "Tell her."

She listened without ever losing her pleasant smile. It was frozen in place. "OK," she said when Rand finished, "how do we know he's really got Lucian?" She turned to me. "Call him, Betts. Then we'll know for sure."

I masked my fear with a dull monotone. "I already tried. No answer. He told me wherever he's staying has poor reception. Maybe that's it."

We all knew better. Things moved in slow motion as if we were all paralyzed. Candy's rictus grin, Rand's pasty complexion, my inertia—none of it mattered anymore. Lucian needed my help.

"Where is he?" I asked. "We can slip away from here without anyone noticing."

"Watch out," Candy whispered. "Arun Rao at six o'clock." She threw back her shoulders, giving him a clear view of perfection.

"What's the matter?" Arun asked her. "Trading up these days? I saw you with that lecher. He's Meg's property, in case you don't know it." He slid his arm around Candy. "Stay close to me. He won't bother you then."

"Not now, Arun." Candy said. "Wait 'til this thing ends." She checked her watch. "Meet you at my place at ten o'clock, OK?"

Arun snarled. "It will have to be, won't it?" He stalked over to the bar and filled up.

"That was close," Candy sighed. "Maybe we should have told Arun."

Rand's eyes widened. "Please. We need to do something. I'll go by myself, if you want. You ladies can stay safe."

Candy rolled her eyes. "Oh, for Christ's sake. You're dramatizing. Where are we meeting him?"

"Around the block on the waterfront," Rand said. "It's faster if we drive. I've got a car outside."

We slipped out the door and into the elevator.

Candy leaned against the door as if her strength was almost gone. "I guess Tony's the murderer," she said. "Too bad. He's really built."

I felt the Glock's substantial weight in my purse. I would use it to save Lucian. "He killed Tommy," I said. "I hope he fries in hell." We exited the front door under the stern eye of one of Chernikova's security men.

"This way," Rand said, steering us toward an elderly Lincoln Town Car. His gait was slow and unsteady. "Do you mind driving, Ms. Ott? I'm not feeling so well."

"No problem," she said, "but this thing feels more like an ocean liner. Ever consider going green, Rand?"

He helped me into the front seat while he sprawled in the back. "Oh, it's not mine," he laughed. "A friend loaned it to me. Turn right on Mass. Avenue. Head toward Fan Pier."

"It's getting dark. I hope you know where we're going. Lucian isn't this far away. He's much closer to CYBER-MED." My fear grew with each block. "Oh, God. How did Tony find out? We never told anyone, just our little group."

"That's a problem," Rand said.

I felt something cold and hard, pressing into my back through the seat.

"Don't move, Miss Elisabeth. I'd hate to shoot you." Rand's voice wasn't weak now. It was vibrant, mocking. "Oh, I took the liberty of borrowing your Glock."

Twenty-Eight

I whirled around, looking for my purse.

"Easy does it," Rand said, "and don't try anything funny, Ms. Ott, unless you want me to blow a sizable hole in your best friend. Slow down and drive into that warehouse." He pointed to a cavernous space that looked abandoned.

"What's going on, Rand? Stop this nonsense." Candy wasn't scared. She was angry.

"I'll take the keys, please, ma'am. You probably figured everything out by now. Right, Mrs. Buckley?"

It wasn't possible. Affable Rand Lindsay killed my friend? "I don't understand. Tony had all that money. You didn't. We checked everyone."

He scoffed, a high-pitched giggle, actually, just like the sound on the tape.

"Tornado has nothing except tons of debt from those rug rats of his."

"But his checking account ..." I was babbling, trying hard to focus on this new reality.

"I gave you that information, Mrs. Buckley. You trusted me. People always do. It's the secret to my success. Tommy trusted me, too. That's why he met with me that night. Such a nice guy. So fair." He snickered.

"Who poisoned you?" Candy asked. "Your partner?"

"Forget it, Candy," I said. "He did it himself. It's the oldest trick in the book. Agatha Christie used it all the time. Throws suspicion off the murderer."

Rand clapped his hands. "High marks, Mrs. B., although I might have overdone things a tad. That crap made me really sick." His air was untroubled, as if we were three old cronies swapping war stories.

"Too bad it didn't kill you," Candy spat. "Bastard! You and Meg Cahill should both fry in hell."

"Perhaps," he said, "but when you two lovely ladies are found asphyxiated in the trunk of Tony's old junker," he spread his hands, "what are we to think? Officer Cohen and Sandman will share your suspicions. They'll find that fifty thousand in Tony's checking account, too."

"I thought you said ..."

"I did. But that sum was added to his private account this morning." Rand shrugged. "Hated to part with it, but chalk it up to the cost of doing business. I've got plenty more. So does my partner." There was that hideous simper again.

"Lucian won't rest until he finds out." It was cold comfort, but I was certain of that.

"Ah, what a man he is. Sandman showed me how to pull this thing off, you know. He trusted me, too, totally bought my act. He was so obsessed about his brother's death that he didn't see the real potential."

He nuzzled Candy's neck with the barrel of the Glock. "I hope you're not counting on some last minute rescue, ladies. That only happens in books and bad melodramas. No one comes around here except junkies and whores. They sure as hell won't help you."

I refused to give up. There were two of us, after all, and Rand was no physical match for us. If I could just distract him long enough to get that gun.

Keep him talking, Lizzie Mae.

I said a silent prayer to Kai and Tommy, begging for help. They would understand that I didn't want to join them now. Not yet.

"Tony knew all about that Mercedes and the lady's dog pictures. How could he?"

"Yeah," Candy said, her voice quivering, "unless you told him, you prick."

"Bingo. I fed Tornado enough information to hang him. Knowing you ladies, I'm sure you shared that tidbit with the divine doctor and Officer Cohen."

He had an enormous, insatiable ego. I had to play to that.

"Pretty clever, I must admit. But you're a decent guy, Rand. Why did you do it?"

He shook his head, more in sorrow than anger. "That's really unworthy of you, Mrs. B. Tommy asked the same thing. Couldn't understand my motive. I did it for the obvious reason, money. Filthy lucre. My days of begging and scraping for tuition money are long gone. See, I hooked up with Terrell Tate at one of those boring fundraisers. She spent hours telling me about her money-grubbing half-sister and how she wanted her dead." He gave that warm, familiar grin. "You know how sympathetic people find me. I agreed to check out Mary Alice Tate's medical info for her. Then one thing led to another and voila, big bucks."

I stole a look at my watch. It was nine-thirty. The event ended a half-hour ago. At least Chernikova had escaped this maniac for now. Besides, Lucian was probably searching for me.

"Do me one favor, Rand. Tell me how you murdered Tommy. Surely you didn't go over to Wellesley after that woman's car."

His face softened for a moment. "You know, I really do like you, Mrs. B. I wish things could be different. OK, if you must know, it was kismet. Just plain old luck. After Tommy confronted me, he gave me an option. Turn myself in, or he would. He actually thought I'd do the honorable thing." Rand hooted at that. "Anyhow, I left a few minutes before him and there it was, a miracle. Some stoner drove up in that Mercedes and dumped it keys and all, can you believe it? Well, I put that thing to good use. When Tommy came out, I followed him. Had to get everything right, you know. Then I gunned that sucker and mowed him down."

I couldn't stop the tears that stole down my cheeks. I didn't even try.

"You should have seen his expression right before I hit him. Priceless! He thought he was such hot shit, but I showed him."

Candy was openly weeping now. For Tommy, not for us. Not yet.

"But Dr. Cahill. How did that happen?" I sighed. "No harm in telling us now. Dead men tell no tales, as they say. Women, too."

Rand smiled. "Believe it or not, I met my partner through a referral. Terrell Tate. We found that we had mutual interests, shall we say. Four more at one million per." He licked his lips. "Made good business sense for both of us."

Candy shivered. "Can't you turn on the heater? It's freezing in here."

"You'll be glad for the cold when you're in that trunk. Won't be long now. My partner's coming to pick me up." He grinned. "You didn't think I'd try to handle both of you by myself. Not smart, and as you know, I'm very smart."

Headlights flashed against the warehouse windows.

"What did I tell you," Rand smirked. "Ask my partner all those questions about motive. You'll love the answer."

We watched a sleek black car drive in. Some foreign make, probably a Lexus. The driver kept the high beams trained on our vehicle. A car door slammed as a figure inched toward us. Rand hauled himself out of the back seat, making a gallant gesture toward his partner.

"Here we go, ladies. Ask away."

We stared into the fleshy face of Carter Cahill.

I was speechless, frozen with disbelief. Carter Cahill, that bumbling ineffectual fool, was the last person I'd suspected. He shuffled toward us, his face as blank as scrubbed chalkboard.

"Come on, Rand. Let's get this show on the road. Meggie will wonder where I am."

He didn't acknowledge us. That bastard acted as if we weren't even there. I couldn't take that. I refused.

"So you bankrolled this enterprise," I said. My voice sounded normal. I was proud of that. "Why bother? They won't be the last ones, you know. She's addicted to it."

Candy caught on right away. "Guess you can't give her what she needs, Carter. Meg spreads them for anything male. Hell, she probably even gave Rand a tumble."

"Shut up, both you bitches! You don't know her, how she's suffered. I had to stop it." He stifled what seemed like a sob. "Meggie loves me. She told me so."

"Hope your money holds out, Carter. Your dear wife has boffed half of Boston, you know." I forced a laugh.

His agitation grew. I hoped Carter wouldn't use that Glock on me. Not Kai's gun.

"I knew from the start you were trouble," he spat. "I should have killed you that first night in the rain. If Sand hadn't interfered, it would all be over now." He flung open the passenger side door and sent me sprawling onto the cracked cement floor. "Well, no matter. Sand can't save you now. No one can."

Rand kept his gun trained on Candy "Out you go, Miss Candy. Scoot now. You're too pretty for a hole in the head."

Candy unsnapped her seatbelt and opened the door. I saw her legs wobble. Who could blame her? We had every reason to be terrified. Only fools rushed heedlessly toward death.

"I have to use the bathroom," Candy begged. Her terror had her shaking.

"Nope," Carter Cahill said. "Use the trunk. That's your new home, your final resting place. You're such a persnickety bitch. Do you good to stew in your own juices."

Rand popped the trunk and made a courtly gesture. "Ladies first. Carter wanted to shoot you right in the head, but you know me, always a Southern gentleman. I prefer a more genteel solution."

The trunk was huge, bigger than most walk-in closets. Plenty of room for both of us. Plenty of space to curl up and die.

Carter had the Glock now. He peered in, regarding us with the disinterest one might show a lab specimen. "I calculated the cubic feet of air in here," he said. "Looks like you have about eight hours." He shrugged. "More or less, depending on how much you struggle. I wish it were summer. You'd cook fast then. Oh, well."

"Sleep tight, ladies. I really enjoyed meeting y'all." Rand snickered as he slammed the trunk and left us alone.

Twenty-Nine

I grasped Candy's hand, counting the minutes until it was safe to talk.

"Don't panic," I whispered. "We'll get out. I promise."

"How?" she whimpered. "Betts, I'm really scared, and I have to go to the bathroom really bad."

"Hold it," I growled. "We'll find a way out of this thing. Just keep cool. If you hyperventilate, you'll consume your air. Mine, too. Come on. Tony Torres has four kids. Maybe he has one of those interior trunk releases. Lots of parents get them."

Candy sniffled. "I've never seen one. What's it look like?"

I'd never actually seen one, but I'd read about them. Pregnant women think about those kinds of things, playing the what-if game. At least, I had. "They usually glow in the dark. Look for a handle, even a cord or button. Come on."

We spent an eternity searching for that damn thing before admitting defeat.

Candy did her part. She was plucky. "What now?" she asked. "It's really cold in here. Wish I'd worn a warmer dress."

"Ah, shucks. If you'd done that, Chernikova would have missed a world-class set of knockers. They mesmerized him."

"Very funny. He's actually kind of cute, you know. Wanted my phone number."

"Who could blame him? OK, there's another possibility. Some of these things have a trunk release cable. It's usually under the carpet near the driver's seat."

"Are you making this up, trying to make me feel better?"

I bit down on my tongue. No time for tears now. "Kai and I got into all these silly hypothetical games. You know, when I got pregnant." I gulped. "You always hear of kids getting stuck in trunks, so we researched it. I know it seems dumb now."

Candy hugged me. "Are you kidding? It's brilliant. You might just save our lives. Come on. What's next, Einstein?"

I used my foot to explore the rest of the acreage. "Wait a second. They forgot to take the tool kit. Use the tire iron, and I'll grab the pliers. Tear that carpet up. Watch your hands. Those staples hurt like hell."

"Hey, I thought of something, too," Candy said. "We can get more air by smashing those brake lights, buy ourselves more time."

"That a girl! Let's get busy."

We crawled over to the driver's side clutching our tools. Lincoln Town Cars are luxury vehicles, and someone really nailed the damn carpet down in this one. I'd send Ford a giant thank you someday soon — if I lived.

"Ow! Fuck!" Candy used a string of four-letter words. "My fingertips are shredded. This better do it."

"Keep working." I couldn't shatter her fragile optimism now. What if Rand or Carter stopped by later to finish the job?

I felt something warm and sticky on my hand. Blood. A small price to pay for freedom. Mr. Lindsay and I had some unfinished business.

It was a tedious, painful process. When Candy found the cable, we both cried.

Everything after that was anti-climatic. We grabbed the cable, fearful of fraying or breaking the damn thing.

"Here. Pull toward the front of the car." Candy's surge of energy redoubled my own efforts. It wasn't easy, and it took both of us. After twenty minutes or so, the trunk popped open. It was heavy, and it plopped back before we could scramble out. That meant repeating the entire process. When it reopened, I held up the top while Candy jumped out. She reached in and returned the favor.

Fresh air. I'd never really appreciated it before. We gulped lungfuls of it and said a prayer of thanks. Then our worst nightmare materialized. Headlights. Someone was coming.

"Grab that wrench," I yelled. "I'll take the tire iron." If those assholes came back for us, I'd take at least one of them with me. We crouched in the only spot that provided cover: behind the big front tires of the Lincoln.

Voices rumbled. At least two of them were male. Probably some of Carter Cahill's henchmen. No matter. I'd die standing on my own two feet. Screw them.

"Ready?" I asked Candy. She nodded.

They had powerful torches. They would see us if they really tried. One of them wrenched open the warehouse door, allowing his companion in first. They moved fast, way too fast for Lardo Lindsay and his puny master. Too bad. I'd rather die smashing Rand Lindsay's thick skull. Tommy would approve of that. Kai, too.

My nose told me Candy had finally relieved herself. She rose to a half crouch, prepared to spring at our enemies. I did the same.

"They're gone," one guy mumbled. "Must have popped the trunk."

I couldn't see their faces, but they looked big. Still, we had the element of surprise. I signaled to Candy. "Get ready."

When the light beam hit us, we sprang at them.

"What the ..." Candy whacked one of their shins with the wrench, leaving the man writhing in agony.

Lucian caught me just before I clobbered him.

Thirty

"Elisa!" He picked me up and swung me around. "Mon dieu, I thought we were too late." He held me tighter than he ever had, raining kisses all over my face.

Candy was a tangled heap, squeezing Arun Rao while he howled in pain.

"You broke my ankle," he yelled. "God, it hurts."

She consoled him in typical Candy fashion until his howls became moans.

"Let's go," Lucian said. "They might send someone, you know." He carried me to the Cayenne, placing me in the seat as if I might shatter. "I thought I had lost you." He took my hand, gently kissing each of my fingers. "What would I do without you? You're part of me now."

"How did you find us?" My teeth were chattering like castanets.

"Arun. Let him tell you." He brushed his lips against my hair, rocking me to and fro as if I were an infant.

Arun had recovered from his earlier upset. He cradled Candy, watching her doze. Then he took a deep breath and told his tale. "I saw you two leave with Rand. Candy had just brushed me off, and I was steamed. Chernikova was leering at her, and she did everything to encourage him. I figured you were going to meet him somewhere, so I followed you."

"What?" Candy's head shot up. "Why didn't you stop Rand?"

"I lost you. It was dark on the wharf. Anyhow, I went back and phoned Officer Cohen. She called Lucian, and we split up. It took a while, but we finally found this place again." He kissed Candy's forehead. "When I saw Tornado's old car, I suspected something was up."

"My hero," Candy said, batting her eyelashes, "wounded in battle."

"You were very brave," Lucian said, "both of you. Femmes formidables. Warriors."

~

Rand Lindsay didn't get far. He gave up without a struggle when the cops stormed his apartment. Francie Cohen laughed about it afterwards. She said Rand was tucked in his bed, wearing the most atrocious nightshirt she had ever seen. He seemed surprised but unafraid when they arrested him, still playing the gentle giant, aggrieved but amiable. Candy and I knew better. All that Southern shit, "Miss Elisabeth, please ma'am, y'all." We'd seen the monster behind that façade and heard that sociopath brag about killing Tommy, murdering the man who tried to help him.

Tommy had a strange appreciation for the macabre. He and Kai probably smirked about the delicious irony of the whole thing from their perch in the hereafter. Hoist on his own petard, that's what Tommy would have joked about himself. Screwing around got him at the end, just as the nuns had predicted.

I knew better. My friend ran afoul of a soulless man who traded dollars for decency. I'd execute Rand Lindsay myself if I had the choice. To hell with lethal injection. I'd stake the bastard to an anthill, pour on the honey and walk away laughing.

He pleaded not guilty when they booked him for kidnapping and attempted murder. Charges for the murders of Thomas Yancey, Jacob Arthur and Ian Cotter were added later after the judge denied him bail. I heard that Rand's attorney plans to mount a diminished capacity defense. Fat chance. Candy and I will be right there in that courtroom, staring into his lying face, sending him straight to hell.

Carter Cahill lawyered up immediately. He was charged as an accessory to kidnapping and attempted murder, pending other murder-for-hire counts. Despite his claims of innocence, Meg immediately filed for divorce, depriving him of the one thing in life he valued. She denied any suggestion that her behavior had sparked her husband's murder spree. One week later, bereft of his darling Meggie, Carter took his own life.

I didn't mourn his loss. I celebrated it. To hell with John Donne and his pompous humbug about one man's death diminishing us all. Carter's obsessive jealousy made him murder my friend. He paid Rand to end the life of someone dear to me, just because he wasn't man enough to satisfy his randy wife. I was glad hell had another occupant.

The Cahill family settled the wrongful death lawsuit I filed against them out of court, as if Tommy's loss could be expunged by a generous check. Candy and I sponsored paid intern positions at Sweet Nothings with part of the money and established the Thomas Yancey foundation. He'd like that, especially since we recruited male candidates to carry on in his name.

My own life was filled with unexpected blessings. Meg Cahill sold her shares in CYBER-MED to Lucian and relocated to Phoenix. Arun Rao became the CEO of CYBER-MED and the proud fiancé of Candace Ott. I think she's serious this time. Sweet Nothings has started a Bridal Blog brimming with tips about autumn weddings in New England.

Six months after our first meeting, I married Lucian Sand on an isolated stretch of Cape Cod beach. I wasn't alone that day. Candy was there, of course, and Della accompanied me down the path wearing her red mountain lead. Others were there, too, their spirits strong and vibrant. We toasted absent friends, knowing with absolute certainty that they were with us, watching everything. I know, even as I focus on the future with my new husband, that they will always be there. Life's rarest gift is a second chance for happiness. I've been given that. It's what Kai would have wanted. He loved me, loves me still, and wants only the best for me.

Lucian is an enthusiastic proponent of large families and dreams of having a son, Thomas Marcus Sand, to carry on his name. That sounds fine to me, too.

I still think of Kai and Tommy with love and tenderness. They're waiting for me, keeping me safe, rooting for my happiness. Someday we'll be together again.

Meet Arlene Kay

Arlene Kay spent twenty years as a senior executive with one of those alphabet agencies that strikes terror into the hearts of all Americans. She cloaked her quirky sense of humor in bureaucratic trappings while crafting word portraits of the snarky characters she encountered in some of the nation's toughest cities.

Since moving to Cape Cod, Arlene strolls the beautiful beaches, plotting mayhem with two Belgian Tervuren at her side. She enjoys hearing from her readers at Kkay3@comcast.net. Read more about Arlene at http://arlenekay.com.

www.ingramcontent.com/pod-product-compliance
Lightning Source LLC
Chambersburg PA
CBHW061603170626
46811CB00001B/301